RIPPLES

by

William J. Millman

SB
Sunset Beach Press

SB

Sunset Beach Press

Manufactured in the United States of America

ISBN: 9781513634449

To the Readers
Everywhere

CHAPTER 1

The cobalt blue sky reminded her of the summers she'd spent with her family up in the Rockies, happy times, times that even now – 30 years later – brought a smile to her face no matter what life brought her way. At that moment, it was bringing laundry: a basket of freshly-washed clothing she was hanging on the backyard line.

Sometimes it was a blessed relief to do something as mindless and time-consuming as hanging clothes, something that occupied her mind and body just enough to prevent dwelling on all the difficulties that had made the previous eight months so trying. First, Jackie broke his leg. Of course, it was something a lot of little kids did, but to see her six-year-old in real pain for the very first time, to see him reach out to her for not only solace but relief and to not be able to do anything other than coo soothing words she hoped would help him cope while struggling to maintain her mask of control – that was hard. Extremely hard. It made her heart tremble just thinking about it.

Then there was her job. Seven years with the same insurance company, the same supervisor, the same cubicle. One day, after years of excellent ratings ("Janice makes the impossible look easy,") she'd arrived (five minutes early, as always) to find a sticky note attached to her computer monitor *inviting* her to visit her supervisor's office. A *sticky note*! Could anything have been more impersonal, demeaning, lacking in any human virtue or nicety? Of course, at that moment she had no idea what would greet her in that office, thinking she might be in line for a bonus, or even a promotion, what with her excellent ratings and the easy, convivial relations she had both up and down the corporate ladder.

But no, it wasn't a promotion, or even a bonus that Jack Lambert wanted to discuss with her.

"Janice, come in, have a seat," Lambert had greeted her, his voice a note too high, his smile an inch too wide, his eyes a shade too cold.

"What's up?" she'd answered, still swimming in a sea of unreal expectations and stunning naiveté.

The smile faded, the voice dropped to its normal timbre, the eyes remained cold. "I know this is going to come as something of a shock," he began, and she remembered a stunning wave of premonition surging through her body, "but there is going to be a downsizing…" She didn't hear much of what he said next, coming as it did through a fog of shock and disbelief, a curtain as real as if it'd been woven of heavy wool. Seems evaluations didn't matter. Good work didn't matter. Money mattered, and as one of the last in her section to be hired, she would be one of the first to go. Oh, they'd provide job-search assistance and a "generous" separation package (why do employers always think generosity is a function of money, and not respect?), but there was no question she could remain with the company.

"I'm… fired?" she barely managed to ask, the words like lead weights squeezing through deadened lips.

"No, not *fired!*" Lambert had answered, his jovial pretense partially reconstituted. "*Downsized!*"

She'd tried to hide the reality from Jackie, though even a six-year-old was perceptive enough to realize that his mother was different somehow, not as warm, not as welcoming, not as *present* as she normally was when she came home from work and took over from the slightly old-ish, slightly priggish babysitter. She'd tried. God knows, she'd tried. Tried to keep a smile plastered to her face, to keep the shock – and even fear – from her voice. But he was a smart little kid and from his reaction she knew he knew that something wasn't right.

It had been seven *months* before she found a new position, as an Administrative Assistant at a small import-export dealer located all the way across town from where their tiny, time-worn house sat. It paid less, the work was tedious (bordering on inane), and she was the only person permanently anchored in the small, cramped office in the back of a cavernous warehouse crammed full of crates and pallets of parts and equipment imported from Asia – China, mainly.

When she'd first begun her new position, the *newness* of everything masked a fact she hadn't even considered when she accepted the job: the sheer isolation of being the only woman, and often the only person, in that huge building for hours at a time. There were other people who worked there, of course, even another secretary, but they were all housed in the low-rise office building next door. No, this warehouse was her domain, and hers alone. She'd imagined how delicious it would be to have all that space to herself, without the nerve-strumming staccato of neighboring keyboards, the constant throat-clearing, bag rattling, and sotto voce phone conversations in cubicles located just inches away, separated by too-thin cardboard covered with noxious polyester mock cloth.

It wasn't. Instead she quickly came to realize that the constant background noise functioned like a cheap motel air conditioner, providing a *texture* to her surroundings, an aural security blanket that prevented her from hearing all the little scraping and creaking noises that generated horror movie images of rats and bats and crazed zombie attackers in her nervous mind. She found herself pausing in mid-document, straining to listen through the shadows and echoing nothingness, to convince herself that the sound she thought she'd maybe, perhaps heard was nothing more than… nothing.

Then too, there were no people. Not literally. From time to time, (actually every day), there were other employees who stopped by to deliver or pick up a pallet of something or another, and required bills of sale or signatures or just a quick chat with the new girl. But they were few and far between. She began to wonder if perhaps the entire operation was some kind of front for an Asian scam, perhaps a trafficking center, or money laundering, or…

She was doing it again. Ever since the father of her child, Jack Senior, had decided to leave town with little advance notice and no forwarding address, she'd found her mind wandering more and more often to the day-to-day hardships of everyday life, and then to the geometrically more difficult and challenging demands of single motherhood. She'd promised herself she would stop the useless and counterproductive rehashing of events long past, making it something of a mid-year New Year's resolution that lasted just about as long and was just about as successful. *'Focus on what you **can** change. Focus on a better tomorrow.'* She wasn't sure where she'd picked up that mantra, perhaps at a pilates class she attended when she still worked at the insurance company and could afford to pay the sitter to stay a little longer twice a week so she could purge her system of all the negative energy she'd accumulated at work before she came home, and so

greet her son with the smile he deserved instead of the snarl he did not.

Speaking of Jackie, she suddenly realized things were awfully quiet in their tiny, two-bedroom suburban rental home. She'd heard one of his Internet kiddie shows blaring away only moments earlier. When had it stopped? She decided she'd better take a quick stroll inside to make sure he wasn't getting into something he shouldn't, either something that would leave her a mess to clean or something that might put him at risk. At his age, either was a real possibility.

She clipped one last blue boy's sock to the clothesline and made her way to the back door. As she pulled open the aluminum screen, she reminded herself for the umpteenth time that the hinges needed oiling and the small hole in the lower right quadrant of the upper screen panel – where Jackie had managed to poke a broom handle through the wire mesh while he was *helping* her clean – needed fixing. She'd have to call the landlord, which she hated doing because he was such a jerk and never repaired anything until after she'd called a minimum of two times…

She'd only taken a step or two inside the kitchen when a rough hand, smelling of tobacco and… was it gin? …collided with her mouth and nose while another hand roughly grabbed her right elbow.

"Make a sound and your kid dies," a deep, rough voice barked in her ear.

Sound? Dies? What was the voice talking about? What was this person doing in her kitchen?

For just an instant, admittedly a very long, very confused instant, she stood at rigid attention, every muscle in her body straining for clarity, every neuron firing as if to blind this

unknown intruder, to send up a flare of distress that would
bring a speedy end to this… affront.

"Do you understand?" the voice asked. It was as if her
brain was slowly defrosting. Now that she could think, a little,
she realized he sounded nervous, perhaps as nervous as she
felt. *Had she heard that voice before?*

She nodded her head, his heavy, stinking hand making it
harder than normal to force her neck muscles to oblige.

His hand slowly pulled away from her face. "Not a
sound," he said.

"Don't hurt him," she whispered, tears beginning to leak
from unseeing eyes.

"You do as you're told, he doesn't get hurt."

She nodded. Jackie was going to be okay.

"How much money do you have here?" he asked.

*Money? She barely earned enough to pay their rent and expenses.
She doubted she had more than…*

"Not much. Maybe twenty bucks or so."

"Let's go get it."

He yanked her elbow so that she pivoted in front of him,
then gave a shove into her lower back. She stumbled slightly,
her legs numb.

"Move it!' he insisted, his tone increasingly on edge.

She dragged her feet through the kitchen and into the
narrow hallway that led toward the bedrooms. As she passed
the kitchen cabinets she noticed they needed a good wipe-
down. It was so hard keeping everything as clean as she'd
prefer, what with all the time she spent at work and now with
Jackie big enough to climb up on the chairs…

Another push in her back.

As they came to Jackie's bedroom she noticed the door was shut. She unthinkingly reached out to open it, to see how he was doing, until the same rough hand slapped her arm away and the voice growled: "Are you *trying* to piss me off?"

"No, no, I was just… He never keeps his door closed," she hurried to explain. She tried to turn back to address the intruder face-to-face, but he shoved her shoulder forward to prevent the move.

"Get the money!"

Her feet moved faster of their own volition, becoming more of an independent conveyance mechanism than a part of her body. The door to her room was open, and she made her way directly to her purse. She picked it up off the chair where it sat unzipped, but before she could rummage through its contents to find her wallet he reached around her and grabbed the bag from her hands.

"Gimme that."

She heard him dump the bag out on her bed and glanced over to see the untidy pile of odds and ends spread out on the bedspread. Removed from their hiding place like that, disassociated from their daily routine, they looked a bit pathetic, a collection of makeup and pens and Kleenex and address books more suitable for the trashcan than a purse. He grabbed the wallet and tore out the emergency twenty she kept tucked inside.

"Is this it?" He sounded angry.

"I barely make enough to pay the rent," she tried to explain. But she stopped; why was she explaining anything to this man, this *intruder*, this lowlife who probably wanted nothing more than to score some drugs with his ill-gotten gains? For the first time, she felt a surge of indignation welling up inside her, an anger at the unfairness, the *inconsideration* of it all. Who did this guy think he was?

"You got any jewelry?" he asked, tossing the pocketbook aside like an emptied fast-food bag.

"Nothing valuable," she said, knowing that she wasn't being entirely truthful.

"Let's see."

He shoved her again and she made her way over to the mahogany dresser they'd bought when they were first married, the first big purchase they'd made as a *couple*. It seemed so long ago… She was nearly there when she looked up and realized she could see the intruder reflected in the matching mirror mounted on the wall, the first time she'd seen more than just his hand and part of his arm. She stopped abruptly, the air sucked from her lungs. He was a bit taller than her, but not much, thin, seemingly young (what made her think so?), and dressed head to foot in black, a ski mask covering his head. She hesitated a second too long and he realized she was looking at his reflection.

"Like what you see?" he asked, his voice as casual as if they had just bumped into each other at a dating bar. Casual and almost *hopeful*.

"Don't do this," she began, her voice quivering despite her best efforts to sound calm, in control. That was what you were supposed to do, wasn't it: sound in control?

He shoved her in the small of the back. "Let's see those jewels." She could tell he wasn't happy, the hopefulness replaced by an authoritative growl.

She took a deep breath and opened the dresser drawer. Her jewelry pouch – a small blue leather bag that one of her necklaces had come in – was easy enough to find and almost embarrassingly light. As she lifted it from the drawer, the intruder grabbed the pouch from her hands and dumped the contents almost immediately on top of the bureau. Her engagement ring – a half-carat princess cut diamond, an old sterling and emerald ring she'd bought herself, two thin gold chains, one pair of small diamond stud earrings and a half dozen costume jewelry studs tumbled onto the maple veneer surface, the sound more like small birds landing than a casino jackpot.

"This is it?" he asked, incredulity stained with contempt coloring his question.

"I don't wear jewelry all that much," she found herself explaining, "and besides, I can't afford much more than this."

He scooped it up in one hand and stuffed it into a pocket.

"If I find out you been lyin' to me," he began.

"No, no I'm not. Really. This is all I have."

"Outta my way," he said, pushing her back towards the bed. He pulled out drawer after drawer and dumped each on the floor at his feet. In moments a small mountain of socks, sweaters, underwear and pajamas lay discarded on the worn pile carpet.

"Arc you shittin' me? You got a Beamer in the driveway and this is all the swag you got?"

"I got the car in the divorce." Why was she explaining anything to him? He was a *robber* for cryin' out loud!

The intruder stood there for several seconds as if weighing his options. Janice saw an opportunity.

"Just take the jewelry, take it and go and I promise I won't call the police. I won't tell *anyone*."

He turned to her, his eyes flashing. "You bet your ass you won't tell anybody! You call the cops, you call anybody, and

I'll come back here and chop that little kid of yours into little pieces!"

He reached out and grabbed her by the front of her blouse. "You understand?!"

"Yeh, I understand!"

"Good, good." He seemed momentarily thrown off balance and for just an instant she thought her nightmare might be coming to an end.

She was wrong.

"Down on your knees," he said.

"What?"

He grabbed her blouse again. "I said, down on your knees!" His voice rose threateningly. "Might as well get sumthin' outta all this," he mumbled, half to himself.

She tried to think of a way out, a way to get away from this madman, but then she thought of Jackie in the room next door and she did as she was told. Her legs trembling, she knelt in front of him. "Please, just take the jewelry and go…" she began but her words were cut off by the sound of his zipper being pulled down.

"Open your mouth," the intruder said.

She swallowed, a wave of horror nearly overcoming her.

"You don't want to do this…"

He shoved his thing into her mouth and grabbed the back of her head.

"Shut the fuck up and suck."

She nearly gagged.

"And it I get one little scratch from those teeth of yours, I'm gonna knock every one of 'em down your throat. Understand?"

She nodded minutely. Time seemed to come to a standstill as she knelt there, afraid to move, afraid to speak, nearly afraid to breathe.

"I said suck!" he ordered after a few seconds. "I don't got all day!"

She closed her eyes and did as she was told. She knew what was happening but it was as if it was happening to someone else, as if she wasn't even there. She heard his grunts and moans, felt his hand push and pull on her hair, but in her mind she was far away from there, in a warm, sunny, safe place.

He must have noticed her vacant look, for his activity gradually lessened and then stopped. He pulled out and grabbed her by her hair.

"Get up!" he ordered. She got to her feet slowly, her knees aching, her brain clearing like at the end of a bad nightmare. "Over there," he directed, pushing her toward the bed. "Get those clothes off."

She froze. "No, please just take the jewelry and go," she said, tears beginning to stream down her face. "I won't tell anybody…"

"I said get them off!" he repeated, pushing her more violently. She fell back on the bed and began to sob, her last vestiges of resistance crumbling before his utter lack of humanity.

"Cut that shit out," he said. "You don't want me to come over there."

She managed to sit up and tried to unbutton her blouse, but her fingers were numb and she did little more than fumble with the cool plastic discs. The intruder stared at her for several long seconds; she could *feel* his glare even though she couldn't meet his eyes.

"For Christ's sake, I don't have time for this," he finally muttered, and in one move stepped to her side and tore the buttons loose.

She let out a little scream.

"You keep quiet!" he growled, hauling her up by the front of her blouse. "You want that kid of yours to come in and watch this?"

She felt as if her heart actually stopped, her chest crushed beneath the weight of his cruelty.

"He's just a little boy…" she began

"Then get out of them clothes. Now!"

She peeled off the torn blouse and slipped out of her shorts. When she was done, she stood before him, one arm across her chest the other covering the front of her panties.

"Well, what're you waitin' for? Get the rest of it off."

"Please, don't do this!" she cried, hoping to reach any crumb of compassion still surviving inside his animal mind. Without warning he backhanded her, knocking her down on the bed.

"Enough of this shit," he said as he pulled a large knife from his pocket and with one flick of his wrist snapped the blade open.

"No, don't hurt me, pleeease," she wailed as he leaned toward her.

He grabbed the front of her bra and cut through the tight elastic in an instant, pulling it roughly from her body. Her hands flew to her breasts of their own accord, her mind so overwhelmed it no longer functioned. Two quick slits in the thin cotton and her panties were tossed aside.

"Now we can do this the easy way, or the hard way," he said dropping his trousers and underwear around his ankles. "Either way, it's gonna get done."

He shoved her onto her back, pushed her knees apart and crawled between them. Before she could even flinch, he was inside her. She wanted to cry out, to howl against the injustice and shame, but no sound would come. She lay there as he did his thing, staring past his bobbing head at the ceiling, scanning every inch of the pebbled white plaster as if it somehow mattered. Her eyes came to rest on a small cobweb attached to one blade of the ceiling fan, a delicate thread that caused her more distress than she could justify.

The attack went on and on, a rhythmic pounding that lulled even as it appalled, the stench of his body and breath occasionally breaking through the cocoon of insentience in which she had managed to hide. To her horror, a familiar wave of warmth began to seep into her abdomen and she heard herself grunting in time with his thrusts. She fought, fought to drive the sensations from her body, to drag herself back to the blankness of escape, the nothingness of self-denial.

And then it stopped.

She opened her eyes slowly.

"Roll over," he said, pulling her by her hip even as he spoke.

She allowed herself to roll, rejoicing in the psychological escape from his immediate presence. For just a moment she could imagine that he was gone, disappeared, as she stared into the welcoming familiarity of her pillow, luxuriating in its softness and familiar scent. Then his rough hands grabbed at her hips and dragged them up toward him. She began to protest, to question, but before the words could form in her muddled brain, before her lungs could propel her thoughts into the room around her, pain stabbed into her from behind, a sharp, tearing, overpowering pain. She gasped, cried out in full-throated agony.

Other than muffling her scream with his hand he ignored her, kept on as if she hadn't made a sound. The pain doubled, re-doubled until it felt as though she would break in half, as if he would stab straight through her.

"Don't wanna get no baby, do you?" he panted after a time.

She did not answer. Wasn't sure if she could formulate a rational sentence. The thrusts came more quickly, more quickly still, the pain folding in upon itself until it was a single burning constant, the only sense that registered, the only reality that mattered.

He shuddered, gasped, and collapsed on her back like some dying fish out of water, gulping for air. Slowly, almost tenderly, he withdrew.

"Now that... was worth it," he said between breaths as he climbed down off the bed. She heard the rustling of cloth and a zipper being pulled up. "You just stay where you are. I'll be getting' out of here now, and you're gonna stay right there, right on that bed for ten minutes. I'll stay around for a while to see if you do like I said. And if you don't? If you try to come out, or call the cops, or anything other than stay right where you are, I'll kill you, kill the kid, and cut the two of you up into little bits. You hear me?"

She tried to nod her head. It was too hard to speak.

"I asked you if you heard me?!" he asked again, louder, anger coloring his words.

"Yes," she groaned.

"Good. Oh, one other thing," he went on, his voice dropping into an abrasive whisper, "you call the cops, and I find out about it, you better hope they find me before I find you." Her brain registered the threat but she felt nothing but emptiness. Footsteps moved away from the bed, and the door opened. She almost allowed her cramping muscles to relax. "Turn around and look at me," he unexpectedly insisted. She struggled to leverage herself onto her side. He held up the knife, pointing it at her as he spoke. "You stay right there. Don't you move!" And then he *smiled* at her. Smiled!

The door closed.

For a long time, or at least it seemed like a long time, she lay there, the throbbing within her the only proof she was still alive. Her mind shut down, thoughts floating like dust in a breeze, swirling in random patterns, signifying nothing. Slowly, so slowly she didn't recognize the process until it was near-complete, the dust settled and consciousness drifted into focus. *'How long, how long has it been? How long should I wait?'*

She listened to her own breathing, felt her own heart beat in her chest. She was still alive. After all that, she was still alive. She strained to hear any sounds from outside the room, but all she could hear was the constant drumbeat of her pulse, so she lay where she was and waited. It took some time, how long she couldn't say, before another thought forced its way through the chaos into mindfulness: *Jackie!* She raised her head, straining in the direction of his bedroom, forcing her breathing to slow, her heart to settle. Nothing. Not a sound.

A cold wave of fear spread like poison. *'No, please God, not Jackie!'*

She forced herself up off the bed and grabbed her blouse and shorts, holding them out in front of her like a protective shield. It took her several seconds to realize the blouse was shredded, limp threads dangling from where the buttons should've been. She walked gingerly to the dresser, each step bringing a stab of torment, and opened a drawer. She took out a t-shirt and pulled it on over her head before stepping into her shorts. It wasn't until she'd finished that she realized her hands were shaking.

She forced her unwilling legs to carry her to the door, where she leaned her ear against the cool wooden surface and listened, listened for any sign of *him*, or of her son. Nothing. Barely able to draw a breath, she gently turned the doorknob and eased the door open an inch at a time. The smallest of hinge squeals made her heart stop in mid-beat. She waited. At first she chanced only an eye, then her entire head emerged into the hallway, watching and waiting to discover if *he* had actually left. She paused as long as she could bear, until her need to know about her son overwhelmed her fear of being discovered. Her pulse thundering in her ears, she slipped out of the room and down the hallway to Jackie's room. His door was still closed. No sound came from inside.

She fought back a sob and turned the handle. The room was dark, the shades pulled. Jackie could only nap during the day if the room was completely in shadow; the dimmest sunlight was enough to keep him awake even if his eyes were shutting on their own. She tiptoed over to his bed, in the gloom just a pile of sheets and blankets. Still no sound. No movement. She remembered how she'd come into his room when he was just a newborn, sometimes three or four times a day, terrified that he would not be breathing, that she would find his tiny still body cold to the touch, his lips and nails blue.

The boy was so burrowed into his covers she had to ease them from his body, pulling one then another as gently if disarming a bomb. Finally, she saw that precious face, eyes closed, his hair a bird's nest of chaotic indifference. She leaned closer, straining to hear... a breath! And another! She nearly burst into tears with relief, but forced herself to stay quiet as she pulled the covers back and tenderly smoothed a single strand of his hair. She stood there in the darkness for several minutes, listening to his breathing, drinking-in the very *nearness* of him. Only when she realized something wet was dripping down her leg did she steel herself with a deep breath and slowly withdraw from the room.

She didn't check her leg; she didn't want to know. Instead she made her way immediately to the bathroom where she turned on the shower full-force before tearing off her blouse and shorts and tossing them into the waste basket. The water was hot, almost too hot, but the sting of the spray reinforced the notion that she was still alive. For the longest time she stood under the steaming stream, letting the water rush over her head and down her back, letting it wash away not only the physical stains but the emotional ones as well. As if it could.

She tried not to think of the attack, not to think of *him*. But it was like trying not to think about a toothache: the harder you tried, the harder you failed. She could feel the roughness of his hand, could smell the rank, ugly stench of his vileness. Suddenly, with no warning, she began to sob,

softly at first and then harder, until her shoulders shook so
hard she could barely catch her breath.

She didn't hear the bathroom door open.

"Mommy?"

She tried to stop the tears, tried to silence the anguished
keening, but it was not like a water faucet, it could not be
stopped with a flick of a wrist.

"Mommy, are you okay?"

He sounded frightened, confused. The sound of his voice
gave her the strength to stop. Like a sputtering outboard, the
wail became a whimper, the whimper became a tiny gulp of
air.

"Yes, yes I'm fine, Jackie. Did you just wake up?" She
tried to keep the pain from her voice.

"I had to pee."

"Go on. Be sure to flush."

She heard him sit.

"Why were you crying?" he asked.

Her mind spun. What to say? "Sometimes people get
sad," she offered. "And so sometimes they cry."

"Why were you sad?"

"Well, sometimes things just don't go the way you'd like
them to."

"Yeh, that happens to me sometimes, too. But don't be
sad, Mommy. Things will get better."

She smiled despite herself. From the mouths of babes…

She heard him pull up his pajamas.

"Don't forget to flush."

"I will."

With the flush and the closing of the door, she was alone
again, alone with her thoughts, alone with her pain. She

marveled at how those few minutes with Jackie had buoyed her, and how quickly the black shadow that enshrouded her had returned. She tried to think, to impose some logic or structure on the attack, but she found it impossible to come to grips with her next step. Call the police? If he found out before they caught him, would he come back?

A doctor, maybe she should call a doctor. But wouldn't the doctor be obliged to report the attack to the police? Were Jackie and she safe in that house? Should she bundle him up and take him... where? To her mother's? She'd have to explain why, and wouldn't she be putting Mom into harm's way? What then – just go on as if nothing had happened, pretend as if today were just an extension of yesterday and a precursor to tomorrow? What to do... ?

If Jackie hadn't been there she would've probably drained a bottle of wine, slipped on her headphones and curled up in an easy chair. The effort to stand upright seemed too much to bear. It was just too hard.

But he *was* there, so she dried herself, ran a comb through her hair (when had all those gray streaks appeared?), and stepped out into a house that seemed like an alien world, a place where once she had felt safe but now felt... vulnerable. Every room promised a threat, every sound an alarm. She forced herself to walk purposefully, to feign a self-confidence she didn't feel.

Jackie was sitting in the kitchen, playing on her iPad.

"Are you hungry?" she asked. He mumbled something that she missed. "Speak up!" she demanded with more force than she'd meant to use. He looked up at her with narrowed, questioning eyes. Did he know? Did he somehow *feel* the disorientation, the utter dislocation?

"I *am* hungry," he said softly. "Will you make me something?"

Make him something. Like what? After what happened, how could she stand there and make a sandwich, or a bowl of Spaghettios? Did he understand what he was asking?!

"Sure. I'll see what I can find," she said, her voice flat, mechanical.

She opened the refrigerator and the brightness of the light inside caught her by surprise. As she slowly scanned the glass shelves she felt a wave of… *blackness* come over her, an undefined sorrow. There was so little on the shelves. So little to choose from… She caught herself as tears began to slide down her cheeks. She glanced over and saw her son staring at her, that same puzzled expression twisting his features.

"Mom?" he asked and she realized she'd been standing there for quite a long time. The alarm bell was dinging furiously.

"Peanut butter and jelly?" she asked, the only unified thought she could ensnare at the moment.

"Yeh. That'd be good. Thanks." He watched her for a few more seconds and then went back to the tablet.

She looked out into the back yard and the sight of the laundry flapping in the breeze brought a lump to her throat. She'd have to bring the wash in soon, she thought, but how soon? Now where was that peanut butter…?

She found it in the cabinet and was lifting the jar out of its niche when the phone rang. She flinched and the jar dropped out of her hand and bounced off the kitchen counter. *'Thank god for plastic,'* she thought as the phone rang over and over again,

"Mom!" her son called out, "Do you want me to answer it?"

"No, no I'll get it," she said with an unthinking shake of her head, making her way to where the jangling tone continued to demand attention. But she didn't pick up the handset. Finally, the voicemail kicked-in.

"Hi Jan, it's Mom. Hoped to catch you in, but I guess I missed you."

"Mom, it's Grandma!" Jackie said excitedly.

Janice stood rooted to the spot as the message continued.

"Nothing much new here. Just was wondering how you and that handsome grandson of mine were doing…"

"Mom! It's *Grandma*!" Jackie insisted, his tone becoming concerned.

"So, give me a call when you get a chance. Hugs and kisses."

Jackie jumped up from his chair and ran over to the phone, grabbing the handset just as the dial tone began to wail.

"She hung up," he said. "Why didn't you answer the phone?"

She looked down at him, wondering why he seemed so concerned.

"I don't really feel much like talking right now," she said, the words dropping from her lips like drying cement. "Maybe we'll call her back… tomorrow."

He stared at her, his look a mix of anger and worry lasting only as long as his attention span. "Okay," he said a few moments later. "Tomorrow."

He grabbed the tablet and took it into the living room where he could play with it at the same time he watched

Nickelodeon. She tried to remember what it was she was
doing before the phone had begun ringing, but all she could
remember was the laundry blowing in the breeze. Then she
saw the peanut butter jar lying on its side on the countertop.

'*Sandwich,*' the thought sputtered through her brain. '*For
Jackie.*'

Her hands moved of their own accord as she went
through the motions of spreading peanut butter on bread.
When she had finished, she trimmed the crust, cut the bread
in half and put the two halves on a paper plate before
carrying it out to her son.

"Thanks, Mom," he said, barely looking up from his
video game.

She watched him sitting there, his little thumbs twitching
like humming birds' wings against the controller, his face a
model of earnest concentration as bangs and booms blasted
over the speakers. She swallowed with difficulty and pulled
herself away from the scene, her eyes tearing once again.

She hadn't taken two steps when his voice called after
her.

"Mom!"

She stopped and turned back to face him.

He was holding the sandwich in one hand, waving it in
her direction. "You didn't put any jelly on it!"

She shook her head numbly. "Must've been thinking
about something else," she said, forcing a meek smile of
embarrassment. "Give it here."

He handed her the plate and returned to his game without
another word, transfixed by the constant stimulation of sight
and sound. She went back into the kitchen, the shock of the
previous hour enshrouding her like a thick fog of uncertainty.

'How can I make a peanut butter sandwich here in the same house where that…. man attacked me?' she wondered. *'How is it even possible?'*

It took some time to locate the jelly and disassemble the sandwich, perhaps quite a bit of time. Everything seemed so… difficult, as if she were living underwater, or pushing her way through quicksand. By the time she returned to the living room, Jackie had moved on to another game.

"Here it is," she announced. "Here's your sandwich."

"I thought you forgot," he said as he took it from her hand. "Did you forget?"

"Of course not. How could I forget *you*?" Her smile felt lopsided.

He smiled back but his look was guarded, questioning.

"I'm fine, really," she said.

He peeled back the top slice of bread to make certain the jelly was in its proper place. When he saw it was, he nodded his acceptance. She felt irrationally pleased.

Without a focal point to anchor her thoughts, she wandered aimlessly through their little home as if rediscovering it after a long absence. It all seemed familiar yet utterly strange, changed in a way she could not elucidate but understood intuitively. Like returning to your old high school for your fifth reunion and realizing that while everything looked the same, it felt different. Not so completely hers, not so welcoming, not so safe.

She stopped at the closed door of her bedroom, determined to go inside yet quaking at the very thought. She rested her hand on the brass doorknob, willing the coolness of the metal into her hand like some talisman. With a deep breath, she turned the knob and pushed open the door. The tainted stench of *him* clawed at her throat, forcing her hand to her mouth to stop her from gagging. A wave of revulsion and anger and shame pushed her inside the room where she tore the soiled sheets from her bed and wadded them into a large ball. She ran through the hallway, out into the garage where she jammed the sheets into a trash can and quickly slammed the lid, as if she feared releasing the evil ensnared in them into another part of the house. It wasn't until the sharp metallic echo of that act faded to silence that she realized she'd been holding her breath. She turned away from the trashcans and threw open the back door, sucking in a gasp of fresh air.

'What now? How can a life so shattered ever return to normalcy?'

She lowered herself clumsily to the concrete steps and began to sob – softly at first, and then not so softly.

CHAPTER 2

When the morning sun fell across her sleeping face, Janice opened her eyes to confusion bordering on panic. Her memories were fragmented, hazy, much as if she'd downed a fifth of hard stuff the night before. Or that's how she imagined it would be, since - except for the months just before and just after her divorce - she'd rarely imbibed more than a drink or two at one time. She shifted her weight as if to roll over and a stab of pain cut through her guts, a pain that validated her remembrance even as it shook her to her core.

Her heart suddenly skipped a beat: *Jackie! Is Jackie okay?*

Ignoring the pain, she jumped out of bed and ran to her son's bedroom. The door was open and his bed was empty!

"Jackie! Jackie, where are you!?" she began to shout, running down the hallway. "JACKIE!"

She stumbled into the living room to find him, an empty glass of orange juice by his side, watching cartoons on TV.

"Mama?" He almost never called her Mama. She followed his wide-eyed gaze and tried to imagine what he was thinking as she stood there in just her ex's old t-shirt, her hair sticking out every which way, her eyes wild with concern.

She forced a smile. "I couldn't find you."

"I've been right here, watching 'toons," he said.

"Yes, well it's getting late. You need to wash-up and get ready for school."

"Just five more minutes?"

It was the same every morning, and every morning she told him *'No, turn it off – now!'* This morning she couldn't bring herself to spoil his fun. "Okay, but just five minutes."

He flashed a big, self-satisfied smile and turned back to the screen.

It was a battle that morning, getting herself going. Nothing was easy; everything seemed a little *off*, almost as if her every movement created echoes in some parallel universe that only she could perceive. But she made her son an English muffin and a glass of chocolate milk, and stayed after him until he got himself into presentable shape for school. She debated whether to go to work but decided against it. She felt just a bit guilty telling the other secretary she was having 'stomach troubles', knowing it was a busy time with too few people, but when she was honest with herself she had to admit there was no way she was ready to go in. Her brain was all over the place and there were things she had to do - the job would have to wait.

She managed to drive Jackie to school without incident – they missed the bus – but without his constant chatter to distract her the drive home was challenging. Twice she found herself drifting across the center line as her thoughts drifted to the attack. By the time she arrived back home she was sweating, her hands cramped on the steering wheel from the emotional strain.

She wanted to just crawl back into bed and forget the whole thing ever happened, but she knew that was as irresponsible as it was impossible. The intruder had been *inside* her. She'd wiped away blood. What if he'd given her an STD; what if he had AIDS? The thought brought a flood of acid into her throat.

She sat at the kitchen table nursing a cup of tea, savoring the quiet, the simple tranquility of being alone. It took her a while to build up the strength, the courage to make the call to her doctor's office. She told the receptionist she'd been feeling sick to her stomach. It wasn't a lie, not really. But she couldn't bear to share the details with anyone just yet, certainly not with someone she barely knew.

The rest of the morning evaporated in simple tasks that nonetheless confounded her. A shower, getting dressed, blow-drying her hair, putting dishes in the dishwasher: every task became a mountain to climb, a challenge requiring every ounce of concentration she could muster. By the time her 11 a.m. appointment arrived, she wanted nothing more than to curl up on the sofa and melt into the cushions. But she was a mother; even if she could be cavalier about her own health, she owed it to Jackie to make sure his mother stayed healthy. So she called the sitter, dragged herself from the sofa to the car, then from the car to the office. Sitting there in the uncomfortable straight-backed chair in the reception area, looking around at the handful of other patients awaiting their appointment, she couldn't shake the feeling that they all knew why she was there, they all knew what he'd done to her.

Angela, Dr. McConnell, was an old friend, going all the way back to college. Janice had been one of her first patients when she'd opened her own gynecology office just a few years after med school, and had been a loyal patient ever since. But despite their friendship, despite the burning need she felt to share the details of what had happened to her, Janice had decided to keep silent about the attack. The pain of keeping quiet was far less intimidating than the pain she knew she'd feel if she shared the horror of that moment. She tried to keep a neutral expression and a level voice when Angela finally came into the examination room.

"Hey there, Janice – has it been a year already?" she asked as she picked up her medical records folder and flipped through the first few pages.

"I… I'm not sure. But like you always say: better safe than sorry." Her sing-song cheerfulness sounded phony to her ears, but Angela didn't react.

"Any problems? Anything bothering you?"

For just the slightest of moments she considered blurting it all out, telling her friend every wretched detail, purging her system of the poison she knew was killing her. But when she looked into Angela's face and saw the calm professionalism there, she balked.

"No, nothing in particular."

"Okay. Then let's get you lying back there on the table and we'll get to it. Assume the position," she said, no hint of levity in her voice.

"Ten four."

Angela kept up a constant stream of chit-chat as she donned the green acetate gloves and organized her instruments. Janice wasn't really listening, her thoughts veering dangerously close to the pain and humiliation of the day before.

"This may feel a little uncomfortable," the doctor said, and despite straining to relax Janice flinched when the cold speculum pushed into place.

"Sorry. Did I hurt you?"

"No, it's okay," she said through clenched teeth.

"Everything looks fine down here," Angela said moments later, half to herself. "Just the usual exam?"

"I… uh, I think I'd like an STD test. And HIV." She felt her cheeks burn.

"Oh. Getting back into the scene, are we?" It was obvious she was joking, but something cracked inside Janice and her forced laugh erupted into a strangled groan.

Angela stood up and moved to where Janice could see her face more clearly.

"Are you all right?"

Janice struggled with her emotions. "I... I..."

And then it all broke loose. As she described the attack and its aftermath, the look on Angela's face morphed from concern to surprise to anger.

"Did he hurt you?" she asked softly when Janice paused to wipe away tears.

"He hit me once." She wasn't going to talk about the other.

"You need to call the police, Janice. If that guy thinks he can get away with it he may be tempted to do it again, to another woman."

"I don't know if I can handle it: all the interviews and the reports..."

"You can handle it. You're one of the strongest women I know. I'll be there with you, if you want."

A warm glow of gratitude pulsed through her chest, at the same time fear and embarrassment gripped her innards.

"Thank you, Angela. You're a good friend."

"We need to support each other, particularly at times like these."

She shook her head. "Everyone will know."

"No one will blame you. They'll know you were attacked."

"But Jackie's friends will know, and worse still, their parents. I don't think I can handle their sympathy, or even the looks."

"Janice, I won't lie to you, it won't be easy. I've been through it with other patients. But you'll get through it, and when you do you'll not only get this creep off the streets but you'll start your own healing. There's nothing as liberating as seeing the schmuck led off to prison in handcuffs."

"I'd pay to see that." The guttural growl in her voice surprised even her.

"So? Do you want to make the call from here?"

Janice knew her friend was right, that she owed it to the community to help put the guy behind bars. But what if he somehow got off? What if he came looking for revenge? And how could she possibly testify before an entire courtroom about the things he'd done to her? It made her short of breath just to think about it.

"I don't know," she said. "I don't know if I can do it."

"I'll be there for you, and we'll get you a counsellor who'll help you through it."

Janice stared out the window, unseeing.

"Jan?"

She knew this would be one of the biggest decisions of her life, and that whatever she decided part of her would be dissatisfied, if not outright disappointed. There was no way to win. But in the end, she refused to be a victim, she refused to let the bastard get away with it.

"Okay. Who do I call?"

Angela had the number for the Special Victims Unit saved in her cellphone. Somehow that made it seem less out of the ordinary to Janice, less of a life-changing event.

A woman answered the phone, surprising Janice. She was professional, maybe a bit curt, but understanding and supportive. In just a minute or two Jan had managed to relive the bare bones of the attack and agreed to come "down to headquarters" to give a more detailed rundown of what had transpired.

When she disconnected the call she felt better, more solid, less likely to crumble and blow away.

"So?" Angela asked.

"They want me to go down there to explain what happened."

"I'll go with you, if you want."

She almost agreed, almost accepted the offer. But something stopped her. Not pride, exactly, not completely. She *wanted* to do this, maybe even needed to. For the first time since the attack she felt like she was in control, if only a little. She was more than just a helpless bystander.

"No, but thanks. I think I can do it myself."

"Yeh, I think you can," Angela said. "You're going to get through this, you know that?"

She forced a crooked smile. "Yeh, I know."

Angela opened a cupboard above the sink and took out a vial of pills, pouring a few into a smaller container.

"Here," she said, offering it to Janice. "In case you have trouble sleeping."

"What is it?"

"Ambien. Just don't take it with alcohol."

"I don't like sleeping pills."

"And I don't normally prescribe them, unless there's a real need."

For a few awkward moments neither said a word. It was as if they'd found a point of equilibrium and didn't dare tip the balance.

Angela spoke first. "They say anything about the kit?"

"Kit?"

From the way her friend nodded with a small grimace, she knew it wouldn't be something to look forward to.

"There's a rape kit. They're going to ask you to let them take a swab. For DNA."

She winced.

"It doesn't hurt." Angela sounded as if she was trying to persuade a child to get her shots.

"You've had it done?" Janice knew she was being petty, but she couldn't help herself.

"No, no I haven't," her friend answered, visibly chastened. "But I've spoken with a number of my patients who have – unfortunately."

Jan nodded. "I'll get through it."

"You'll get through all of this, honey, I promise you. And anything I can do, you let me know, okay?"

Janice didn't know if it was her friend or her doctor talking to her, but it didn't matter. She'd decided to go after the bastard who'd done this to her, and that was that.

*****

She had planned on going back home and having a cup of coffee after the visit to Angela's office, but with the visit to the police station hanging over her she quickly realized she wouldn't be able to relax at all until it was done with. So with nothing but a deep breath and a steely promise to do as she'd promised, she drove the short distance to the police station, her mind awhirl with thoughts and emotions she could neither banish nor control. It was a plain brick building, probably constructed in the Fifties or Sixties with the telltale small windows and stainless-steel cut-out lettering that probably looked spiffy and innovative back then but now looked like nothing more than a sterile, outdated government outpost. She parked in the small lot next to the building, thankful that only two of the twenty-something spots were occupied.

As she walked from her car to the station, she realized she had never entered a police station before – not for any reason. Certainly not as a victim. She felt an eerie sense of unreality as she walked up the concrete steps, a feeling of disassociation from everything surrounding her. As soon as she stepped through the heavy glass doors, she had second thoughts. The quiet, sterile room she entered was completely unlike the bustling city precinct offices she'd seen in all the TV dramas. She hesitated just a second to gain her bearings, but a middle-aged woman sitting behind a desk marked *Information* didn't let her indecision overwhelm her shaky determination.

"May I help you?" the un-uniformed woman asked sweetly.

"I…uh…" she glanced around to see if anyone was listening-in, but no one else seemed aware of her existence. She shuffled closer to the receptionist and dropped her voice to scarcely more than a whisper. "I'd like to report a crime?" She sounded unsure to her own ears.

"Okay. What kind of crime?"

Janice felt her face flush. She leaned in closer to the woman and barely whispered, "A rape."

She didn't know what she'd expected, perhaps shock or pained sympathy, or… something out of the ordinary. Certainly not casual acceptance.

"I'm sorry to hear that," the woman said even as she rifled through some papers to find a form. "Were you the victim?"

She had to swallow to say the words. "I was."

"Were you hurt? Do you need any medical assistance?"

"I've been to my doctor."

"Good, good. Your name?"

Janice gave it to her, spelling the last name to be sure it was entered correctly. Everyone seemed to want to spell Greyson with an *a* instead of an *e*.

"Very good. If you would just have a seat and fill out this report, I'll get someone out here to talk with you in just a few minutes." She handed Janice the form on a battered clipboard with a cheap Chinese pen clipped to the top. Janice took it as though in a dream and half-sat, half-collapsed into one of the molded plastic chairs. The information was basic: name, address, and what happened? She wasn't sure how much detail to provide and started to tell everything at first until she decided to stick to the basics, assuming the details could all come out in the interview. She was in no mood to repeat everything twice.

She'd just finished making a couple of editorial changes to her brief declaration when an interior door opened and an attractive young woman about 28 came striding out. Janice didn't know how she knew, but perhaps it was the simple white blouse and navy-blue pants – she was a cop.

"Mrs. Greyson?" the woman asked.

"Yes, that's me."

"Mrs. Greyson, I'm Officer Daniels. I understand you were attacked."

"*Raped*," she said with emphasis. Suddenly it was important the officer understood.

"Yes, I'm terribly sorry. Are you done with the data sheet?"

Her eyes led Janice to the form in her hands. "I didn't know how much detail to include…"

"Don't worry, you can tell us all about it inside."

"*Us?*" It just slipped out. She'd been hoping she could speak to only the one officer.

"My partner and me. Don't worry, he's a good guy."

It was as if she was joining some club or secret society. "Okay."

"Can you follow me, please?"

The officer led her back through the same door into a larger room that more closely resembled the prototypic police station from TV. A half-dozen desks buried beneath dozens of manila files sat crammed into the limited space, with old-style metal file cabinets surrounding them like some kind of rusting fortification. Only one of the desks was occupied, by an older man with short graying hair and cold blue eyes in a round weathered face.

"Mrs. Greyson, this is Detective Willard," Daniels introduced.

The Detective pushed himself away from his desk like an overburdened cargo ship leaving port and struggled to his feet. She tried not to stare at the prodigious beer gut.

"Mrs. Greyson," he said as he extended his hand. "Can I get you anything to drink: coffee, water, a soda?"

"No, no thank you."

"All right then, have a seat." He motioned to a worn black leatherette-covered office chair that wouldn't have looked out of place in a garage. She sat and looked around the office as he dug through some files. Officer Daniels pulled up a second chair and sat midway between her and Willard.

"So," Daniels began, "why don't you tell us what happened."

Janice took a deep breath and launched into the story. At first, she felt as if the lump in her throat would make any thorough explanation impossible, but as she got going the words picked up a momentum of their own and began to rush from her in a torrent of fear and anger. It wasn't until she was nearing the end of her statement, until the stream of words dwindled to an awkward trickle, that she realized the two cops hadn't said a single word during the entire fifteen-minute ordeal. She felt flushed, sweaty, and her throat suddenly seemed impossibly dry.

"Sorry. Didn't mean to go on like that," she apologized when the sudden silence at her stopping seemed louder than her words had ever seemed.

"No, no, not at all," Daniels said. "That was just what we needed to hear." She glanced over at her partner. Janice thought she caught a raised eyebrow prompt.

"Yeh, that was good," Willard agreed.

Janice felt an incomprehensible sense of pride at their halting praise, a feeling that immediately generated an equally incomprehensible feeling of embarrassment. *My emotions are all screwed up,'* she thought nervously as she stared down at her fingernails. The polish was chipped; she pulled her nails into her palms and tucked them out of sight.

"Could I get that drink now?" she asked, her throat a scratchy mess.

Daniels jumped up agreeably. "Sure thing. Water okay?"

She nodded. For the first few seconds after Daniels left, Janice and the Detective sat in complete, awkward silence.

"How are you doing with this?" Willard asked out of the blue. "I mean, have you been able to handle it all okay?"

Part of her wanted to yell at the guy, "What the hell are you talking about?! Of course I'm not *handling* it okay!", but the other half realized he was trying his best to be understanding and comforting and so she swallowed her contempt.

"Yeh, okay, I guess. It's a lot to handle."

"I'm sure it is." They returned to self-conscious silence for a few seconds until Daniels came back with a plastic glass of cool water.

"Here you go."

Janice drank deeply, both to soothe her throat and to avoid saying anything more until she'd settled her nerves.

"I was just asking her how she's handling all this," Willard explained, sounding somewhat apologetic.

"And?" Daniels followed-up, her gaze panning to *The Victim.* That's how Janice thought they viewed her.

"Okay. It's... hard."

"I'm sure it is. You've spoken with someone – doctor, counsellor?"

She nodded.

"Good, good. As painful as it may be, talking it out seems to help."

Janice forced a wan smile and nodded.

"Well, one thing I can tell you is that we're gonna do all we can to get the bastard who did this to you," Willard chimed in. "Make sure he can't do it to anyone else."

"That would be good." What else could she say?

"Are you willing to look through some photographs, see if maybe you recognize anyone?" Daniels asked.

The idea of seeing the intruder's face again made her queasy, but that's why she was there, wasn't it?

They sat her in front of a computer monitor and showed her several dozen photos of "previous offenders," and when she didn't recognize any of them they dragged out a couple of old, dog-eared photo albums and repeated the process. All the men looked similar somehow. She thought it was probably their eyes. Most seemed dull, even dead, as if the spark of humanity that made them living things had sputtered or gone out. It sent a chill through her body.

But none of them looked familiar.

"Are you sure?" Willard asked. "Take your time."

She glanced at the photos once more, to be polite, but she was already sure. Did he think she could possibly forget that face?

"Nope, sorry. None of these either."

The two cops exchanged a glance that probably spoke of disappointment. "Okay, no problem," Daniels said. "Could you give an artist enough details to make a sketch?"

"I think so."

Willard excused himself and a few minutes later Daniels took her to a where her partner stood beside a different computer where a young woman was visible on-screen sitting at a desk somewhere.

"Ms. Greyson, this is Emily. She's the police sketch artist at South Branch."

"No budget for that sort of thing here," Willard explained. From his intonation she assumed he thought that was a bad thing.

After minimal pleasantries, they got down to it. Janice had done enough Facetime and Skype to feel comfortable chatting with a virtual artist, but somehow it still seemed somewhat futuristic and flimsy. But as the session continued her confidence grew. As soon as the introductions were over, Emily's photo shrank to just postage-stamp size in the upper right-hand corner while the rest of the screen was filled by a blank page where the intruder's image would grow. And grow it did. Led by very specific questions and proddings from Emily, Janice recreated *his* face feature by feature, beginning with the general head shape and evolving through hair, eye and skin color, scars and blemishes, and finally tattoos.

The final portrait was eerily reminiscent of the man. Not exact – it didn't have the rancid odor of the man and didn't give off the threatening energy that had nearly taken her breath away. But close enough. A trained police officer could recognize him if he saw the image, or at least she hoped so.

"Is that him?" Daniels asked when the sketch was complete.

She nodded. She felt as if her voice might crack or explode so she kept her mouth shut. As she stared at the sketch his eyes stared back and it was all she could do to remind herself it was only an image, only a series of body part

line drawings melded into a reasonable likeness. He couldn't
see her. He didn't know where she was. Right?

"We'll find him," Willard spoke up, his voice causing her
to start. "Don't you worry about that."

"Good job, Emily," Daniels said.

"Helps to have a good witness," the young computer
artist said, and Janice wondered if she was just being
patronizing or if she really was a good witness. On second
thought, it didn't really matter as long as they caught him.

"What now?" she asked.

"Well, we take the sketch you two just worked-up and
send it out to all our contacts throughout the country."

"And with any luck, someone sees this guy and we grab
him."

"No, I didn't mean with him. I meant with me." She
knew she sounded self-centered and whiny but she didn't
care. She was rapidly growing tired of always giving. She
wanted something back.

"How do you mean?" Daniels asked. She sounded
guarded, as if she expected some kind of dressing-down.

"Am I done here? Is there anything else you guys need?"

Daniels' face relaxed. "Oh, no, I don't think there's
anything else…" She looked over to Willard who shook his
head.

"Other than the kit," he added just as the officer was
about to give the all-clear.

Janice winced. She'd hoped to somehow avoid the final
indignation of another, cold, anonymous test at the hands of
a physician she didn't know. She *hoped* it would be a
physician.

"Oh, right," Daniels said. "Has someone talked to you about the collection of DNA evidence?"

"Just my personal doctor."

"Did she run any tests?"

"A couple." She suddenly felt too shy to share the intimate details of the nasty diseases Angela would be testing for.

"Could we have her name and contact info, please?" Willard asked. "We might need to piggyback on some of those swabs."

"Piggyback?"

"It's been a day since the attack," Daniels explained gently. "We don't know how much... evidence remains."

"Ah. Of course." She gave them Angela's name and looked up her phone number on her cell. "And the *kit*?"

"You'll have to go down to Mercy General," Willard began. "Just ask for the Rape Investigative Unit. They're very familiar with the procedure."

"But I'm not." She tightened her lips into a thin slash of displeasure.

"It's nothing to be overly concerned about," Daniels chimed in, literally stepping between Willard and Janice to stop the verbal jabbing. "I've had it done myself."

"You were *raped*?" Janice asked before she could stop herself.

"Training," the female officer admitted. "But I went through the entire procedure."

*'Not the **entire** procedure,'* Janice wanted to say, but she bit down her reply. "And?"

"A nurse or doctor takes a quick swab, asks you a few questions. That's about it. Shouldn't take more than ten minutes."

"Once you get seen."

Daniels dipped her head in tacit agreement. "Sometimes, if they're really backed-up, you might have to wait a while."

"Is it really necessary?" She was nearly sure it was but hoped there might be some wiggle room.

"It's the only way to link the guy to the crime with nearly incontestable evidence."

Janice wondered whether Willard knew what *incontestable* meant, or if he was just parroting a phrase he'd heard a thousand times before. She quickly lowered her eyes in embarrassment for categorizing the Detective. Would she want them to think of her as just another frightened, undependable victim? Probably partly responsible for the attack. No, of course not.

"Can I just go down there, or do I need an appointment of some kind?" she asked as an unspoken apology.

"We'll let them know you're on your way," Daniels said. "Will you be heading down there straight from here?"

She thought about it for an instant. "Yeh, I want to get it over with."

"Good. Then we'll tell them to expect you."

Janice did her best to push away all the pain and hurt and fear for a few seconds and thanked the two cops for all their help.

She was about to leave when one last question forced its way into her consciousness. "Do you really think you'll catch him – the intruder?"

"We'll catch him," Willard said. "Almost always do."

All she heard was *almost.*

"Don't you worry about that," Daniels quickly jumped in. "Let us take care of him."

"But what if he comes back to my house?" It was a thought she'd sublimated for twenty-four hours, but one she couldn't shake. Whenever she closed her eyes it was the first picture to come to mind. The last thought before she got out of bed. What if he *returned?*

"That rarely happens," Willard said. Daniels frowned.

"We'll ask the Captain to send a patrol car to look in on you several times a day," she said.

Janice nodded. It wasn't much; it wasn't enough. But it was something.

Daniels walked her out to the front door of the station, virtually ordering Willard to stay behind. Not that he needed much encouragement.

"You take care of yourself, hear?" he said just before he headed for the break room and a cup of coffee. Or that's what she imagined.

The lady cop seemed relieved.

"Anything we can do for you, even if you just feel like something's not quite right, you give me a call, okay?" she said, handing Janice her business card.

"Thank you. I hope I won't have to."

"So do we."

They shook hands and then Janice was on her way through the parking lot to her car. The day had grown warm and she felt waves of heat rise up off the asphalt. She tried to reflect on her time in the station but it only came back to her in bits and pieces, like a dream she'd just awakened from. *'Must still be in shock,'* she decided. She opened the door to her car and sat in the stifling heat for longer than was necessary, thinking: Would it ever be like it was *before*? Would she ever put this behind her?

She hadn't been to the hospital in a while, not since Jackie had fallen and broken his leg. Seven stitches as well. Looked worse, with all that blood.

The GPS guided her through the center of town with hardly a turn required, owing more to the paucity of routes than the capability of the machine. Her mind was so occupied she barely registered the passing sites and so was caught by surprise when the disembodied voice announced, 'You have arrived.'

She walked into another brick building from the same architectural era as the police station, a time when the town still had high hopes of growing into something more than a crossroads, a stopping point on the East-West highway for a bathroom break and a quick bite to eat on the way from somewhere more important to somewhere else more important. The flickering fluorescent lights and institutional smell made her head swim.

"May I help you?" the young black woman at the reception desk asked. Janice realized she'd probably been standing there longer than she'd been aware.

"I, ah…" she began, cozying up as close to the window as she could get without appearing suspicious, "I'm here for the Rape Investigation Unit."

"Ah. Your name?"

Janice spoke so softly the woman had to lean toward her to catch the breathy words.

"Why don't you have a seat. I'll get someone out here as soon as possible."

More molded plastic chairs. This time, several of them were occupied – an older man with a lost, glazed stare; a young mother, not much younger than herself, with a child about five or so who coughed ceaselessly as Mom fussed ineffectually, his face bright red and distorted; a teen, maybe a bit older, holding his arm as if broken. He groaned every now and then.

She ignored the green-tinted talk-show people on the busted big-screen TV, going through their normal gyrations as they issued ill-informed pontifications to over-caffeinated audiences that hung on their every ill-advised word. She thought about checking her cell phone like everyone else in a public space these days, but she was afraid what she might find and stared out the small, dirty windows at the parking lot outside instead.

"Ms. Greyson?" a woman's voice stirred her after a short (was it short?) while.

She identified herself and was shown into a small examination room off the main emergency room corridor. Just before the door closed behind her she saw the panicky eyes of the young mother with the sick child and the angry eyes of the teenager - who'd arrived before she had and was in more pain besides - reaching out to her, criticizing her for cutting in line. She felt chagrinned, but after all, what could she do?

The nurse who took the swab was professional, gentle, and about as warm as a bag of hail. Somehow Janice had thought the personnel at a hospital would be more caring and empathetic than those at a police station, but it turned out that people are people no matter where they work: some are naturally compassionate, while most look upon a customer as just one more bump in the nasty dirt road that leads to the end of the work day. At least it was over quickly.

"When will you have the results?" she asked, more to make small talk with the taciturn employee than because she really cared. It would be ready when it was ready and it would help catch the guy or it wouldn't. She realized she was slipping into benumbed cynicism but couldn't muster the energy to fight it.

The best she could do was focus on Jackie; she needed to get home and take care of her son. She'd told the sitter 'a couple of hours.' She'd probably be getting worried.

CHAPTER 3

Officer Daniels found Willard dipping a doughnut into his coffee in the break room. The heavyset Detective barely acknowledged her existence as she made her way to the coffee machine. It smelled like burnt socks, again.

"So, what d'ya think?" she asked as she poured some of the oily sludge into her stained smiley face mug.

"About the girl?" he mumbled, his mouth full of crumbling dough.

'No, the fucking Pope!' she wanted to answer, but she had learned that sarcasm only worked with people who cared what you said to them. "Yeh. What d'ya think?"

He put his mug down heavily, as if the weight of his answer had someone been transferred to the battered ceramic cup. "Waited too long for the sample. We'll be lucky to get any useable DNA."

"Oh, I don't know. I think we may get lucky."

"That's you all over, Daniels. Just one big bundle of optimism."

Hardly. In fact, she was one of the least optimistic people she knew, so far as her day-to-day dealings with 'the public' went. She couldn't remember if she'd been so cynical when she joined the force, or whether twelve years pursuing the scum of the earth had made her that way. Probably a little of both.

Sometimes she looked at the photo of her Police Academy graduation and wondered if the smiling face that looked back at her was actually her at all. Seemed more like a ghost, or maybe one of those alternate universes. She certainly looked a hell of a lot younger back then, more like a kid than a woman. Certainly not like a street cop.

When she'd announced to her parents she was skipping college to join the police force, their initial response was shock tinged with disbelief. "Sure you are," her father had said with a bemused shake of his head. "Kids. Where the hell do they come up with these hare-brained ideas?" Her mother's face had collapsed into a sink hole of desperation. "Honey, are you sure you want to do something like that?" Her anguish had almost shaken Daniels, but the decision had been made. Actually, had been made months before.

She'd decided to become a cop after she'd watched a news report about an officer somewhere who'd created a Boys & Girls Club to help some of the gangbangers he'd met on his beat. At first they'd thought he was nuts. But by the time of that news piece, the Club had gained some 60 members and most of them were planning on graduating from high school. For the first time she realized that being a cop didn't only mean chasing bad guys and getting drunks off the roadways. She could help, help the kids who could change the community, change the world.

She smiled into her cup of coffee. *Did I really believe all that crap?'*

Twelve years later she struggled to make it through the day on more occasions than she'd care to admit, barely tolerating all the macho, sexist, racist bullshit that flowed through the headquarters like some toxic river of hate. As a woman, she'd had to play the game, appearing every bit as macho as the toughest ex-Marine who cracked heads and laughed about it over beers at the local cop hangout. But all the while she maintained a small sliver of her true self, walled-off from the testosterone-fueled mayhem of day-to-day patrolling. It was days like this one, and cases like this Greyson thing, that reminded her what really mattered. She could help this woman, help her get through the trauma that even now threatened to derail her perfectly fine middle-class life. The main thing was to find the asshole who raped her.

To that end, she made a call to Mercy to goose the system into producing a report on any identifiable DNA they were able to salvage that morning. She knew it was a longshot, despite her feigned optimism with Willard. Oh, they might find something, maybe even pull a reasonably full sequence. But the odds of matching it with some scumball already in the system were small, despite all the movies suggesting it was nearly a slam dunk. But if she didn't stay on their asses down there at the hospital, it could be a week or more before they even sent the results.

So she called.

"Jesus, Daniels," one of the RIU nurses said when she heard the request, "we just scraped her this morning. Give us a couple of hours at the minimum."

"Just let me know when you've got it," she'd answered. "Day or night, call." She knew the 24-hour bit would circulate through the staff down there in matter of minutes, and anyone who gave a damn would push the tests through the system as quickly as possible. Past the indigents and druggies, past everyone except the very rich and connected. If a cop showed interest in a rape case, the hospital staff usually played along and made things happen. Daniels might not be the most popular cop in the precinct, but she was a woman and so were most of the hospital people who ran the tests. Occasionally the lack of a Y chromosome paid off for her.

It was later that afternoon, after five in fact, when the phone on her desk rang. It was the hospital. Not only had they been able to pull some decent swabs, but they'd struck paydirt in the computerized DNA archives: Daniel Lee Archer, a 23-year-old who'd been busted for B&E not six months earlier.

Daniels typed the ID into her own computer and out popped the history and mugshots. Kid didn't look like much in the photos, not at all the monster the victim's report had suggested. But evil is in the eye of the beholder, she figured, and for Mrs. Greyson this SOB was the devil incarnate. She printed out the basics of a new file and plopped it down on Willard's desk just as he was pulling on his sports jacket to head home.

"What's that?" he asked, not so much with curiosity as hostility.

"Mercy matched the DNA on the Greyson perp. B&E conviction less than a year ago. Twenty-three-year-old named Daniel Lee Archer."

"Yeh? Got lucky, huh? I'll take a look at it tomorrow."

Part of her wanted to grab him by that ugly ass tie of his and pound his face into his desk until he saw the error of his ways, but the rational part realized she was more pissed off at the perp than Willard and nothing much would likely be accomplished overnight anyway. Besides, pissing him off would only make everything so much harder down the road.

"I'm gonna request a warrant," she said.

"Aren't you going to wait for the independent lab to reconfirm?"

"I got a feeling he's the one. I'm putting in the paperwork."

"You do that. If your luck holds, maybe he'll be sitting in his living room when they pop him."

Maybe. But the odds weren't good.

CHAPTER 4

As she pulled into her driveway, Jan was struck by how small and grim her house looked in the dim twilight. Or was it just her frame of mind? Twenty-four hours after the attack and, if anything, she was feeling even worse than she had in the immediate aftermath. Then she was largely numb, still hopeful that he would be quickly caught and punished. Now... she didn't know. The numbness had worn off and the full impact of his attack had fully set-in. The police weren't going to catch him quickly, or not as quickly as she wished. Maybe never. The thought of that possibility, the disgusting sensation of helplessness, had crawled deep into her gut and lay there like a ticking time bomb, ready to explode without warning or reason.

She opened the door and Jackie's smiling face and squeal of pleasure caught her by surprise and nearly knocked her back on her heels. How could anyone be so happy in a world so bereft of fairness and reason?

But one hug, one "Mommy!" and the ice that encased her heart shattered into a million pieces. She struggled to keep tears from forming.

"How's my boy?" she called out, hoping to dispel any unanswerable questions before they could arise. She hugged him so hard he wiggled furiously to escape the crush of her emotion.

"There you are!" the sitter called out as she strolled into the entryway. "I was beginning to worry."

"I'm so sorry. I got caught up in all the paperwork – the police, the hospital..."

"It's okay, I understand. How did it go?"

She shrugged and was saved from further commentary by the insistent tug of her son's hand on her arm.

"Mommy, mommy, we drew a dragon. A purple dragon!"

"He did a really good job of it," the sitter said. "He definitely shows artistic ability."

Jackie beamed.

"Come on, Mom," he said, pulling furiously on her arm. "Come see."

She let him pull her along, all the disappointments and fears of the previous few hours sloughing off like so much dead skin, not that the scars weren't all too visible from her point of view. She laughed and admired his work, giving him another big hug, but for all her efforts she could not shake the cloud that engulfed her, that followed her every step and haunted her every thought. It was if she were watching her own life through a gauzy filter, a filter not only of sight and sound but of emotion as well. She felt... sodden, heavy, the effort required to accomplish the simplest of acts nearly overwhelming.

She thanked the sitter even as she parried the obvious worry in her eyes and expression.

"Are you okay?" became an opening for complaints about the police interview and the hospital tests. She could see her dissembling almost achieving its goal, almost convincing the rumpled woman sitting at the kitchen table of Janice's sound mind and strong spirit. Almost, but not quite. Even in her lessened state, Janice could feel if not fully rationalize the concern in the woman's chatter. It was as if she was afraid to leave Janice alone.

After a polite twenty minutes or so, she brought the farcical theater to a halt.

"Can I give you a ride home?" she asked, even though the sitter had shown no eagerness to leave.

"Uh, no, no that's okay. I drove over."

For just an instant Janice was embarrassed, not having seen the familiar red VW Bug parked in front of the house. But the embarrassment passed before she could answer, and the sitter had nowhere to go but home.

Janice played with Jackie for the next couple of hours, each of them needing the reassurance of the other's presence. Jackie was uncharacteristically clinging, only allowing her out of his presence to use the bathroom, and that with some objection. If she had ever wondered whether the invasion had affected him as well, she had her answer.

For dinner she cooked his favorite – macaroni and cheese – and after an evening of online children's shows and a broadcast repeat of Sesame Street, she carried him to his room at long past bedtime. Even as his eyes were shutting of their own accord, he fought against sleep with the fervor of a drowning man, jerking awake from time to time as she read from one of his favorite bedtime books. Finally, at nearly 11 pm, he fell off to sleep.

She sat on the side of his bed for many minutes after that, staring down at his sleeping face with pride, love, and not a little worry. What would she do if anything ever happened to him? How could she live? Why would she even consider it?

She left his door ajar just a crack, enough to provide some light if he should awaken during the night but not so much that her movements would provide any reason for wakefulness. She walked stealthily back to her own bedroom, but after just one step inside she stopped as if struck. The sense of the previous night, the memories that assaulted her, literally paralyzed her legs. Her heart thundered and she felt a wave of anxious nausea sweep through her gut.

'*Nope, not yet,*' she decided, and grabbing her long flannel nightgown off the hook on the back of the door, she hurried nervously to the spare bedroom. A single bed and old battered bureau looked lonely and abandoned in the otherwise empty room, but the close confines appealed to her just then. She exhaled a breath she didn't realize she was holding and began to close the door behind her. It was only when the sound of the door latch clicking into place echoed throughout the silent house that she realized what she was doing and opened it back up several inches. She leaned her head out the half-open door and listened intently for… what? *Anything.* Any unexpected sound from anything that shouldn't be there. The hum of the a/c was the only noise to besmirch the quiet.

Brushing her teeth, a task so commonplace, so often repeated that she had never even thought about it before, became a tense struggle to finish as quickly as possible – to turn off the running water before it could provide aural cover for anyone who might try to break in. Even after she'd dimmed the lights and pulled the covers up to her chin, sleep danced just out of reach as her exhausted body performed a tug-of-war with her over-active mind. She tried to read, but the words didn't stick and she found herself re-reading sentence after sentence.

Just as sleep finally began to overtake her tattered defenses, just as her focus shimmied and swam, she heard a sound. '*What was that?*' She held her breath, listening so intently the muscles in her shoulders began to ache. '*There: was that it again?*' For just a second she toyed with calling 911, but as she played the potential conversation in her mind she saw the problem with calling an emergency number to report a possible *sound*. Hardly urgent.

The only other solution held no real attraction, however. Getting up out of her nice warm, seemingly safe bed to check the house offered little reward and evident downside. Yet she couldn't just lie there...

She half-sighed, half-groaned and threw her legs over the side of the bed. She grabbed the flashlight she always kept on the side table and slipped her feet into her comfy lambswool slippers. With one last grunt she was up and moving.

Why is it that everything at night seems so much more sinister than during the day? We all know the location of virtually every item in our homes, yet under the coherent beam of an LED flashlight it all looks like an alien spacescape. Furniture looms out of shadows; darkness encroaches on either side of the beam like some deathly fog.

Janice made her way as carefully and quietly as her anxious legs permitted, out of her bedroom and down the corridor toward the living room. She'd only taken a few steps when she heard the same noise, only closer and more distinct. Without thinking, she flicked off the flashlight and stood very still in the middle of the hallway, her thoughts racing her heartbeat. She was just about to admit to hearing things when a dim shadow appeared beyond the corridor wall, coming her way. She screamed, a blood-curdling yell followed almost immediately by a crash and the sound of breaking glass. Her hands shaking, she managed to turn on the flashlight to reveal Jackie, his eyes as wide as platters, a bowl of spilled milk and cereal lying in the middle of the hall. He looked about to cry.

"Mom – are you crazy?!" he yelled.

She squeezed her eyes shut and opened them with a forced smile.

"Sorry, champ," she said, moving toward him with the slow measured steps of a rancher approaching a spooked calf. "Didn't expect to see you this time of night."

"I got hungry," he mumbled, seemingly close to tears now that the adrenaline had burned off.

"Did I scare you?" she asked, bending down to give him a big hug.

"A little."

"Well you certainly scared me, I can tell you that."

He stared into her face as if searching for something.

"Did you think it was *him*?" he finally asked.

"Who?" She knew, but didn't want to admit it.

"The guy, the one who broke in."

In a split second she debated whether to lie to protect him or tell the truth to make him aware. She decided on the latter.

"Yeh, I guess I thought it might be him."

"You think he's going to come back?" The quiver to his lip made her heart melt.

"No, buddy, I don't think he's going to come back. I was just being a scaredy-cat."

The quiver stopped. "Made a mess, didn't I."

She glanced down at the slow spread of milk with the flotsam and jetsam of multi-colored edible animal forms. "Not so bad. I'll clean it up for you. Still want cereal?"

For the first time some life came back into his face. "Will you get it for me?"

"Please…"

"Please." He scrunched up his nose and tilted his head with a familiar begging expression.

The smile that spread across her face felt real, intrinsic, not some mask she needed to protect him. It felt good to smile, really smile.

"Go hop into bed. I'll bring it to you."

Unexpectedly, he reached up and gave her a big hug.

"What's that for?" she asked.

"Just because," he said, and in that echo of his father she felt a stab of... loneliness? Maybe more like nostalgia. She mussed his hair and sent him off to his room with a gentle shove.

She flipped on the kitchen lights and with a headshake wondered why she hadn't simply done the same when she first heard the unexpected noise. She decided it was to keep from seeing too much too fast – if it was something bad, maybe it wouldn't cause so much pain if she saw only a piece at a time. As she poured first the cereal and then the milk, her eyes glanced into the inky blackness just outside the kitchen windows, a blackness that whispered of unseen threats and incontestable evil. She shook off the chill that ran through her body and quickly carried the cereal to her son's room.

"Here you go," she said, setting it down on the side table next to his bed. He was looking at his iPad and barely looked up at her.

"Thanks, Mom," he muttered.

"What ya' lookin' at?"

"Just stuff." His focus was, as usual, nearly total. Sometimes she'd call to him while he was busy surfing and he literally didn't hear a word she said.

She was going to ask what kind of *stuff* but decided to just peek over his shoulder instead. She was taken aback to see a martial arts video of some kind, two slim Asian men throwing each other to the ground, blocking chops and kicks, and generally emulating all the old Bruce Lee moves.

"Wow. Those guys look pretty tough," she said. "What is that – kung-fu?"

Her son looked up at her in disbelief. "*Taekwondo*, Mom."

"Ah, right. I didn't know you were interested."

"Just looking."

"Any reason in particular?"

"Just in case."

"In case of what?"

"You know – in case *he* comes again. I can protect you."

She swallowed the lump in her throat that suddenly threatened to choke her. "That's very brave of you, but he won't come back again." She tried to sound confident.

"Why not?"

She hesitated. "Because he knows the police are watching our house. He doesn't want them to catch him."

"Will they – catch him?"

His face was so open, so hopeful, she didn't dare share her fears. "Of course they will. They always catch the bad guys."

"What about Lex Luther? They never catch him."

She didn't know whether to laugh or cry. "This guy isn't Lex Luther. They'll catch him. Now why don't you turn that off and finish your cereal. It's way past bedtime."

She bent down and gave him a kiss on his forehead before starting back to her own room, pausing in the doorway to take one last peek before partially closing the door. As she walked through the darkened hallway her son's words about the intruder's possible return kept echoing through her mind: "Why not?"

Why not indeed…

*****

She lay in bed staring at the ceiling for what seemed like hours, her mind racing. The attack replayed in a dozen differing scenarios – what she *could* have done; what she *should* have done. Eventually she couldn't stand the confines of her covers and so made her way to the bathroom where she opened the medicine cabinet and took out the sleeping pills Angela had given her. She read the warning dismissively: how many people took a sleeping pill and then tried to drive farm machinery? Still, she swallowed the pill with some reluctance. If anything *did* happen, she wanted to be sharp, on her toes…

She didn't know how long she'd been asleep – it might have been minutes, maybe hours. But with a gasp of recognition she found herself wide awake again, sitting up in bed. *Was that glass breaking?*

As she reached for the flashlight, she was surprised to realize she wasn't wearing her nightgown. When had she taken it off? Her anxiety about taking the pills resurfaced; she'd have to be careful. The floorboards were cool underfoot, but the chill she felt came from the sense that someone was inside the house, a feeling that both unnerved and motivated her. Should she call the police? Not this time. This time she wasn't going to be a victim, wasn't going to cower in some corner waiting for the cops to arrive – or not.

She opened her closet to search for something heavy and grabbed a baseball bat that leaned against the back wall. *'When did I put this here?'* she wondered even as she took a couple of short, choppy swings to test its heft. She felt a surge of power, of control. *This time it's going to be different. This time, I'll dictate the rules.'*

She threw open her bedroom door and marched down the hallway with *attitude. 'Just let him show his face. I dare him.'* The fact that she was stark naked did not bother her, did not enter into her thoughts. She was focused, determined. Nothing and no one was going to stop her…

A hand reached out from the spare bedroom and clamped tight across her mouth while another grabbed the bat and tossed it dismissively off to one side. *'Where had he come from? Was it the same guy?'* The odor that wafted past her nose answered the second question: the sour reek was unquestionably from the same intruder. She struggled to break his grip, but it was as if he were made of stone – he didn't waver, didn't weaken, but began to drag her back into the bedroom. She kicked, she bit at his hand, but still he dragged… and dragged… and dragged her deeper into the shadows. How could it be? How could he drag her so far in the limited confines of the small bedroom? She tried to twist away from him but the next thing she knew she was on the bed and he was on top of her and she saw those eyes, those wild, crazed eyes and she knew what he was going to do. She tried to cry out, but no sound came. It was happening again! It was happening…

Janice awoke drenched in sweat, her breaths coming in short gasping pants. It took several long seconds for her vision to clear and several more to gain control of her wits. It was just a dream, just a drug-induced nightmare! There wasn't anyone inside the house, no one threatening them. She was safe. Jackie was safe. She began to sob, both from relief and from the realization that the dream had come from within her, from the fears she harbored, from the doubts she'd been unable to dispel.

By the time she'd stopped her hands from shaking the green numerals on her bedside alarm clock read 3:42 and she knew it would be difficult if not impossible to get back to sleep before she needed to get up at 6:00. She threw back the covers and turned on a light, the brightness seeming as unreal as the dream. She could feel where her sweat-drenched nightgown stuck to her skin; in one impulsive move she pulled it off over her head and threw it into a corner.

It would almost be funny – her, standing stark naked in the middle of her room at quarter to four in the morning, her matted hair sticking out every which way, her red-rimmed eyes staring like some madwoman's. But she couldn't make herself laugh, or even smile. In fact, it was all she could do to keep herself from crying – again. It seemed like that was all she wanted to do. Cry. Or shrivel up in a tight little ball and hide in some dark corner somewhere, where no one could find her, where *he* couldn't find her.

She sat heavily on the bed, eying her reflection in the dresser mirror like some virtual horror show, a living nightmare. *How could this be? How could it happen to her?*

Whether it was the sleeping pills or the hour or everything from the previous days combined, she suddenly felt like a desiccated husk, absolutely exhausted, empty, drained of even the energy to cry. She let herself drift back into the mattress, her world spinning slowly like a dying merry-go-round, and with the lights still shining brightly she closed her eyes and slept, a deep, dreamless sleep.

*****

She awoke to a loud pounding.

Her head encased in a cloud of spent-sleep fog, she struggled to sit up in bed and focus. *What the hell is that?'* Her first thought was that Jackie had gotten up and was building something. But the sound was too loud, too urgent for that kind of pounding. She considered letting it go, letting it pound itself out. But the urgency pricked her curiosity. She threw on a sweatshirt and shorts and stumbled out to see what was going on.

The glare from the open front door nearly blinded her, but even that wasn't enough to quell the lance of fear that stabbed at her insides.

"Jackie – I told you never to open the door..."

"It's Grandma, Mommy! It's Grandma!"

As her eyes adjusted to the morning light, she could make out her mother kneeling by Jackie's side, giving him a big, grandmotherly hug. She struggled awkwardly to her feet and stood facing Janice, a look somewhere between trepidation and hopefulness trapped in her eyes.

"Mom?" This was so unexpected, so out of context, she didn't know whether to feel angry or pleased.

"I don't suppose you'd believe I was just in the neighborhood?" The smile wavered, as if melting under her daughter's stunned glare.

"No, but that doesn't mean you need to stay there in the doorway. Come in, come in." She stepped forward and grabbed her mother's rolling suitcase before she could object.

"You're looking good." In fact, her mother was looking, for the first time ever, her age. Her hair had turned entirely gray – or she'd stopped dyeing it, and her 5' 2" frame was slightly more rounded than the last time she'd laid eyes on her. Of course, that had been… was it two, no three years earlier. Could it be that long?

"You look tired," her mother shot back. No filter there.

"It's been a rough couple of days."

She could see the pain spread across her features like a slow-motion mudslide. "I know. That's why I'm here. I got a call from Angela… Don't be angry!" For just a moment Janice didn't know what to say, how to react, and in that second her mother stepped forward and threw her arms around her in an all-encompassing bear hug unlike any she'd experienced for quite some time. Despite the surprise, she would have made it through the moment except for the short husky-voiced message whispered in her ear. "I love you."

With that, the damn broke. She found herself sobbing uncontrollably into her mother's shoulder, all semblance of adult conduct and propriety out the window.

"It's alright, honey. Everything will be alright," her mother cooed, patting her lightly on the back. The tableau reminded her of many similar moments when she'd been a little girl.

"Mommy, why are you crying?" a tiny, anxious voice asked.

She pulled away from her mother, who gave ground only grudgingly. She wiped at her tears with the backs of her hands and tried to sniffle away her runny nose.

"It's nothing, sweetie," she said, bending down to hug him. "I'm just glad to see Grandma."

"Me too!" he said, all sadness and worry chased away in a twinkling.

"Why don't you show her the puzzle you've been working on," she said, "while I take Grandma's bag to her room."

"Grandma has a room?"

Despite the shakiness that still plagued her knees, a smile erupted before she could reason it away.

"She does! She'll be staying in the spare room."

"How long, how long, Grandma?" Jackie, asked, pulling her along by the hand.

Jackie's mother looked back over her shoulder with a questioning glance.

"I'm not sure, sweetie. A few days anyway."

"Yay!"

Janice surprised herself by agreeing with the sentiment.

*****

With Jackie monopolizing most of her mother's time, *the talk* Janice knew was coming was – thankfully – delayed until after Jackie was put to bed. She kept to her usual nightly tasks, feigning ignorance of the impending heart-to-heart until it could be ignored no longer.

"Honey, Jan – would you like to sit down and talk a little?" her mother asked once the house had eased into the gentle quiet that presaged an attempt at sleep.

'*Not really,*' she wanted to answer, but she knew full-well her mother would not give up until *the talk* was a fait accompli and so caught herself before she could blurt the truth. "Sure Mom. Can I get you a cup of tea, or anything?"

"No, I'm fine. Come here, sit next to me." She patted the sofa cushion.

Janice smiled agreeably even as she sighed inside.

"So, how are you doing – really?" she asked even before Janice had found a comfortable spot from which to withstand the siege. "Angela said you were pretty shook up when you came in to see her."

"Good. I'm doing good."

Her mother's look became an unapologetic stare. "Really? Because it would be completely understandable for you to feel…" She searched for a word.

"Conflicted?" Janice offered, feeling just a tiny bit of satisfaction in tweaking her mom.

"Yes, conflicted. You've been through quite a lot."

'*More than you know,*' she resisted saying. "I know, Mom, but I'm okay."

Before she could react, her mother had taken her hand in her own and was patting it reassuringly. "It wasn't your fault. Sometimes bad things happen to good people."

A strangled growl of sarcastic disregard was twisted into a clearing of her throat, not without considerable effort. "I know, Mom."

"It's nothing to be ashamed of."

Her jaw twitched. "Uh huh."

"Would you like to talk about it?"

Janice took a deep breath through her nose and exhaled slowly through her mouth. "Not really."

"They say it's important for victims to talk, so they don't keep it all inside."

"I've talked to Angela, and the police – I'm getting it out."

"But are you talking to them about your feelings? About all that's happened?"

Part of Janice wanted to bite her mother's head off. Another part, however, had to admit she hadn't shared her deepest feelings with anyone, nor could she deny that it might be cathartic. But her *mom*?

"What can I say?"

"Anything. Everything."

She rolled the words around in her mouth, almost like dice before a crap shoot. "It's hard, Mom."

"Take your time."

She did. And then a little longer besides until it began to feel as if an electrical charge was building between the two women, a charge that might damage, or even kill one or both. But like all charges, once accumulated the energy had to go somewhere. So she spoke.

"I feel… dirty. Ruined. As if… as if he took something I can never get back."

Her mother looked ready to cry. But she didn't. Instead, she barely whispered, "What's that, honey?"

Tears pooled in the corners of her eyes but her voice never wavered. "My confidence. My soul. My ability to live in this world without thinking that any moment, no matter

where I am or what I'm doing, something bad may happen.
For no reason. Just because."

She spit the words with a venom she hadn't
acknowledged lived within her. And damn it, it *did* feel good
to get it out! Until she saw her mother's face.

"I'm… so sorry," her mother said, her pain clear and
deep.

"It's okay, Mom," Janice said, taking her mother's hand
and squeezing it reassuringly. "I'm getting through it."

She was caught off-guard when her mother wrapped her
arms around her shoulders and held on for dear life. A casual
bystander might think it was the older woman who'd
experienced the attack, not Janice.

"What can I do?" her mother moaned, her pain a living
presence.

"It's enough that you're here. That's all Jackie and I need
– just your being here."

Through the tears streaming down her face, her mother
smiled. "Whatever I can do…"

"I know, Mom. I know."

*****

By the time she managed to persuade her mother to go to
bed, Janice was utterly exhausted. It felt like a fire had swept
through her body, leaving nothing but a black smoldering
hollow. She forced herself to brush her teeth and wash her
face, more out of habit and pride than desire. She went so far
as to take the sleeping pill bottle from the medicine cabinet,
but after a good ten seconds of wavering, she put it back
without opening it. The previous night had been enough to

convince her that pills weren't a miracle cure. She'd just have
to get to sleep on her own.

Easier said than done. As tired as she was, sleep would
not come. It felt like a pulsing current ran through her brain,
providing just enough energy to keep her awake but nowhere
near enough to fuel any productive activity. So she read, a
junk paperback she kept in her bedside table for just such
sleepless nights. Normally, five to ten minutes would be more
than enough. That night, after thirty minutes she put the
book down in frustration, the urge to sleep as distant as ever.

Five minutes of staring at the walls brought the usual
sense of mounting frustration that drove her from the bed
and out into the kitchen. She tried to move as quietly as
possible, both to avoid waking her son and mother and
because she wanted to be able to hear any strange sounds
over the thud of her own footsteps. And then there was the
knife. She'd slipped a kitchen paring knife into her robe
pocket, just to be safe. She wasn't exactly embarrassed by the
precaution, but she'd rather not have to explain it to either
Jackie or his grandma in the middle of the night.

The hum of the refrigerator and the warm glow of the
light that popped on when she opened the door provided
surprising reassurance. *'Am I losing it?'* she wondered when
she caught herself standing in the open fridge, staring at
everything and nothing. Spurred into action, she quickly
chose cereal and milk, despite an internet report she'd read
that said the tryptophan in milk really didn't help with sleep at
all. She didn't care what they said. She'd always found it easier
to sleep with a little food in her stomach. Not too much –
that usually resulted in uncomfortable sleeplessness – just
enough to soothe and pacify. Maybe milk and cereal were just

placebos, like a teddy bear or pat on the head. Whatever it was, it worked for her.

She padded slowly back to her bedroom, taking pains to hold the cereal bowl steady; the carpet was stained enough already. She stopped outside her son's door to listen to his gentle rhythmic breathing, a warm feeling radiating throughout her body. She'd been doing that ever since he'd been a tiny baby. One night her husband had caught her standing there, seemingly doing nothing in the middle of the hallway late at night.

"What's up?" he'd asked, the tone suggesting worry, or at the minimum confusion.

"I was just listening to Jackie sleep."

"Listening to him *sleep*?"

"Just breathe, actually. It's like a listening to a breeze in the tops of the trees – you know?"

"Ah."

She could tell he had no idea what she was talking about, but he was either too polite or too tired to continue the discussion. The reminiscence brought a tightness to her chest, the pain of warm memories gone cold.

She took one last peek at Jackie before continuing on to her room. Eating the cereal filled some time as well as the empty space in her stomach, but it did not bring-on sleep. In fact, the memories of her ex- exacerbated the tenseness that kept dreamland at bay, as each remembrance prompted another, and another, and each memory brought forth the emotions tied to it: some good, some bad, all sleep-killing. Finally, sometime in the middle of the night (she didn't dare look at the clock for fear the lateness of the hour would further stimulate her thoughts), she drifted off to sleep with visions of flashing red and blue emergency lights dancing in her head.

*****

Maybe her mother's visit was helping.

She slept through the night without a single nightmare. At least none she could remember. Of course, she'd been so exhausted it's possible she slept the proverbial *sleep without dreams* the books and movies always speak of. No matter. Whatever the reason, she awoke feeling much better than any day since... Well, since.

Jackie and her mother were already awake and playing out in the yard by the time she dragged herself into the kitchen for some breakfast. Breakfast. She had an *appetite*.

"Mommy! Mommy!" Jackie called out. He came running, with Grandma in close pursuit. He gave his mom a huge hug around the knees before she could even brace for his impact.

"Seems like someone's glad to see you this morning," her Mom said as she straggled in behind.

"Not as much as I'm glad to see him!" she called out, lifting him up for a sloppy kiss to his belly that elicited the hoped-for hysterical giggles.

"And looks like someone's feeling a little better," Grandma continued.

"Sleep works wonders." *Even if it's only a few hours,* she thought. "And you? How'd you sleep?"

Her mom signaled *comme ci, comme ca* with her hands. "Fell asleep okay, but got up a few times during the night."

"You're not here often enough to feel comfortable. Give it a day or two and you'll feel more at home." She didn't realize until she'd said it that her mother might take her words as implied criticism. She didn't.

"Tell that to my bladder."

"What's a bladder?" Jackie piped-up.

"It's a body part inside *here*," Janice said, using the opportunity to tickle Jackie until any thoughts of definitions disappeared beneath peals of laughter.

"What can I get you for breakfast?" her mother asked, moving solicitously toward the fridge.

"Sit down, Mom!" Janice ordered with a bleary smile. "I'll get something once I'm awake."

"Not even a cup of coffee?"

Janice surrendered to the inevitable. "Sure. That'd be great."

Her mom clearly knew her way around the kitchen despite her infrequent visits, as she went straight to the right cupboard for the mug and then to the silverware drawer for a spoon. "What's on the schedule today?" she asked as she made her way to the well-used black and stainless-steel coffee maker. Janice offered no coaching on its use, since although it had been eight years since they'd gotten it for a wedding gift it was so complicated Janice rarely used it for anything beyond plain old Black Java Americana.

"I'm not sure. I'll probably call the policewoman working on the case to see where things are…"

"And where are they?"

Janice glanced purposefully at her son – who had begun playing with a Star Wars figure and was ignoring the two of them.

"I think we're just waiting for the test kit results to come back. To see what evidence they provide."

"Aren't they already looking for the guy?"

Janice began to answer, then realized she had no idea if the police were actively searching for him.

"I don't really know," she said. "I'll have to ask them."

"You do that. The police have so many cases these days, there's no way yours will get the attention it deserves unless you stay on them."

Janice's eyes widened. This was her *mother*? The sedate, sometimes nearly comatose parent who didn't seem perturbed by almost anything that came her way? She was nearly as impressed as surprised.

"I will."

"Your work is okay – with you taking some leave, I mean?"

"They told me to take as much time as I needed."

"Don't take that literally. They probably mean a week or so. Beyond that, I'm guessing you'll be hearing from them."

"I don't expect to be out too long. A few days, maybe. A week at most." In truth, she hadn't thought much about returning to work. It wasn't in the front of her brain these days. Somehow the prospect of returning to that dank old warehouse, surrounded by nothing more personal that pallets and shipping crates, did not beckon to her. Quite the opposite. When she thought about work – which was not often – she felt queasy, just this side of nauseous. The idea of spending so much time *alone*, in that big empty space… that was even more disturbing. Her palms got sweaty just thinking about it.

"Well, if you need me to be here when Jackie gets home from school…"

Hearing his name, her son looked up at them with worried, expectant eyes. It was clear he'd been hoping he'd be overlooked.

"Speaking of which," Janice said, trying to hide the fact that she'd forgotten it was only Thursday, "you need to get to your room and get ready."

His grumble of objection matched his expression: utter disappointment.

"Do I *have* to?"

"Yes, you *have* to. Now come on, lickety-split!"

Grimacing as if carrying the burden of every unfair decision ever made, Jackie grabbed his space figure and started down the hallway.

"No Star Wars," Janice called after him.

His pout would have brought a smile if she wasn't so distracted.

"He seems to be doing pretty well," her mother said softly.

"He's a kid. And that's one reason I'm sending him back to school so soon. Angela thought it would be better for him to be around his friends than sitting here stewing."

"Like you?"

"Have I been *stewing*?"

"Haven't you?"

Janice bit back the reply that had jumped into her mouth and thought for a second. *Of course* she'd been stewing, or whatever you wanted to call it. She'd been *attacked*, for cryin' out loud! What did they expect her to do – just go on like nothing had happened?

"Maybe. But I have a good reason," she answered.

"Of course you do, honey. But so does Jackie."

The feeling of dissociation she'd been wafting in and out of came thundering back - with attitude. *Jackie feels bad? He doesn't even know what happened, not really. What does he have to feel so bad about?*

Followed immediately by the guilt. *How can I think such a thing? What has happened to me?*

Apparently all this played out on her face, because her mother's expression turned from loving concern to shaken in a matter of seconds.

"Are you okay?"

She almost lied, almost said exactly what she knew her mom wanted to hear. But she couldn't, not again. The lies would eat her alive.

"I don't know. No, I'm not okay, Mom. Ever since it happened… my head's not right. I find myself thinking the most terrible things, and I can't seem to stop it. It's like I don't know who I am anymore."

"Have you thought about seeing a psychologist? Just to help you get through this bad period," she hurried to add.

"I don't know…"

"Ask Angela. I bet she could suggest someone."

One part of her wanted to tell her mother to mind her own business. Another considered throwing herself to her knees and holding onto her mother's legs like she used to do when she was an infant. She did neither.

"I'll give her a call," she said, though whether she really intended to or was just saying it to keep Mom happy, she wasn't entirely sure. Her mother reached out to smooth her hair, and before she could think it through, Janice recoiled. The look on her mother's face made Janice feel ill.

"Sorry, Mom," she said, taking her mother's hand and holding it to her chest. "It's just..."

"You don't have to explain," her mom said.

But she did, if only to herself.

*****

"Any preference of a man or a woman?" Angela asked when she called later that afternoon and asked for a psychologist recommendation.

"Doesn't matter," she said. But almost immediately she changed her mind. "A woman," she corrected. "A woman would understand better, I think."

"Maybe. What's most important is that you feel comfortable with whoever it is. Let's see..." Janice could hear her clicking through a list on a computer. "Yes, here's someone I think would be perfect for what you're looking for: Theresa Thurman." She gave her the phone number.

"Do you know her?"

"No, not personally, but I've heard a lot of good things about her. She specializes in... these kinds of situations."

The hesitation cut Janice. Of course people would be hesitant to say the wrong thing. But somehow it almost hurt worse that they didn't believe she could handle it.

"Should I tell her you suggested I call?"

"Can't hurt, I suppose. But try to get an appointment as soon as you can."

"Why?" Janice asked, the laughter in her voice forced. "Do you think it's an emergency?"

"No, of course not. But in my experience, it gets easier and easier for someone to justify not calling as time goes on.

Your motivation is probably never going to be stronger than it is right now."

Janice winced internally. If this was the best she could hope for, she was worried.

CHAPTER 5

Dr. Thurman's office was located in one of those 1970's mini-malls of doctors and dentists that seem to spring up on the periphery of hospital complexes. The ones with the koi ponds and hissing electric fountain pumps. She tried not to judge as she approached the office door, though the urge to turn and flee was strong.

As she sat flipping through The Journal of the American Psychiatric Society, a slick, dense compendium of all things psychological, she kept having flashbacks – of *that* day. It wasn't the first time she'd revisited that horror, but the impending chat with a credentialed, intimidating stranger seemed to have increased both the number and intensity of the *reminiscences*. The door to the waiting room opened and when her eyes returned to the Journal, Janice realized she'd been reading the same page for the past fifteen minutes. This realization only compounded the associated physical and emotional reactions, leaving her heart pounding, her palms sweaty, and her thoughts swirling in a grotesque whirlpool of fear, confusion and guilt.

She heard a voice and looked up, more from reflex than conscious motivation. She saw a young woman in a conservative but expensive-looking outfit staring at her. "Mrs. Greyson?"

Janice realized the woman had been calling her name. *For how long?*

"Yes, I'm Mrs. Greyson," she said, rising from her seat with some difficulty.

The young woman held the door for her and then led her back to the more elegantly decorated rooms beyond. "You're younger than I expected," she found herself saying, to break the awkward silence more than anything.

"Oh, I'm not the doctor," she said with the slightest hint of guilty pleasure. "I'm her assistant, Elaine."

"Oh, I'm sorry. I just thought…"

"No problem. Here we are." She stopped at a spacious room with tastefully-patterned wallpaper, a huge Persian rug covering most of the dark hardwood floor, and two dark brown leather chairs that looked like something out of a London men's club. "Make yourself comfortable. The doctor will be with you shortly." She smiled but did not wait for a response.

Janice eyed the two facing chairs suspiciously, trying to determine if her choice of which to sit in would somehow give the doctor an insight into her mental state. She could see no advantage, or disadvantage, of choosing one over the other, but before she could come to a decision her eyes roamed to a covey of diplomas on the wall opposite one of the chairs. She looked briefly at the door before sliding over to see what was what. Middlebury for undergrad. Columbia for her medical studies. Looked solid. Certainly not fly-by-night. Then a few certificates and diplomas… yes, solid. Very solid.

She was just finishing her inspection when the door opened, startling her. She quickly turned to face a woman of perhaps 50, greying hair, with a smile both welcoming and evaluative.

"I'm always wondering whether I should get rid of all those old diplomas," she said, closing the door behind her. "What do you think – too much?"

"No, not at all," Janice said. *Was this another test?* "Good schools."

"Yeh, good schools. But after all these years, I sometimes wonder what – if anything – they have to say about me at this stage of my life. Theresa," she continued, striding over with hand extended, "Thurman. You're Mrs. Greyson?"

"Janice," she said. The woman had a strong grip, authoritative. She tried to match the pressure.

"Ready to give this a go?"

She wasn't, not really, but didn't feel she could say no. "I suppose so."

"Have a seat," the doctor said, indicating the chair that faced the wall with the diplomas. "Have you visited with a psychiatrist before?"

'Visited.' Interesting choice of words. "No, never."

"Well, it's a lot less intimidating than you'd think from all the movies and TV shows you see. Mostly, just chatting."

"That's a relief." She smiled, not entirely without reason. The doctor seemed nice, normal.

"I can imagine." She brought out a digital recorder. "Mind if I record our sessions? I can take notes if you prefer…"

"No, the recorder's fine."

"Good, good. We want you to feel relaxed, or as relaxed as you can be. How are you feeling right now?"

And so it begins.

*****

An hour later, (or more accurately 56 minutes), Dr. Thurman drew the session to a close.

"I think that's enough for one day, don't you? Anything else you wanted to discuss?"

"No, not really," Janice said. Their chat had been somewhat painful, as she'd expected, but nothing she couldn't handle. The more significant question was whether all the talking would help get her past *the incident.*

"So, what do you think?" the doctor asked as if she were mind-reading. "Worthwhile?"

"I don't know yet. Let's say I reserve judgment."

Dr. Thurman nodded. "Good answer. I'm always a little skeptical when patients leave after our first session singing hosannas."

"Can I hum?"

The doctor smiled. "Joking – that's good. When would you like to get together again?"

Janice made an appointment for the same time the following week. She didn't want to come across as too needy, but she wasn't at all sure she could go longer than a week without another assault by the thoughts and feelings that had been keeping her awake at night. Dr. Thurman didn't reveal any reaction whatsoever.

"Good. See you then."

As she walked out of the therapy area and back through the waiting room to reconfirm her appointment, she couldn't help noticing the expectant – or was it pitying? – expression of the two people waiting their turn. She smiled as if to say, *'it's not so bad'* and finished her business with the receptionist.

The feel of sun on her face and the breeze in her hair helped buoy her thinking, but she'd barely closed the car door when a familiar voice whispered in her inner-ear.

'Was that progress, or is all this psychiatry stuff just mumbo-jumbo?' the voice asked. She immediately tried to distract herself with some basic meditating, but the doubting whispers were insistent.

'Why didn't you tell her the truth?' quickly morphed into *'What are you hiding?'*

She turned up the radio and tried to focus elsewhere, but it was like trying not to think about a pink elephant: the more she tried, the pinker it became. She was startled when she pulled up in front of her house, since it had seemed she'd been driving for only a few minutes.

'Get it together!' she chastised herself, but when it came right down to it, she had no idea how to start.

CHAPTER 6

Jennifer Alice Bodecker was her name, though since the
birth of Jackie she had been known in her daughter's home as
Grandma. She still found it both amusing and confounding
that her identity was so dependent on the perception of
others. Fifty-three years of one identity disappeared at the
moment of the little guy's birth. Not that she was
complaining, exactly. She had looked forward to this next
stage of her life ever since her youngest, Eddy, had moved
out. That was twelve years ago. Now Jackie was the central
star in her universe, the point around which she and
everything else revolved. Just the thought of him brought a
warm glow to her chest, a need as real as she imagined
addiction must be.

But now, *this*. She had never entertained the possibility of
such a thing occurring to someone she knew, least of all to
her *daughter*. It was as if the sun hadn't risen one day, or the
ocean waves fell flat. Impossible. Worse yet, she feared for
the impact on Jackie. Yes, she knew she should hold the
greater portion of her concern for Janice, but somehow she
focused on the repercussions to the little guy. Janice was an
adult, a grown person. Heck, she hadn't listened to her advice
or followed her suggestions for years now. Maybe since
college. She'd figure it out.

Jackie was another thing entirely. Only 6 years old, he
hadn't yet developed the tough emotional exoskeleton that
protects most people from the bumps and bruises of
everyday life. He was an innocent, not in any way responsible
for the horror that had befallen his mom. Not that Janice was
responsible, of course. Well, not overtly, anyway. She'd

warned her daughter a million times about dressing like a
streetwalker, and chatting with everyone she met as though
they were best friends. Had the chickens come home to
roost? She didn't know. But somewhere deep inside, in a
place she dared only visit in her darkest moments, she feared
it might be true. Perhaps her daughter had given off *signals*,
unintentional vibrations that had led to the attack. She'd
never suggest such a thing, of course, but that didn't mean it
couldn't be true.

Now Jackie would carry the burden of the attack, the
terror he couldn't explain, the nightmares that seemed all too
real. What could she do about it? She was just *Grandma*, after
all, the smiling face on Skype, the reassuring telephone voice,
the occasional fawning visitor. What did he think of her? Did
he even realize how much she cared about him, how *essential*
he was to her well-being, her sense of self? How could he?

With Janice out meeting her psychiatrist, Jackie was all
hers, not just a responsibility but a reason to be. Not that
Janice wasn't a good mother. Probably better than she'd been
at the same age. It was only that she'd *learned* so much over
the years, from her own mistakes and those of her friends.
No young mother could possibly know as much as she did, or
could possibly give as much of herself. With her husband
gone, there were only the two kids – and now Jackie. She
remembered all too well what it'd been like to balance a job, a
marriage, and her own needs, with the needs of her children.
Now she could concentrate all her attention on her grandson.

She glanced at him musing over a tableful of puzzle
pieces, his look of deep concentration so endearing she had
to stop herself from cooing. He was an angel, an absolute
angel.

*****

As soon as Janice walked in the door, her mother knew something was not right.

"How'd it go?" she asked hoping to elicit something deeper than evasion.

"Okay. How were things with you two?" It was clear she wasn't eager to share.

"Good, good. Jackie's been working on that puzzle almost the entire time you've been gone."

"Really? When I'm home I can rarely get him to focus on anything for more than a few minutes at a time." She walked to where he was still working away.

Maybe that's because you always have the TV on, the computer running, and your cellphone in your hand,' her mom felt like saying. But she didn't. "Maybe he's just in the mood."

Janice gave him a big hug. "Mommy, I'm working!" he said, wriggling from her grasp.

"Oh, I am *sorry!*" she said, but her smile was half-hearted.

"What did you guys talk about?" her mother pushed.

"Oh, you know, pretty much what you'd expect."

"And it helped? I mean, do you feel any better?"

She stopped to think. "A little, I suppose. But I'm not expecting miracles. This will take a while."

Her mother watched Janice closely. Was she being honest, or trying to keep her from worrying?

"What?" Janice asked.

"Nothing. Just looking at my beautiful daughter."

"You know, Mom, this is probably going to go on for quite some time. You can't keep worrying about me every minute of every day."

"I just want you to be happy."

"I *am* happy... most of the time." Okay, so maybe that was a little white lie. *Some* of the time?

Jennifer wasn't buying it. She'd seen her daughter's expression when she didn't know anyone was looking: the pensive, far-away look, her lips moving in a private conversation with no one. She could hide her feelings from most everyone else, but not from her mother.

"Well I'm glad to hear it," she said. There would be plenty of time to press Janice to cut herself some slack. For now, better to go along with her pretense. If it was pretense.

Just then, the phone rang. Janice answered it.

"Hello."

"Ms. Greyson? Officer Daniels here."

"Ah yes, Officer Daniels." Her stomach dropped. "What can I do for you? Do you have any news?"

"As a matter of fact, I do. We've put out the APB we told you about for this guy, Archer."

"Any leads?" She tried to keep her voice level.

"It's still early. But if he's still in the country, we'll find him."

Her thoughts whirled. "What then?"

"Well, then we'll bring him in – once we find him, of course – interrogate him, give the evidence to the DA's office, and see if they'll press charges."

"Is there a chance they won't?"

"I wouldn't think so, but you never know."

The phone suddenly seemed terribly heavy. "Will I have to testify against him?"

"That would be the DA's decision, but probably so. The more evidence against him, the stronger the case."

She thought about walking into a courtroom, facing that animal... she closed her eyes in anguish. "Mrs. Greyson?" Apparently she had been silent longer than she'd realized.

"I'm here."

"We'll be with you every step of the way."

"I appreciate that." Her thoughts darted every which way: *What will happen when he gets out? What if they can't find him?*

Now it was the policewoman's turn to hesitate. "How are you doing?" she asked, tentatively.

Was it that obvious? "Okay, I guess. I'm just a little shook-up. I mean, I've got all these questions, like how much time will I have to take off from work? Will we be safe if he knows I'm going to testify against him? I'll need to make sure my son is taken care of."

"Let's get him behind bars first, then we'll see how it all plays out."

She exhaled a great sigh. "Yes, of course, it's just that..."

"I understand, believe me. Try to stay calm. Easier said than done, I realize, but this may be a long slog."

"How long?"

She shrugged. "I've seen cases take over a year, particularly if the perp won't take a plea deal."

"A year!" She'd never dreamt it could take so long. How could she survive all that time?

"You'll be okay, I'm sure of it."

She forced a smile. "Surer than I am."

*****

Actually, Officer Daniels wasn't. Surer than Janice. But she felt the woman needed reassurance and so she gave it. Is there anything wrong with that?

She hung up the phone with a shake of her head.

"What happened – your kid's hamster die?" one of her fellow cops asked when he caught her sitting motionless with a look of worried concern.

"Nah. Rape victim. Just explaining the routine."

"Ah," the other cop said understandingly, "one of my least favorite conversations."

"One of many."

The cop's eyebrows shot up. "Aren't we in a cheery mood."

"Not a whole lot to be cheery about."

The cop nodded. "Don't let it get to you."

"Yeh." Good luck with that. It was an occupational hazard – getting involved with the victims, trying to ease them through the many twists and turns in a legal system that seemed more accommodating to the perps than their prey. It was one of the things she hated about the job: the way everyone seemed so concerned about the rights of the accused and nobody seemed to care two licks about the poor people who got robbed, or mugged, or raped.

When she'd first joined the department, as a raw rookie right out of the Academy, she'd thought she had a pretty good idea of how things worked. She knew cops sometimes stretched the rules. Sometimes stomped all over the *Constitutional rights of the accused.* But it wasn't until she'd spent a few years among them that she realized they came up against some dumbass rule or reg nearly every day. Sometimes more. Forget fifty shades of gray. Working as a cop was more like a thousand shades. She was starting to slip into the funk that seemed to come upon her more and more often recently, when Willard came strolling up to her desk waving a sheet of paper.

"Bingo!" he said, tossing the paper onto the desk.

"What?"

"Got the bastard," he said. "The one who raped that Greyson woman. Report came in from the independent lab."

"DNA match?"

"99.9. No way this one walks."

Daniels knew he was referring to two recent suspects, both ID'd in lineups, who got off when the DNA didn't support the charges. Their lieutenant had made a big deal out of it, probably because the media had done the same. Front page stuff. "Jump to Judgement?" the headline read. They had reason to be skittish.

"Got an address?"

He nodded. "Don't know if it's current, but thought I'd cruise out there to take a look. Wanna come?"

He knew she did, but it was this Detective-Officer thing. Most of them felt the need to spray their territory, particularly with a woman cop.

"You bet. When you going?"

"Not doing much right now. You?"

And so they piled into one of the old shitbox unmarked cars and headed out to scout the address. At first they kept their own counsel, each lost in thoughts about the crime, or the investigation, or whatever. But as they drew closer, Daniels focused in on the task at hand.

"Think this guy will put up a fight?"

"He's got a couple of priors, so it's possible. But I'd guess he comes in without a peep, unless he's not even there."

"How do you want to handle it?"

"Just tell him what we're there for and throw the cuffs on him."

"And if he doesn't want to cooperate?"

"You itchin' for a fight?"

Daniels started to deny it, but stopped herself. *Was she?* "Not exactly itching, but can't say I'd be disappointed if he has to be 'subdued'."

"Just keep it under control, okay? I don't want to get involved with those IA assholes if it can be avoided."

Internal Affairs? What did he think, that she was going to beat the crap out of the guy for no reason? What the hell...

"Don't you worry, Detective. It'll be by the book – as always."

Conversation dropped off again, neither willing to revisit such touchy territory. It wasn't until they pulled up in front of a rundown building in a rundown neighborhood that the communication resumed.

"What're the odds he's there?" Willard asked as he pulled the car to a stop in a red no-parking zone.

"You're in a red zone."

He feigned looking out the windshield at the painted curb. "Not parking. Just making a pick-up." With that he threw open the door and dragged his substantial bulk out of the seat. She had no choice but to do the same.

The apartment building looked like dozens of other 1970's concrete structures whose glory days were long-past: five stories, small windows, balconies not really big enough to do anything with except maybe dry clothes - as a number of residents seemed to have discovered.

"Looks like TJ," Willard said.

"Or Juarez, or Santo Domingo or Tegucigalpa," she said, "which is where most of the folks who live here probably come from."

"Great. You habla?"

"Un poquito."

"Good. You can interpret."

As they walked toward the entrance to the building she heard several sliding glass doors slam shut.

"They know we're here."

"They probably knew when we were two blocks from here."

Despite having experienced it many times before, Daniels was still put-off by all the graffiti staining the walls to the entranceway.

"You'd think they'd keep their own buildings clean."

"Gangbangers. They don't give a damn about anything."

A woman about 40 with a young kid no more than 3 or 4 walked past, her stare anything but welcoming.

"Buenos Dias," Daniels said.

The woman hid behind hunched shoulders and hurried out the door. "Was it something I said?"

"Probably should've changed into civvies. That blue uniform won't win us any popularity contests."

"As if they couldn't spot you a mile away with that flat-top and JC Penny suit," she countered.

"Men's Wearhouse, I think." She couldn't tell if he was proud or pissed.

They took the elevator up to the third floor, the acid stench of urine a constant companion. A small group of little kids, probably 4 or 5 years old, were playing in the hallway, their screams and laughter a welcome contrast to the grim, dimly-lit corridor with holes punched in the drywall every few feet. As soon as they stepped out of the elevator, the kids scattered like startled doves. Suddenly the dim passageway turned silent, oppressive.

"It's like they're all waiting for something," Daniels whispered.

"Us," Willard said. "They're waiting for us."

They found the apartment where Archer supposedly lived, or had lived, and knocked on the door with the authoritative drumbeat they'd learned way back in training. *'Make it clear who's in charge from the very first,'* the trainer had said.

They heard the sound of muffled voices through the scarred metal door. A shadow passed over the peephole. Willard whipped out his badge and held it up to the hole.

"Policia," he said, loud enough to be heard not only through the door but for a good distance up and down the corridor.

Slowly, with trepidation in every move, the locks clicked open and the door swung back. An older woman, dark complexioned but probably Latina, stood facing them with several small children huddled behind her.

"Si?"

"Do you speak English?" Willard asked, his question another blow, another display of control.

"A leetle," the woman said, her voice shaky.

"Mejor en Espanol?" Daniels asked.

"Si, gracias."

"Ask her if Archer lives here," the Detective said.

"Conoce a un Senor Archer?"

The look on her face said all that was necessary. "El no esta aqui."

"She says he's not here."

"Not my question."

"El vive aqui?"

"A veces. Cuando mi hija esta."

"Donde esta ella?"

"Trabajando."

"Cual es su nombre?"

"Alicia."

"What's she saying?" Willard asked. She could tell his patience was fraying.

"She says sometimes Archer stays here when her daughter, Alicia, is home, but now she's working."

"Does she expect him tonight? And if so, when?"

Daniels asked the woman. "She says the daughter should be home around 5:30. She doesn't know if Archer will come tonight."

"When was the last time she saw him?"

The woman hesitated before answering. "A couple of days ago," Daniels translated.

"Can we come in – take a look?"

"Is that necessary?"

"You gonna take her word for it that he's not inside?"

She shook her head distractedly and relayed the request. The woman looked like she wanted to say no, but she crumbled under their combined glare.

The apartment was small, just one bedroom, but it was clear that several other people lived there. The small kids, their expressions ranging from excited bemusement to sheer terror, huddled behind the older woman like chicks behind a momma hen.

"Lo siento, no vamos a quedarnos aqui mucho tiempo," Daniels said even as her partner plowed straight through the tiny living room and drew his service revolver before cautiously opening the closed bedroom door. The kids all clucked nervously.

"Clear!" Willard called out a few seconds later. Daniels smiled at the kids, who stared back nervously. Willard holstered the gun as he made his way back, poking here and there with a gloved hand and shoe. His frown only deepened with each step.

"What a pigsty," he muttered. "Don't translate that."

"I had no intention of doing so, Detective."

He pulled out a business card and offered it to the woman. "Tell her to give us a call if she sees or hears from Archer. We just want to talk to him."

Daniels translated, then turned back to her partner. "You don't think she'll buy that, do you?"

"Who knows? Can't hurt to try."

The Officer apologized once more, bid goodbye to the kids – only one of whom returned her smile – and followed the Detective out the door.

"I have a feeling we won't be seeing Archer around here anytime soon," Willard said as they made their way back to their car, untold eyes watching their every step from the shadows.

"Not likely. But you never know. People do stupid things sometimes."

"Sometimes?"

CHAPTER 7

It had been four days since the incident, four days without much sleep, four days of nightmares – both sleeping and waking. Janice let her hand fall on the squawking alarm clock, hitting it perhaps a bit too hard in her sullen stupor. She knew she wasn't ready to go back to work, knew she really needed to talk to the shrink again, knew that neither she, nor Jackie, nor anyone else directly involved had *moved past* it. *Moved past* – just exactly what did that mean, anyway? Bypassed? Worked-through? Or just forgot about? No matter what it meant, she hadn't been able to do it. Oh, from time to time, for maybe a few hours in an afternoon, she'd managed to think about something, anything other than *it*. But then she'd see something, or hear a news report, or just forget to *move past* and the next thing she knew a lump had welled-up in her throat and tears were pushing at the corners of her eyes.

Damn it! Perhaps more than anything she hated the weakness this whole ordeal had revealed. She'd always thought of herself as a strong woman. A strong *person*. But now... now she wasn't so sure. It's easy to be tough when there's nothing threatening your ordered, safe, mundane existence. Not so easy when you see those eyes and hear that voice in your head every minute of every day.

She wasn't entirely sure how Jackie was handling it either. She couldn't separate how he felt about what had happened from how he felt about how she was reacting. It must've been hard for him, not understanding, only sensing her fear and anger.

And then there was her mom. Did she look older, more fragile, or was that just her imagination, her guilt? Was it even fair to drag her through all this? Sure, she'd come on her own, but Janice wasn't sure how she could have made it through the previous few days without her – babysitting for Jackie, listening to her blubbering daughter drone on and on about her screwed-up thoughts… It was too much to absorb, almost too much to tolerate.

But she had only two choices at this point: roll over and hide her head under the pillows, or suck it up, pull herself together as best she could, and go back to work. Jackie was already back at school and her mom would stay at home to answer any calls and keep the wheels turning. For an instant it was a real battle between the two options, but in the end she just couldn't force herself to hide a minute longer. She threw the covers back and stumbled to the shower.

The steaming slash of the shower felt good, a hedonistic penance that punished even as it rewarded. She caught herself staring at the mirror, trying to see through the swirling fog at the reflection of the bathroom door, thinking without thought that she couldn't let down her guard in case someone – *him* – came in unexpectedly. The thought embarrassed her, yet even as she chastised herself she felt the crawl of fear, realized she was still on edge, still waiting for… something. She tried to tear her eyes from the mirror, tried to force herself to act as if it was just another shower, just another moment in a life that was no different than it had been five days earlier. An event is singular, her conscious mind argued, it exists for the time it is allotted and then it is gone. It is the repercussions that linger, the ripples of thought that keep it alive past its time. If a tree falls in the forest… But if it falls and no one remembers, its impact in this world ceases to exist. A fallen tree is not a falling tree. A woman who *was* attacked is not a woman who *is* attacked.

By the time she stepped from the shower, she was afraid to look at her hands for fear they'd be shaking. Instead she focused on the towel, its softness, its reassuring familiarity. My god, who'd have ever thought a towel could be life-affirming!

If she thought her morning could only improve from there, she was quickly proven wrong. She had to get dressed. Normally she'd just flip through the hangers of whatever was clean and ironed, choosing the color and cut that struck her fancy for the day. But today wasn't just another day. Today she would have to face her fellow workers, if only when they all punched in and traded lies over coffee first thing in the morning. She needed to look… restrained, under control but solitary, willing to do what was needed as long as it didn't require idle socializing. She didn't want to chance blurting the details, or worse, breaking down for no apparent reason. They'd all know soon enough. Once *he* was arrested and charged it would hit the papers, and even if some of the media tried to keep the victim's name out of the public eye, there'd always be one that would revel in the revelation. And after the first, the others would have to go along – or lose their audience. So it was only a matter of time before they'd all be looking at her differently, thinking back to this day. *'Ah, so that's why she was like that,'* they'd say.

And so the dilemma of choosing an outfit. She flipped through one after another, considering and then discarding possibility after possibility. It was as if making a decision – *any* decision – might set-off unseen after-effects that could damn her future life, and not just hers but Jackie's and her Mom's, and… She sat heavily on the bed, her head spinning. *'Catch your breath,'* she ordered as her heartbeat roared out of control. *'In, and then out. In, and then out.'* She wiped tiny pinpricks of sweat from her forehead. Was she having a heart-attack? She considered calling Angela, but she felt foolish: she was just picking an outfit, for cryin' out loud!

Focusing on that thought broke the cycle; her heart began to slow even as her head cleared. She pushed herself to her feet and grabbed the nearest blouse and skirt from their hangers. Screw it! She would wear what she would wear and if any of them didn't like it, that was *their* problem! In a cold fury she pulled the clothes on and buttoned and zipped as if donning armor for a joust. She glanced at herself in the mirror, shoved a few strands of hair aside with her sweaty hand, and stormed out of her bedroom headed for the kitchen.

"Looks like someone didn't get up on the right side of the bed," her mother said reservedly as her daughter stormed past her on the way to the coffee machine.

"I don't care what everyone else thinks," Janice muttered as she slammed drawers getting her mug and spoon.

"About what?"

"You *know* about what!" Her eyes were black bullseyes rimmed with red.

Just then Jackie appeared from the hallway, stopping to stare with the look of a spooked deer.

"Are you okay, Mom?" he asked cautiously.

Janice swallowed. *What was she doing?!* "Yeh, sure I am, Jackie. I just need my morning coffee, that's all."

He looked to his grandmother for reassurance. She forced a tepid smile. "What would you like for breakfast, honey?"

Janice cradled her coffee in her hands, her anger at her fellow workers morphing into self-hatred. *How could she do this to her son? Hadn't he been through enough already?* She walked over to where he'd taken a seat at the table, his tablet already spitting out the raucous inanities of some kiddy show. He seemed hypnotized. When she tried to smooth his ever-present cowlick, however, he flinched. That tiny movement, barely noticeable under normal conditions, seemed at that moment an unspoken chastisement, criticism by the one person whose unshakeable support she'd always taken for granted. It hurt. It hurt a lot.

She glanced up to see her mother's pitying look and her anger flared again.

"What?!" she said, much too loudly with way too much attitude. Jackie looked up for just a second before the show drew him back in.

"Nothing," her mother answered, her concern bleeding through the mock nonchalance. Janice wanted to set her straight, to let her know that she was doing just fine, thank you very much, but she couldn't bring herself to do it. Mainly because she wasn't doing just fine, thank you very much, but also because she knew her mother was only trying to help. She couldn't know how deeply the pitying looks cut, or how susceptible she still was to even the smallest jab.

"Would you like me to make something for dinner?" her mom asked, breaking the internal monologue.

"Huh? Oh, yeh, thanks, that would be great," she managed.

"Anything in particular?"

She barely caught herself before she went off. "No, whatever you want."

"You guys still like spaghetti and meatballs, don't you?"

Spaghetti and meatballs. Janice was locked in a seemingly unending battle with a memory that flayed her very soul, and her mom wanted to talk about pasta.

"Yeh, good. That would be good. Thanks, Mom."

Before Jennifer could move into any other mundanity, Janice made her move. "Gotta get going," she announced. She bent down and kissed Jackie on the cheek. "You all ready for school?" she asked, knowing the answer.

He looked up at her with exasperation bending his lips into an attempted sneer. "Do I *have* to?"

"Yes, you have to. Now turn that thing off and get your little butt moving." When he hesitated a second too long, she added, "Now!"

This time the flinch was accompanied by a look, a look of surprise tinged with hurt. He turned the tablet off and pushed away from the breakfast table.

"Take your bowl to the sink," she said before he could take a second step.

"Mom!" he objected, glancing at his grandmother for support, but he was on his own.

He grabbed the bowl and half-placed, half-dropped it into the sink. He stormed off without so much as a goodbye.

"He's still trying to find his way," her mother said with cloying sincerity.

"Aren't we all. See you around 5." She didn't wait for any further interaction, wasn't sure she could handle it. She went outside, hopped into the car, and waited for Jackie to straggle along. After checking that he had his lunch and homework despite knowing her mother had probably already done the same thing - she turned the key and put the car into gear with a purposeful snap of her wrist. Her foot hovered above the gas pedal, just awaiting the all-clear to stomp it to the floor. At the last second, she caught sight of her dark narrowed eyes in the rear-view mirror. The stomp became a gentle coaxing, and she rolled slowly into the tributary stream of commuters heading toward the city.

*****

The twenty-minute trip to Jackie's school was uneventful, though her continuous stream of conversation sounded forced even to herself. Jackie, thankfully, seemed oblivious to her stress and ran off to his classroom with his usual happy abandon. She waited until he disappeared into the tidy brick building before continuing on to work, nearly on autopilot - until she reached the parking lot. Then with a suddenness that caught her entirely off-guard, that familiar feeling of dread seeped into her consciousness like steaming effluent into a mountain stream. It was as if something was pinning her to the seat, something so big, so overwhelming she could barely draw a breath. She eased the car into a space and managed to drop the transmission into Park by some sixth-sense. She was lost, blown about like smoke in the wind, unable to focus on anything beyond the darkness, the sense of impending doom. She dragged a breath into her lungs, then another. Her hands slowly unclenched from the steering wheel, and with a superhuman effort she turned off the ignition.

She sat very still, hoping it would go away, forget about her. Ever so slowly, like ice melting on a cool spring morn, she felt the weight lift from her chest; she took a full breath. *How long can this go on?'* she worried as she checked her reflection in the rearview mirror. It was as if she were staring at a familiar stranger, or maybe at one of the statues in Madame Tussaud's – similar features but dead as wax inside.

Two more deep breaths and she opened the door. The blast of warmth and bright sunshine momentarily disoriented her, forcing her to stagger back and shield her eyes. When her vision finally cleared the huge metal grey warehouse loomed in front of her, seemingly even bigger and greyer than she remembered. *'One step in front of another,'* she coached herself. *'You can do this.'* She staggered across the lot until her hand rested on the steel push-bar to the front door. She felt the coolness of the metal battling with the warmth of the sun, and for several seconds she literally couldn't move a muscle.

"You going in?" a voice erupted behind her, sending shockwaves through her body.

She turned too quickly. Her head swam. "Yeh, yeh, sorry." It was Jerrard, a forklift driver about 45 years old with thinning brown hair and a gap between his front teeth.

"Sorry – didn't mean to scare you." When she didn't reply immediately, he pushed on. "You've been out a few days, haven't you?"

"Yeh." She struggled to say something more, but couldn't force the words.

"Well welcome back. Or maybe I should say *condolences.*" The gap seemed to widen as he flashed his wittiest smile.

"Thanks – for either."

He held the door open for her. "After you."

She couldn't tell if he was just being friendly or if he had ulterior motives. Or was that the *incident* talking? She smiled and nodded once, rushing ahead without waiting for further exchanges.

"No need to hurry," he called out to her as she pulled away. "Andy's never in at this hour."

She answered back over her shoulder, without breaking stride or slowing. "I just need to do some errands before getting started."

He seemed to take that at face value as his echoing footsteps faded away. She was half-way across the warehouse floor before she let her adrenaline ease. The machinegun clatter of her heels slowed to a measured drumbeat. She could hear muffled voices up ahead in the break room and despite having no interest in either coffee or gossip, she headed straight for the door.

Heads turned and the chatter momentarily dropped. She felt as though they were staring and wondered if they saw some psychic Scarlett Letter or if she was just worked up from her contact with Jerrard.

"Hey, you feeling better?" another of the guys – was it Pedro? - asked.

"Yeh, thanks." She went straight to the refrigerator and made believe she was stashing something there from her lunch bag. Nobody followed. Conversations continued. She felt color rise into her cheeks. *'I'm being ridiculous,'* she thought. *'They don't care where I was or what happened. It' just another day to them.'*

She made her way out into the main room without any further interaction and settled behind her desk. She signed-in on her computer, took a look at her personal emails to be sure Daniels or Willard hadn't sent anything, and was more relieved than disappointed when she found nothing from either of them. In just a few minutes the coffee klatch broke up and all the guys went to their various machines, leaving her, as usual, alone in the cavernous structure. At first, she had some success convincing herself that everything was back to normal, that memories and repercussions of *that* day were finally coming under control. She kept busy, distracting her thoughts with as much work as she could handle, or as much as her wandering mind permitted. Correspondence that had lain in the bottom of file cabinets for months became a priority; old emails flew into new files or virtual oblivion. She was doing it. She was getting back to normal.

And then the phone rang. It was Officer Daniels.

"We've got a good lead on your attacker," she said, her voice so matter-of-fact that Janice felt like screaming. "We think we may pick him up this afternoon."

"Great! What do you need from me?" She hoped it was nothing, but doubted she'd be so lucky.

"For now, just stay near a phone so we can call you in if we get him."

"Call me in?"

"Yeh, for a lineup. We'll need you to identify him."

"But you have his DNA…"

"DNA evidence can be challenged. It's better to have a positive ID as well."

"Challenged?" She'd convinced herself that the legal part of all this would be short and sweet.

"There can be questions of sample degradation, chain of custody, lab mistakes, etc., etc. Lawyers are basically snakes – anything to get an acquittal."

Janice felt her throat begin to swell shut. "So, I have to pick him out?"

"That's right – but don't worry. You're in a darkened room behind a one-way mirror. He won't see you."

"But he'll know I'm there."

"Well, yes. I mean, he'll know it's you who's ID'ing him."

Janice struggled to draw a full breath. "But he can't get out, can he? I mean, they won't let him out on bond, or whatever?"

"Not likely. Not with a rape charge. But I have to be honest; it's up to the judge. It's very unlikely, but not one-hundred per cent impossible."

"Yes, well, you don't have him yet, do you?"

"Not yet, but we've got a pretty good lead. We'll know better this afternoon."

"Then we'll face all this when you capture him."

"Right. No sense getting all wound up about something that hasn't happened yet."

Janice was quiet for a long moment, her thoughts in a flutter. "Right. Okay, thank you for calling."

"I'll keep you informed."

Janice held the phone in her hand until the dial tone finally penetrated her daze. Then she hung up and hurried to the bathroom.

*****

Officer Daniels' frown was visible from all the way across the police headquarters bullpen.

"What? She gonna be a problem?" Willard asked.

"I don't know. Maybe. She's definitely feeling the pressure."

"Maybe we should go pay her a visit after we get this Archer asshole."

"*If* we get him."

"Even if we don't, it might pay to chat with her a little bit. Get her head right."

"I don't know. What if we spook her even worse than she already is?"

"How many victims have we interviewed – a couple hundred? We got this."

Daniels wasn't at all sure, but she didn't have a better idea. "Yeh, okay. We can give it a try."

"Let's get the perp first. That'll make everything easier."

*****

They'd received a tip on Archer, one of nearly a hundred they'd received since they released his old booking mugshot to the local TV stations and uploaded it to the social media outlets. It was amazing how many more responses they got now that they used Facebook, and Twitter, and all those other Internet sites. In the good ol' days it was just the three local news channels, and even then you sometimes had to fight the news director to get on the air. Now, a couple of keyboard clicks and… Voila! Instant notoriety.

The person who'd called was a young woman, a not-unusual occurrence in the world of snitching.

"These guys think they can just play with their woman and then walk away for another one," Daniels said as soon as she heard about the tip. "She sounded pissed."

"I wonder if it was that Alicia. Maybe she got tired of the bum hanging out there."

"Or maybe some of those kids were his and he doesn't hang out there enough," Daniels said.

The tipster told them Archer would be at the Eastside Café, a little diner-esque spot not too far from where Alicia lived, for lunch at 1 pm. Willard and Daniels decided to be there as well.

The neighborhood was not much better than where his girlfriend lived, but at least there were a number of Latino businesses lining the busy boulevard and the clientele didn't scatter when the two cops got out of their very obvious unmarked police car.

"It's almost like being in the USA," Willard muttered as they made their way to the café.

"Not every Latino's an illegal," Daniels countered. It was the same argument pretty much every day.

"Yeh, just 90 per cent."

The diner was crowded, both at the dozen or so small tables lined all around the periphery of the one room, as well as at the counter in the center. Faces looked up as the two cops entered, most with only casual interest.

Willard nodded to his left. "You take that side, I'll take this one."

Without waiting for a reply, he started off to his right. She hated when he did that: gave her orders without waiting to see what she thought of them. Sure, he was a Detective and outranked her, but that didn't mean she was an idiot. Sometimes she had good ideas, sometimes better than his. Actually, most of the time better than his.

She was still steaming when the door to the restrooms at the back of the room opened and a familiar face emerged. She stopped where she stood and eyed him to be sure. At first he didn't notice, but all too quickly the look she'd seen so often in crooks who realized they were about to be arrested appeared. Not exactly surprise. Most of them knew it was only a matter of time. More like denial tinged with fear. Oh yeh, definitely tinged with fear. Just then Willard saw him as well, and stepped around a crowded table to confront him.

"Daniel Lee Archer," Willard began reaching behind his back to draw his service weapon, "you are…"

Archer bolted. Ran right at her, knocking her backwards into four young diners who'd been watching the scene develop as if it'd been the premiere of a new cable show. She barely got her gun out of its holster before she smashed into the table, sending glasses, plates and silverware flying and customers screaming. Archer made straight for the exit, crashing through anything and anyone who got in his way, unintentionally creating just enough chaos to get him out the front door before Willard could push his way through all the bystanders who were too busy taking cellphone video to realize they were letting the guy get away.

"Go! I'll be right behind you!" Daniels screamed when the Detective glanced in her direction.

As it turned out, she took a few seconds to disentangle herself from the table, its contents and the four diners, apologize profusely (if somewhat bluntly), and wipe the biggest pieces of the foursome's lunch off her uniform. By the time she was on her feet and ready to pursue, the exit was so blocked by spectators she had to pull her badge and start screaming, "Police! Out of the way! Police!"

Whether it was the tone (and volume) of her voice or the fact that she rolled through them like a 16-pound bowling ball, she managed to get outside in time to see Willard hoofing it down the street in pursuit of a younger, fitter, faster perp who was clearly pulling away.

She stopped, evaluated the situation, and immediately called it in. There was no way they were going to catch Archer by themselves.

"Got'a suspect on the run!" she radioed, trying to keep her voice calm yet energized enough to communicate the urgency. She gave them Archer's name, description, and location, then jogged off in the direction they'd disappeared. She was hoping the perp wasn't carrying a gun.

It didn't take her long to catch up to the panting Detective, bent nearly in two trying to catch his breath.

"Where'd he go?!" she called out, hoping she might still have a chance of running him down.

"How the hell would I know?" Willard growled between wheezing breaths. "Little bastard's… fast, I'll give him that much."

Daniels knew the perp didn't have to be too fast to outrun a tub of lard like Willard, but she didn't think it would be in her best interest to share her opinion.

"Which way?"

Willard flicked his head straight ahead.

"I'll be back," she said as she broke into a jog. "I called in the reserves!"

The street was unnaturally empty; word had apparently spread quickly. Still, Archer was nowhere to be seen and so the officer kept on the same path, hoping he'd done the same. After two blocks, still no sign of him. She was just

about to turn back when the scream of two black and whites
brought her up short. One of the two screeched to a stop
right beside her.

"What's his 10-20?" the young officer driving asked
through his lowered window.

'Must be a rookie,' Daniels thought. "Not sure," she
answered, "my partner thought he was headed that way." She
pointed down the street.

"We'll see what we can see. You okay?"

"Yeh, fine. Go see if you can flush him out."

The car sped off in a squeal of tires, a cloud of exhaust,
and the renewed wail of the siren. Daniels considered
continuing on a short ways, just to be a good sport, but
decided against it. She already had a stitch in her side, Willard
looked like he might drop dead from a heart attack, and the
perp was likely long-gone. She turned around and started to
walk slowly back toward where she'd last seen Willard.

She'd only gone a short way, less than two blocks, when a
familiar shape materialized from an alleyway not twenty feet
ahead of her. Archer saw her at the same moment she saw
him. She reached for her gun and he took off running.

"Stop – Police!" she called out, as if he didn't know who
she was. She broke into a fast jog, but she knew within the
first five seconds she wasn't going to catch the little bastard.
Willard was right: he was too fast. She saw him speed around
the corner of an intersection maybe 100 yards ahead.

'Hell, he's history,' she thought, holstering her weapon. She
slowed to a tired stroll. It probably took her less than a
minute to reach the intersection, so the last thing in the world
she expected when she turned the corner was to see Willard
hauling Archer to his feet, his hands cuffed behind his back.

"You got him!" Daniels said, the obvious seeming her only choice given the circumstances.

"Ran right into the fat pig," Archer snarled through bloodied lips. "Or he'd never've laid a hand on me."

"Dream on. We always get assholes like you, sooner or later."

"Read him his rights?" Daniels asked.

"Be my guest."

She recited the admonishment against self-incrimination in the bored sing-song voice of a cop who's said the same thing a thousand times.

"Yeh, right," Archer spit.

One of the black and whites appeared just then and took him off their hands. As he was being sandwiched into the back seat of the car, he couldn't resist one last challenge.

"You ain't got nothing on me. I'll be out before you get off-duty."

"You'll be lucky if you get out before I retire," Willard shot back. They all saw the impact his riposte had in the perp's expression, which changed from cocky to concerned in a millisecond.

"I hope they lock that little asshole up and throw away the key," the Detective said as they watched the car drive away.

"I just hope they get a conviction. With the courts the way they are these days, who knows?"

CHAPTER 8

She was in the process of shutting down her computer and locking up when the phone rang.

It was Officer Daniels. "Got him," she said.

"Archer?"

"He tried to run, but we got lucky."

"Is he... in jail?" She almost couldn't formulate the words.

"He is. And with any luck, he'll be there for quite some time."

"With any luck?"

Daniels cursed her sloppiness. *Watch what you say!* "Like we told you before, he'll get a hearing. Probably won't make bail, but you never know."

"You said it was very unlikely!" Daniels could hear the panic.

"It *is* unlikely."

"When will we know?"

"Not sure. Probably within a few hours, unless they can't get him in front of a judge until tomorrow."

No response.

"You okay?" the officer asked Janice.

"Yeh, yeh, I'm fine," she answered with that far-away distracted voice Daniels had heard so many times before. The legal system was not conducive to clear thinking or pleasant dreams. It was a meat-grinder that caught victims as well as criminals in its gaping maw. "What happens if he gets out?"

Daniels knew she meant 'what will happen to me?'

"Probably nothing to worry about. Unlikely he'd go back to

your house." She hated the required vagaries, the practiced half-truths that hid more than they revealed.

"He said he'd cut me and my son into pieces if we called anyone." The small flutter in her voice alerted the officer that the woman was close to cracking.

"He just wanted to intimidate you," she said with confidence she didn't feel. "Besides, I'll call the Prosecutor's office and let them know he said that. Another reason to keep him locked-up."

Another long pause. "Then what?"

"Like we told you, we'll call you in to identify him in a lineup. Probably in a day or two."

"Do I *have* to identify him?"

"We can't *force* you to come in, but like we explained, it adds credibility to the charges."

"I don't know…"

"Look, we'll cross that bridge when we come to it. For now, you can rest easy knowing he's behind bars."

"For now."

Yeh, for now.

*****

The warehouse never seemed any bigger or emptier than when Janice turned the lights out. Every little sound seemed magnified, echoing in the darkness like distant thunder before a storm. She forced herself to go through her usual routine as if it were just another day, an effort that was doomed to failure from the very beginning. The more she tried to ignore the feelings of dread that seemed to ooze from the shadows in every corner of the building, the less she was able to control the prickling unease that crept up the back of her neck. Just as she was locking her desk and was about to set the alarm and leave, the phone rang. She nearly swallowed her tongue.

It was a longtime customer checking on a shipment. She had to restrain herself from jumping all over him. As it was, she knew she was being unnecessarily snippy and short with the poor guy, but she couldn't help it. She wanted out. Right then. As quickly as she could, she provided just enough information to satisfy his curiosity while all the while her eyes scanned the far reaches of the warehouse, her ears straining for any unexpected sound. By the time she finally hung-up - barely two minutes later - she was sweating, the self-imposed tension utterly draining.

'Let me out of here!' she insisted as she activated the alarm and hurried out the back exit. The sun had fallen below the rooftops and the shadows had grown long and threatening as she made her way around the huge building to where her car was parked. Every day she faced the same dilemma: park in front and have a short walk to start the day but a long walk to end it, or vice versa. Somehow she usually succumbed to the allure of the short early morning stroll and put off the nerve-wracking perimeter sprint until end-of–day. It hadn't mattered much until the attack. Now… it mattered.

The main problem was that she was almost always the last to leave. The forklift operators, the warehouse stockers, even the managers usually hit the road at 4:31, at the latest. She rarely got out of her little corner cubicle until 6, sometimes – like this night – even later. What seemed during the day like nothing more than a large, ugly, 1970's-era monstrosity became an evil entity, a hulking nightmare ready to collapse upon her with unspeakably vile consequences.

By the time she jumped into her car and locked the door, she was sweating, her heart was pounding, and her thoughts... well, better not to examine those too closely. It wasn't until she saw the dark umbra of the warehouse fade to nothingness in the rearview mirror that she was able to focus on her driving and let its unspoken threats fade as well. Not that she could stop the thoughts. Nothing but non-stop, fully-involving work could drive them from her consciousness. And even then, just for a while.

She turned the radio as loud as it would go to try to blast the black thoughts into oblivion, but they sneered at her feeble attempts and raised their own volume to match. When would it ever end? When would it be over?

A flash out of the corner of her eye and her foot hit the brakes reflexively. The tires screamed in an uncontrolled skid and she felt the car slide sideways into the intersection. Time slowed as she awaited the crunch of metal-to-metal contact; she braced for the impact she knew was coming. Screeching brakes, a horn's blare: she closed her eyes and waited. And waited...

When she opened them again she saw a white van stopped mere inches from her driver's side door, a fat, red-faced driver screaming what she could only assume were obscenities at her through his windshield. She mouthed *'I'm sorry'* to him and waved feebly. She re-started the stalled car and – after checking carefully in all directions – continued on through the intersection, her mind numb with fright and relief.

*****

"You look like hell," her mother said as soon as she stepped through the door. Janice knew it must be bad for her mother to swear, but she didn't care.

"It's been a hell of a day," she answered, only after the fact glancing around to make sure Jackie wasn't close-by.

"Want to talk about it?"

Actually, she did. But not just yet. "Where's Jackie?"

"In his room. Reading one of the books I brought with me, last I saw."

"Let me say hi and change. Then I'll be back."

When she opened the door to her son's room she found him sitting on his bed, propped-up against a stack of pillows on the headboard, reading as intently as a third-year grad student. The sight made her smile at the same time it reminded her how quickly he was growing up. It took him a second to realize she was there.

"Mommy!" he cried, jumping off the bed and running to her with arms open wide.

She gave him a crushing hug and kissed the top of his head. "What were you reading?"

"It's this really cool Star Wars story – one they haven't even made into a movie, yet!"

His enthusiasm for all things Star Wars was legendary, though she was somewhat taken-aback to learn he was now reading the books. It had been all videos and computer games up til now.

"Sounds great!' she said. "You hungry for supper yet?"

"I'm right in the middle of a good part," he complained. "Could we eat a little later?"

"I think that could be arranged," she said, secretly thrilled she'd have a chance to unwind a bit before taking-on dinner. "I'll call you when it's ready." He was back reading before the door closed.

She changed out of her work clothes and into one of the loose-fitting casual outfits she favored for at-home wear. She glanced at her reflection in the bedroom mirror and shook her head resignedly. It was worse than she'd thought. She looked five years older, the circles under her eyes not half-disguised by the concealer she'd applied so carefully that morning. Her hair stuck-out on one side and her mascara had run a little from both eyes. *'Night of the Living Dead,'* she mused, only half in jest. With a deep sigh she opened her door and walked back to the kitchen, where she dug around in the fridge looking for something to transform into dinner.

"What're you doing in there?" her mother called out from the living room. "I've got your glass of wine already poured out here."

She had to smile. Her mom knew her all too well. "Seeing if we have anything to eat for supper," she answered.

"Already have some chicken marinating in that blue bowl. Thought I'd grill it with a baked potato and a salad."

Janice wanted to hug her. "Thanks, Mom. Can I get you anything?"

"I'm fine. Come on out – have a seat. Relax a bit."

Janice could hear her mother's trademark care-giving voice, but for once it didn't annoy her. She did as she was told, too tired to argue.

"Tough day?" her mother asked as she collapsed onto the couch with a satisfied groan.

"Not good."

"Drink some of your wine. It's good for what ails you."

Janice didn't object. She felt rather than tasted the Cabernet slide down her throat and nearly moaned with pleasure as the first sedating waves of alcohol crashed upon the sharp-edged rocks of her battered mind.

"So?" Her mother was not going to let it go.

"It's just... I don't know. I guess I still haven't worked through the repercussions of the attack."

Her mother screwed-up her face in evident displeasure. "It's been less than a week!" she finally said when she couldn't restrain herself any longer.

"I know. But..."

"No 'but'!" Her mom took a deep breath to calm herself. "You need to give yourself time. This isn't a stubbed toe or toothache. Isn't that what your psychiatrist said?"

"Psychologist." She knew she was being petty but couldn't resist.

"And?"

"And, yes, she said it might take a while to work through it. *But,*" her voice increased by several decibels, "I want it over. I want everything back like it was." She knew she sounded naïve bordering on juvenile.

Her mother's face relaxed into pure sympathy. "I know you do, honey. We all do. But it's not so simple."

'How would you know?!' she wanted to shout. She ground her teeth instead.

"You've had a terrible shock, physically, emotionally, every which way. I have no idea how long it'll take to *work it through,* but you need to be patient. It'll come, but maybe not as fast as you'd like it to."

Part of Janice wanted to snap at her mother's well-meaning interference; part wanted to hug her for caring. The internal conflict was too much, mixed in with the near-accident, the wine… everything. She tried to hold it in, but the mixture was more potent than she'd thought. Before she knew what was happening, tears were streaming down her cheeks and her mother was hugging her around her shoulders.

It all spilled out then: the warehouse, the near-accident, even her paranoia that the intruder would be granted bail and get out, his threat hanging over her like an emotional guillotine. The more she talked the more the tears flowed and the tighter her mother held her. By the time she finished, in what seemed like an endless confessional torrent, she fell back against her mother's shoulder, drained, exhausted.

"My poor girl," her mom cooed, the first words she'd spoken for a very long time. Her hands stroked Janice's arms, reminding her of when she'd been a small child and had sought refuge in those same arms from any number of injuries, real or imagined. The tears had stopped. "You're a strong wonderful young woman. You'll be back, even better than before." She didn't need to explain *before* what.

Incredibly, Janice believed her. Only a mother can say something so… distant, and make it seem like a sure thing.

"Feeling a little better?" her mom asked.

She smiled, not forced, or tentative, but a real, honest smile. "Thank you, Mom." She hugged her back, the warmth of her mother's body seeping into her own.

"Hey, what d'ya say we go get Jackie and get an ice cream cone somewhere? My treat."

"*Before* dinner?"

"Just this once."

"Sure. Why *don't* we?" Janice said, wiping the last vestige of tears from her eyes with the backs of her hands.

They half-pushed, half-pulled themselves off the couch and – with one last silent hug – headed down the hall toward Jackie's room.

It would be better now. It already was.

*****

The next day dawned brighter, if only a little. For the first time in days Janice didn't think of *'it'* as soon as she opened her eyes. Instead, she remembered Jackie's laughter the night before, and the relative normality of her conversations with her mother on the way home. A smile crept across her lips, an alien creature desperately welcomed. She hesitated getting out of bed, fearing the aura of normalcy might vanish if she left the consoling confines of her covers. But leave them she did, and not even a hot shower and two cups of coffee managed to dissipate the glow that emanated from every pore of her being.

Until, that is, mid-morning at work. Everything was going along fine, no unusual problems, no overly-solicitous coworkers, not even too many complaints from the usual whining clients. Until 11:07 am. The phone rang at exactly that hour, as it had many other times that morning, but when she picked it up she knew almost immediately that her happy, forward-looking optimism was about to be shattered.

"Eagle Transport," she answered.

"Janice, it's me, Officer Daniels."

At first Janice couldn't answer, her breath a sodden lump in her throat. "Officer Daniels," she finally managed to croak, "to what do I owe this unexpected call?"

"I hate to bother you at work like this, but like I told you, we need you to come in to ID the perp."

"ID the perp?" She'd heard the lingo on all the TV cop shows, but she wanted to be very sure she understood exactly what Daniels meant.

The Officer got the message. "Sorry. We need you to identify the guy we've got in custody. From a line-up. There'll be a half-dozen or so men that fit his general description, and we'll ask you to pick him out."

There was a long pause. "I thought it wouldn't be for a day or two." She sounded like a wounded little girl.

"Yeh, that's what I thought too. But his pro-bono lawyer is already pushing for a bail hearing, so we need to get moving."

"I thought he wouldn't get bail!" The very thought both angered and sickened her.

"Unlikely, but possible. He doesn't have any major priors, so some judge might think he doesn't pose a flight risk."

"But he *raped* me!" Now the anger was coming out full-force.

"Yeh, yeh I know. It stinks. In a perfect world, he'd stay behind bars until his trial. But, this ain't a perfect world."

You're telling me,' she thought. "So, when is this... line-up?"

"Can you be down here at one? Maybe you can stretch your lunch hour..."

An hour and a half. "Will he be able to see me?" she asked.

"The perp? Nah. You'll be behind a one-way mirror. All he'll see is himself, and the other five or so guys."

Her thoughts bounced crazily. "Yeh, okay. I can be there," she answered as soon as she could formulate the reply. "Is there parking?" The question sounded too mundane, almost comical.

"What? Oh, yeh, sure. Park in the lot right next to the Department. I'll get you a visitor's pass."

Another long pause. "Okay. Then I guess I'll see you at one."

"Good. And Janice?"

"Yeh?"

"Don't let this wind you up. He won't see you, he won't hear you, he won't even know you were here."

Until they charge him,' she thought. *Then he'll damn well know I was there.*'

"Yeh, sure. Anything else I need to know?"

"Nope. Just bring your glasses if you need them to see at a distance."

"I don't wear glasses."

"Then you're all set. See you at one."

"Right." Before she could say anything else, the dial tone exploded in her ear. She returned the phone to its cradle as if it were a venomous snake about to strike. In fact, it already had.

*****

The downtown police station was neither new nor ingratiating. It featured the drab gray poured concrete exterior so popular in the early 70's, the look made even more gruesome by the tiny glass slivers that passed for windows. None of that made much of an impact on Janice as she arrived mid-day. Her thoughts were focused on the line-up and nothing else. If she could have mustered the self-consciousness to analyze her feelings she would have been forced to admit she had none - she was basically numb. She put one foot in front of the other and forced herself to walk into a bad dream come to life.

A slightly overweight cop in his late 50's or early 60's sat behind a counter just inside the entrance. She went up to him like a prisoner approaching the noose.

"Ah, I'm here for a line-up?" she said with barely enough force to be heard over the radio playing some kind of Latin music just inches from her left arm.

The cop looked up at her with an expression of bemused indifference. "Victim or perp?" he said without so much as a hint of a smile.

The question momentarily stunned her. "I... ah... I'm supposed to identify the bastard who raped me."

The smart-ass look on the cop's face faded slightly. "Oh, right. Daniel's case. I'll call her to come get you. Just wait a second."

Janice tried to ignore the hot red blotches forming on her cheeks as the cop picked up the phone and dialed an extension.

"Yeh, your witness is here for the line-up," he announced. "I'll tell her." He hung up the phone. "Officer Daniels is on her way. She'll be out in a few jiffs."

"Thanks," Janice said, though she was tempted to say considerably more.

She turned and looked around her at the sterile reception room: a half-dozen battered plastic chairs of three different designs, two snack machines, and a message board with so many overlapping slips of paper it looked more like a leaf pile in late October.

"Ms Greyson?" the familiar voice startled her back to awareness.

"Officer Daniels!' She tried not to sound like a drowning swimmer reaching for a life preserver, but was only partially successful.

"How you doin'? You ready for this?"

She wasn't at all sure if she was, but she wasn't going to let anyone know either. "Yeh, I'm good. Thanks."

"Good. It'll only take a few minutes. Relatively painless." She smiled, but the word 'relatively' hung in the air.

Daniels led her back through narrow, noisy corridors to a modest room somewhere in the bowels of the building. If the reception room was stark, this was downright barren. Two chairs - likely nabbed from the three reception room sets - and nothing else. One half of one whole wall consisted of a darkened window. Janice knew intuitively it was a one-way mirror.

Daniels reached for a wall switch and suddenly another, larger room appeared on the opposite side of the mirror.

"The suspects will be standing in there. Like I said, six or so of them," she explained. "You'll be able to see them, but they can't see you. For them, it's just a mirror."

"But they'll know I'm here, won't they," Janice said, more a statement than a question.

"Doesn't matter. They can't see you."

"But he'll know it's me. The one who did it, I mean."

Daniels shrugged. "I suppose. But we don't announce who's in here. He'll just be guessing."

"Uh huh…" She looked around anxiously. "They won't be able to hear us, will they?"

"No, of course not. But better to keep your voice down anyway."

She wasn't sure if she'd be able to say a word.

"Ready?" Daniels asked. She nodded.

The officer touched another switch as she spoke into a microphone. "Let's get this moving," her voice boomed over a speaker somewhere outside the room. "Bring 'em in."

Once more she felt tiny pinpricks of tension sweep across her body as the muscles in her chest constricted. From behind a metal door came seven young men, each of them a rough - in some cases, *very* rough - approximation of the man who attacked her. She caught herself holding her breath as they shuffled in, their expressions ranging from sullen to confrontational. When her attacker appeared, she felt a stab of cold fear in her guts, a reaction that angered as much as sickened her. A male officer arranged the seven in front of numbers painted on the wall behind them.

"Ok, eyes up - look into the mirror!" Daniels barked into the mike. Most did as they were told. *He* barely glanced up, a self-assured smile on his lips. "Now turn to your right," Daniels continued. "Now, your left."

There was no doubt in her mind. It was *him*, with no sign of regret, or fear, or anything other than sheer, utter contempt shining through his narrowed, dark eyes. It seemed to Janice as if he were trying to peer through the mirror, to pierce the barrier that separated the two of them. She drew back against her will.

"Do you see the guy who attacked you?" Daniels asked.

She wanted to shout, to condemn him to everyone within earshot. But her mouth was dry and her reply came out more like a frightened gasp. "Yeh. Number 3."

"You sure?"

"I'm sure."

"Okay." She patted Janice on the arm. "Well done." Pushing the button on the microphone, she directed the cop shepherding the seven men, "You can let 'em all go, Mike. Except Number 3."

Her attacker stared at the mirror long and hard, his smile unwavering. But Mike the cop grabbed him by the elbow and ushered him out of the brightly lit line-up room.

"What now?" she asked.

"Now we file the charges, and you go back to work, or wherever."

"And *him*, what happens to him?"

"He goes back into an 8x10 holding cell."

"And he stays there until the trial?"

The Officer shifted her weight from one foot to the other. "Most likely. But in the end, that's up to a judge."

"They wouldn't let him out, would they? I mean, you said he might get bail…"

"We'll ask that he be held without bond, but I've seen some crazy stuff down here…"

Janice nodded solemnly. What could she say?

"You just go back to work and let us handle all this," Daniels continued. "Live your life. Don't let that scumbag ruin your day."

"Yeh, okay," Janice said, feigning a weak smile. *'Easy for her,'* she fretted. *'He doesn't know where she lives.'*

Daniels walked her out to the reception area, maintaining a constant upbeat monologue that Janice really didn't hear.

"So, you gonna' be ok?" the cop asked when they'd arrived in the midst of a half-dozen other civilians wearing the same distracted look of utter confusion.

"I'll be fine." She had no idea if that was true, but that's what Daniels wanted to hear. So she said it.

"Good, good. I'll keep you updated."

Janice found herself nodding, her mind racing.

Daniels gave her shoulder a little hug. "Drive careful."

And then she was alone, surrounded by strangers, but alone. She walked woodenly out into the bright sunshine and climbed into her car.

*****

It had taken a while - most of the afternoon actually - for Janice to process what had happened that day, but eventually the demands of her work overwhelmed her fears and she settled back into her usual routine. By the time the end of the day rolled around, she was actually feeling something close to relieved. Good thing, since she had promised herself she wouldn't bring her neuroses back home with her. No need to make her Mom and Jackie any more upset than they already were.

They went out for dinner - if you could call MacDonalds dinner, but since that's what Jackie wanted, that's where they went. They'd just come back into the house, laughing at some silly little joke Jackie had made, when the phone rang. Janice tried not to flinch, tried to hold onto the good thoughts that had nested in her mind since coming home, but the thoughts fluttered anxiously as the shrill electronic shriek repeated and she found her heart thumping with an adrenalin rush she could neither block nor control.

Her mother must have seen her reaction. "Want me to get that?"

"No, that's okay. I'll get it."

She picked up the phone with tingling hands. "Hello?"

"Janice. It's Officer Daniels." She didn't sound happy. The tingling swept through her entire body, ultimately curling up in a quivering ball in her stomach.

"Oh, hi Officer. This is a bit of a surprise."

"Yeh, well, we've had a development and we thought you should know about it."

"A development?"

"Archer – your intruder. He made bail."

For a long moment there was no sound but the rasp of her breathing. "But, I thought you said there was almost no chance…" She couldn't keep the fearful whine from her voice.

"His high-powered pro-bono defense attorney from one of the big downtown firms apparently talked about his *ties to the community* and convinced the judge he wasn't a flight risk."

"But what he did..!"

A pause. "Yeh… well, I'm afraid there's more."

Janice steeled herself as best she could.

"He's claiming that it was consensual. He says he knew you, and you went along with it."

"That's ridiculous! I never met that man and I certainly didn't *go along* with anything!" The whine had morphed into indignant disbelief.

"I know that, but the judge had to weigh the various claims."

"They never even called me to testify!"

"It was a bail hearing - they usually don't take witnesses. And they had your statement." Daniels sounded like she was just going through the motions. Maybe she was as stunned as Janice.

Janice didn't know what else to say. She was lost. The warm reassuring hand that landed on her shoulder brought her back to reality, if that's what you could call it.

"You okay?" her mother whispered.

She nodded, none too convincingly.

"We're going to send a black and white out there to drive past your house every few hours," Daniels went on. "Let everyone know we're keeping an eye on you."

Every few hours? "Did he say anything about coming here?"

"No!" the officer answered definitively. "It's just a precaution. To put your mind at rest, you know?"

Her mind was anything but at rest. "Yes, okay, thank you for that. Is there anything we should do?"

"Just keep all your doors and windows shut and locked, and keep your phone nearby. Do you have an alarm?"

Not reassuring. Not reassuring at all. "No, no alarm."

"No problem. I'm sure he won't go out there – the judge warned him against any further contact. Just go about your normal routine and try not to think about the jerk."

Pink elephant. Pink elephant. "Yeh, I'll try to do that. Thanks for calling."

"You're welcome. Let's talk again tomorrow."

As she hung up she nearly collapsed against the kitchen counter.

"What is it?!" her frightened mother asked, her support the only thing keeping Janice upright. Thankfully, Jackie was already hard at play in his room. She didn't want him to see her like that.

"He's out," she managed to whisper. She didn't need to say who. Her mother knew immediately.

"But…" she began before catching herself, "he certainly won't come anywhere near you. That would be crazy!"

Almost as crazy as… raping a woman in her own home in the middle of the day. Her mother's confidence was not transferable.

*****

Hours later, with Jackie sound asleep in her bed (he'd been coming to her bedroom nearly every night since the intruder), and her mother ensconced in her own room (probably reading or listening to talk radio), Janice allowed herself one last glass of wine and a few moments of solitude to think things through. She settled down on the worn living room couch, moving one of Jackie's toys aside with unconscious familiarity, and stared into the darkness as she sipped her Chardonnay.

*What did I ever do to deserve this? My whole life I've tried to be the kind of person my parents would be proud of, and yet here I am, huddled in my living room, scared half-out of my mind, waiting for this asshole to come finish the job he started. I've had lots of friends, more like acquaintances I suppose, who've lied, cheated, you name it, and their lives have been pretty much normal. At least from the outside. I guess no one really knows what goes on behind closed doors. Not even **my** friends. But none of them have had to put up with anything like this! And why* *me? Of all people, how did he pick me? I know life isn't fair, but this is… bullshit!'*

Without warning, tears began to stream down her face once again. At first she tried to rub them away with a vicious swipe of her hand, furious that she'd let some deranged maniac get to her, shake her to her very core. But her anger lasted only moments before the flood of emotions - the pain, the embarrassment, the fear - overwhelmed her determination and she deflated into a quivering ball, her pathetic whimpers heard only by herself.

Which is where her mother found her a half-hour later, asleep, her empty wine glass tipped on its side in a damp spot on the rug. She debated waking her and sending her to her bedroom, but on second thought decided to let her sleep where she was. She unfolded a blue afghan she'd made herself and draped it over her daughter's body. Then she dabbed at the wine stain with a wet paper towel, turned off the lights, went back to her room and tried to sleep.

CHAPTER 9

Officer Daniels sipped her third cup of coffee as she reviewed the Greyson file at her precinct desk. Usually she didn't let a case get to her like this, keeping her awake even when her eyes were so heavy at night she could barely force them open. But for some reason this one got to her all the way, touched her somewhere inside she thought she'd walled off completely. She'd dealt with other rape cases, plenty of them actually. All of them made her angry, all of them made her want to take a scalpel to the offending body parts of the perps. But most of the others… well, she wouldn't say they *deserved* it, but most of them put themselves in a position where it could happen: too drunk, too friendly, whatever. It was rare that a victim seemed to be picked at random, minding her own business in her own home, a true innocent insofar as anyone could be called innocent these days. Worse of all, it made her realize 'There but for the grace go I.' And that scared her.

She knew she'd been putting in too much time on the case. Even Willard had noticed. But she wanted to nail the bastard. For Greyson, sure, but for herself and every other woman out there as well. No guy could really understand what a rape did to the victim. *What the hell, just get on with it,'* seemed to be the general opinion of most guys. Not all, but most.

What if it'd been them? What if some bigger dude had corn-holed *them*? She'd seen some tough guys crack-up completely when their jail-time had included an unplanned poop-chute party. But when it happens to women? Then the empathy was sorely lacking. She needed to make up for that, no matter what Willard - or any of them - thought. This guy was going down.

"That Greyson case *again?*" her partner's voice intruded. Had he stressed the last or was it just her imagination?

"He made bail."

"And? Two-thirds of the judges out there don't give a damn about the victims. You know that."

"There's no way that asshole should've been turned loose. Janice is scared he's gonna come looking for her."

"That's what they all think. But they hardly ever do."

"And if he's the one who actually does?"

Willard shrugged his hefty shoulders. "Bad luck. Nothin' to be done about it."

She wanted to scream at him: *"What's wrong with you, you stupid moron?! Don't you care about these people?"* But she was pretty certain she already knew the answer to her own question: No, by and large, he didn't give a damn. To him, and many more like him, they were just faceless 'chumps', in the wrong place at the wrong time. But Janice had been in her own home. Are you a chump if you do everything right and still get screwed?

*****

Although her desk was piled-high with manila case folders and reams of paper that gushed from each one of them, Daniels decided to ignore their silent entreaties and go pay this Archer jerk a visit. She should've told Willard; he *was* working the case with her – in theory. But she knew he'd give her crap about spending so much time and effort, so she conveniently *forgot* and headed out on her own. She made a token attempt to enlist one of her male counterparts on the way out of the building, but he wasn't available and she didn't want to waste any more time begging for backup.

In order to make bond, Archer had to give the Court an address where he could be located. Daniels knew it was probably a dead-end - either the apartment of a friend or a location he pulled out of his butt. She was going to check it out anyway. There was always the one in ten chance he'd been stupid enough to give a real address. Besides, she didn't have anything better to go on.

Not surprisingly, the apartment building was a run-down wreck surrounded by buildings equally decrepit, if not more so. The area had been an Italian immigrant community 60 years earlier. Now, it was the home of poor, largely illegal Latinos, with a smattering of blacks too poor, too old, or too lazy to move a few blocks uptown. It was the kind of place Daniels and her fellow cops visited much too often; usually for domestic violence calls or gang banging. She parked the car in plain sight, hoping the visibility would provide some semblance of security. One of the other beat cops in her command had parked on a side street in a similar neighborhood just a couple of weeks earlier, and they'd stolen everything but the steering wheel: tires, radios, even the seats. Probably a gang wanting to embarrass the force. None of that stuff would bring enough cash to justify the risk, but any opportunity to make the cops look bad was an opportunity too good to pass-up.

A handful of young punks hung out on the street corner, all of them eyeing her with a mix of hostility and brazen disrespect. "Hola, Muchacha, que pasa?!" one yelled out. "Goin' to get your oil changed?" another added. The raucous laughter echoed through empty streets; Daniels ignored them. She purposely kept her pace steady and her eyes locked on the doorway straight ahead of her. Street punks were like sharks: they could smell fear.

She stomped her way up the unpainted stairway, making no effort at stealth or subtlety. Both would be lost on the inhabitants of that dump. It was kind of like giving rattlesnakes plenty of notice: less probability of getting bit if you didn't surprise them. That was her theory, anyway. She felt eyes on her as she walked down the hallway to the apartment listed on Archer's papers, but didn't bother to acknowledge them. She did allow her hand to brush against her holster, just to reassure herself that her service revolver was ready and waiting if needed.

She knocked on the door with enough force to show authority, but not so much to suggest she was pissed-off or scared.

The door opened a crack. "Yeh?" a young woman answered, peering through the thin opening.

"I'd like to speak with Daniel Lee Archer," she said, trying to keep her voice modulated.

"He ain't here."

"Does he stay here?"

"Sometimes."

"Has he been here lately?"

The young woman's eyes narrowed. "What you want to know for?"

"I need to talk to him. Like I said."

"Well, he ain't here, and I don't know where he is."

Daniels started to tell the woman she should call her if Archer showed up, but the door slammed shut before she could get the words out. She shook her head. "Typical," she muttered. She considered pounding on the door again until the woman answered and took her card, but decided it would be a waste of time. She turned and started down the hallway. She hadn't gotten more than halfway back to the stairway when a door opened just ahead of her and to her left. Her hand strayed to the holster once more. It was an older woman, probably pushing 70, although in those projects it was hard to tell how old anyone really was.

"Yo' lookin' fo' her brutha'?" the women whispered conspiratorially, nodding her head toward the apartment Daniels had just left.

"You know where he is?"

"Ain't been here fo' three days or so. What he done now?"

"That'd be between me and him." She slid a business card from her pocket. "If you see him around, you give me a call?"

The old woman took it, glancing at the card perfunctorily before sticking it under her bra strap for safekeeping.

"I think on it," she said, before closing her door without another word.

Daniels sighed and started back down the stairway to the street. She got a lot of her tips from people like the old woman, but she probably gave out a hundred cards for every call she got back. She guessed the odds were 50-50 with this one. Not something she could - or would - count on.

Just as she was coming down the last flight of stairs, three of the punks who'd been hanging on the street corner slid into the doorway, their wiry muscled bodies black cutouts against the bright afternoon sun outside.

"Muchacha! Fancy meeting you here," one called out.

"That weren't long enough for a decen' oil change," another added.

Daniels slowed gradually to a stop, just a couple of steps from the blocked exit. She felt the fight-or-flight adrenaline rush she'd come to know so well over the years, and her hand landed instinctively on the butt of her pistol.

"Don't you boys have anything better to do than block doorways?" she said with as calm a tone as she could muster through a pounding heartbeat.

"Oh, I imagine there's a few things we could do," the seeming leader of the trio said. "Can't you think of some things?" he added to his buddies.

"Oh yeh, we can think of some things," another said, his stare icy cold despite the forced smile.

"Then why don't you just mosey along and *do* them," the officer said.

The leader of the group took a step to the side and waved his hand majestically.

"After you," he offered with a hint of a bow.

She hesitated a heartbeat, then decided that any indecision could prove catastrophic and continued down the last steps.

"Good decision," she growled as she reached for the panic bar on the metal exterior door.

Her hand never made it that far. One of the young thugs grabbed her arm and twisted it behind her back while another threw a bony mitt of a hand over her mouth, stifling the pained scream that tried to escape her throat. She reacted instinctively, kicking back against an exposed shin while flailing with her free elbow trying to catch a nose or jaw. She heard a shouted profanity as her steel-reinforced boot struck home, but the elbow struck only air; pain shot all the way up her neck as her other arm was bent back past horizontal.

She felt powerful arms grab her legs moments before she was thrown dismissively down on the concrete floor. A hand tore at the front of her uniform and then slipped roughly inside her bra, the calloused palm pawing painfully at her breast. She heard rather than felt her belt being unfastened, the sound giving her strength to kick out against the arms pinning her legs to the floor. But it was not enough. There were too many of them, and they were too strong. She began to steel herself for the inevitable, even as she continued to fight as best she could. Her fury was nearly spent when bright light flooded into the landing and a powerful voice shouted: "Turn her loose! Get yo' fuckin' hands up in the air before I blow yo' fuckin' heads off!"

In that instant, the force of the attack dissipated, even as the hands stayed pretty much where they'd been.

"Yo' makin' a big mistake, bro'," the presumptive leader of the three threatened in a voice much too calm for Daniel's liking.

"Not as big as you three if yo' don't get up and get the hell outta here - now!" The final order was yelled with such vehemence that Daniels flinched. More importantly, the three gang-bangers jumped up and darted out past the young man's drawn pistol without so much as a sideward glance in his direction. The last guy hesitated as though he might say something, but the new arrival pointed the gun at his head and in just a few heartbeats he was gone too, despite a sullen glare that would've committed mayhem if it could've.

Daniels took a moment to make sure nothing was badly hurt, then struggled to sit up, pulling her uniform top back into place.

"You okay?" her savior asked, standing over her like Ali over Liston.

"Yeh, I'm fine," she growled with less empathy than she might have. She winced at her lack of civility toward this man who'd risked his own safety to protect hers. For the first time she actually looked at him: a youngish black male, maybe 30-35, tall, well-built, with cornrow braids dangling past his shoulders. To be honest, if she'd seen him on the street she'd probably roust him as a gang member.

"Wasn't too bright, comin' in here on yo' own," he said, sticking the pistol in the back of his belt like some 30's gangster.

All the thank-yous bubbling up in her mouth suddenly turned to stone, even though she knew he was right.

"Wasn't too bright to come in here and save me either," she said instead, before catching herself and adding in a tone bordering on gratitude, "but I'm glad you did."

He smiled down at her and reached out a hand. "Come on, get yo'self up and get outta here. They jus' might go get some more of they's homies and come back to finish the job."

The thought roiled her guts, but she took a moment to finish buttoning her blouse. She was a police officer, and no group of punks was going to shake that persona. At least not so anyone could tell.

"Officer Daniels," she said as soon as she'd brushed off her uniform. Her savior took the proffered hand and shook it with a nod of his head. "Nice meetin' yo'. Now yo' need to go."

"And you are?" she pressed.

"The dumb-ass who come to yo' rescue. Now, if yo' ain't goin', then I is." He turned and opened the metal door to the street.

"Hey," she called after him. "Thanks again. Really."

He nodded solemnly. "Ain't nobody deserve that shit. Not even a cop."

Before she could react he'd slipped out the door, leaving her standing in the dimly lit stairwell with no one within earshot. She tried to tell herself that what happened didn't matter, that it was just another staircase, but as hard as she tried she couldn't quite convince herself. After a few seconds to give her rescuer time to get away and give herself time to pull it all together, she slammed her hand against the panic bar and walked out into the brilliant sunshine. She glanced around casually to make sure none of her new *friends* were lying in wait and then forced herself to walk a half-beat slower than normal to her car. She knew there'd be people watching her. Maybe none of the punks, but probably someone who knew them and would give them the play-by-play of her departure. She was determined to show them their attack had failed to shake her, no matter that her knees felt like they could give out at any moment. '*Screw 'em,*' she thought, sliding into the black and white. '*They ain't shit.*'

But when she looked in the rear-view mirror before pulling out of the parking space, the eyes that stared back were dilated and dancing.

CHAPTER 10

She didn't want to open her eyes.

Not because she felt so bad after draining the bottle of wine the night before, although the all-too-familiar sensation of a queasy gut and a blossoming headache reinforced the urge. No, it was a more general feeling, a sense that if she could only lay there on the couch for a day, or two, her eyes glued shut, maybe all the bad crap that had been swirling around her those last few days would somehow blow away, or dissipate to a gentle breeze from the black-edged tornado that had been wreaking havoc on her life ever since *that* day. But she knew it was just a childish daydream, the sort of fantasy that little kids relied on to make it through bad times. Now she was the adult, and she had to be strong to help Jackie.

With an ill-suppressed groan, she forced herself up to one elbow and looked around the room. Her mother must've spread the afghan over her after she'd passed out, and the faded wine stain on the carper looked like she might've given that a quick once-over as well. Janice would have to thank her.

The smell of coffee and... was it oatmeal?... both repulsed and invigorated her. Mom must already be up and in the kitchen. Janice sucked in a deep breath of stale air. No time to hide. No time to feel sorry for yourself. She forced herself to her feet and stumbled out into the brightly-lit kitchen.

"Rough night?" her Mom asked cheerily as she squinted into the brilliant early morning sunlight. "Have a seat. I've got some hot cereal and coffee, if you can handle it."

"Coffee would be great," she muttered as she collapsed into one of the well-worn chairs surrounding the kitchen table. '*I gotta replace this set,*' she thought as she struggled to refocus her eyes. '*Looks like crap.*'

"You going to work today, or taking a day off?"

"Do I look that bad?"

"No! No, of course not, but maybe a day to yourself is just what you need."

"I don't think my boss would see it that way. No, I'll get it together."

As Jennifer spooned steaming oatmeal into a bowl, she glanced over at her daughter. The sight was not reassuring. "You know, you don't have to be a superwoman with all this. It's okay to just be a normal, everyday person."

Janice raised her eyes to stare at her mother without moving her head. "What's this? I didn't realize you'd become a shrink in your spare time." The jibe was not particularly light-hearted.

"Don't be like that. You know I'm right. Making believe that everything's okay doesn't make it that way. You need to give yourself time to heal."

Janice felt the defensiveness leak out of her. "Yeh, I know Mom. And I appreciate the concern - I really do. But I've got to do this my way. And for now, that means trying to keep my life more or less normal. Including going to work."

Her mother placed the cereal and a cup of coffee on the table in front of her. "Whatever you want to do, just know I've got your back."

Janice fought back tears as she grabbed her mother's waist and pushed her face into the warmth of her stomach. "I know you do, Mom. You always have."

Just then footsteps approached from the hallway.

"What's the matter, Mommy?" Jackie's voice called out. "Are you okay?"

He ran over and wrapped his arms around her shoulders, and for a few moments the three of them fell against each other in a heaving scrum of emotion.

"Yeh, yeh, I'm okay Jackie," Janice said, pulling away from his grasp to surreptitiously wipe her eyes. "Just wanted to give grandma a hug."

"Are *you* okay, Grandma?"

Jennifer forced a smile. "Of course I am, Jackie! I'm here with my best girl and my best guy - how could I not be?"

"Then I'm okay too," he announced with such surety that even Janice had to smile. She gave him a big hug and kissed the top of his head.

"Hey!" he protested, squiggling free. "What's for breakfast?"

*****

The drive to work was less distracted than the ride home the night before, but Janice still had to strain to keep her focus on the road and not in her head. It was a constant challenge to push the negativity from her thoughts while she knew her attacker was out there somewhere, doing what, no one knew. Every time she caught her focus wavering, she turned up the radio a notch and sang along. By the time she reached the warehouse, the music was blaring and she was singing at the top of her lungs.

The silliness of it all made her feel a little better, and she stepped from her car with a sense that maybe everything would work out okay after all. Maybe she just needed to let the system do its thing. Maybe...

Out of the corner of her eye, she saw movement. It wasn't close-by -- maybe thirty or forty feet away, at the corner of the biggest warehouse on the property. As she turned she saw a taunting smile, white teeth gleaming from the darkest shadows. It was *him*, she was almost sure of it!

And then it was gone.

Her heart began thundering as if it would burst through her chest; the ground suddenly shifted beneath her feet.

'It can't be! He wouldn't dare,' she tried to convince herself, but she knew the self-deception before the thought even coalesced. Caught midway between her car and her office, she froze. It was as if her mind could no longer communicate with her limbs. Finally, her eyes still glued to the corner of the warehouse, she forced her legs to carry her back to her car. She locked all the doors and started the engine before pulling her phone from her purse, spilling half its contents on the floor mats.

"Officer Daniels! He was here, the bastard was here!" she screamed into the mouthpiece when the policewoman answered.

"Whoa, whoa, calm down. Is this you, Janice?"

"Yes, yes! But he was here, at my work!"

"Archer?"

"Yes! The SOB was standing in the shadows when I got here this morning!"

"Are you okay? Did he do anything to you?"

"He *smiled* at me. He wanted me to know he could get to me whenever he wanted."

There was a moment of silence on the other end of the line. "He *smiled* at you?"

"He was hiding in the shadow of the warehouse and when I got out of my car and started walking to my office, he just stood there and smiled!"

Another, shorter pause. "Did he say anything? Make any hand motions?"

"No! He just smiled!" She could hear the panic in her voice. She sounded... unhinged. To her credit, Daniels kept her cool.

"We'll have to get a restraining order. Can you get down here today?"

"I've got to work! I've taken too many days already."

"How about on your lunch hour again?"

Janice stopped to consider the idea. "I suppose. How long will it take?"

"I don't know - depends on how quickly we can get a judge to issue the order."

"Okay, but *about* how long? An hour? Two?"

Janice could almost hear the cop weighing the possibilities on the other end. "If all goes well, around an hour. Maybe a little more."

"Okay, yeh, all right. I'll bring my lunch with me and eat it while we're chasing down this judge. Will that work?"

"Should. And Janice, stay calm. We'll stop this creep."

"Can you assign a guard to make sure *he* doesn't get to me?"

A *long* pause. "I can make the request… but I can't make any promises. They don't like to provide protective details."

"But he knows where I *work*! What if he finds out where I live? I have a six-year-old son!"

Janice fought the sob that welled in her throat. She barely suppressed it.

"I'll make the point," Daniels said, but she didn't sound confident.

Janice took a deep breath and let it out slowly. "Okay. Thanks. I'll be down there around 12:30."

"Good. I'll try to get a staffer to book a meeting with one of the sitting judges. As soon as you get to the parking lot, call me on this number." She gave her private cell number. "I'll come right out."

"Yeh, good, good. And Officer - thanks. I'm sorry to be so… shaky."

Daniels was still far from solid herself after the previous day's extracurricular activity. But Janice didn't need to hear any of that.

"You're doin' fine. Just hang tough. That bastard Archer picked the wrong woman when he picked on you."

Despite Daniel's seeming confidence, Janice couldn't stop her hands from shaking.

*****

True to her word, Officer Daniels was waiting patiently when Janice arrived at the downtown headquarters building. What Janice hadn't expected, however, was Daniels' partner Willard accompanying her.

"Ms. Greyson," he greeted her with a nod of his head.

Officer Daniels could see the look of consternation in Janice's eyes. "I've got to run - got called to testify in a case that wasn't supposed to come up for another week or two. Detective Willard will see you through the process," she explained.

"But..." Janice began, only to be cut-off by Willard.

"No worries. I've been through all this a dozen times or more. We'll be in and out in less than an hour."

"Sometimes it's that fast," Daniels said, "but sometimes all the paperwork takes a little longer. Just stay patient."

"I'll try."

With that the officer patted her on the shoulder and looked to the Detective. "Give me a call when you're all through down here, okay?"

"Yeh, sure. They gonna let you keep your phone turned on in the courtroom?"

"If not, I'll get the missed call notice and call you back as soon as I can." She smiled reassuringly at Janice. "Just stay calm."

Janice didn't have time to answer before she turned, her spit-shined shoes beating a staccato rhythm on the hallway linoleum.

"Gets a bit wound-up sometimes," Willard muttered, half to himself.

"She's worried that Archer is free and stalking me," Janice explained bluntly. "I am too."

"And you have every reason to be! Why don't we go get a restraining order to keep that asshole at a distance?" His enthusiasm seemed forced, rehearsed.

She nodded half-heartedly. She didn't feel as comfortable, as secure, as she had with Daniels. *'Maybe I'm just used to her,'* she thought. *'Willard's probably good at what he does.'*

The overweight detective led her through the sterile hallways of the Judicial Building, hallways frequently crowded with victims, criminals, lawyers and cops. Quite the circus, one which might - on some other day - have made her smile. Not this day.

Willard eventually opened a door marked 'Chambers' and stepped aside for Janice to enter.

"May I help you?" a receptionist asked as soon as she stepped into the small outer office. She sounded dis-interested, just this side of hostile. As soon as Willard came in, however, her attitude changed dramatically.

"Detective Willard!" the middle-aged woman greeted him as if he were some long-lost friend. "Haven't seen you down here for quite some time."

"Been out catching crooks," Willard said with as much Dirty Harry inflection as he could muster, which wasn't much.

"Hope you don't expect to find any here today!" the woman chirped. Both she and Willard chuckled. Janice had to restrain herself from commenting.

"Got a meeting with Judge Monahan. Request for a restraining order."

The receptionist looked at Janice for the first time since Willard had come in. "For you?"

"She's got a perp nosing around her," the detective took it upon himself to explain. "A real jerk."

"Then let's get you in there!" She picked up the phone and pushed an intercom button. "Your Honor, Detective

Willard here for an RO request." She listened for a few
seconds before hanging up. "She's running just a few minutes
late," she explained. "Have a seat and she'll be right with
you."

Willard raised his eyebrows in a 'what can you do?'
expression of mild exasperation before sitting heavily in one
of the four brown leather chairs lining the opposite wall.
Janice eased herself into the chair next to him.

"Can I get you anything - Coffee? Water?" the woman
asked, her question seemingly directed at Willard.

"Not for me. You?"

Janice shook her head. "No, thank you." She didn't know
why but she felt too nervous to drink, fearing she might spill
all over herself or the furniture.

They sat there for a while, probably only ten minutes or
so, but it seemed like forever as Janice flipped through an old
People magazine, her eyes barely focusing on all the celebrity
drivel. None of it stuck.

She jumped when the phone rang on the receptionist's
desk.

"You can go in now," she announced a few seconds later.

Janice thought she saw Willard wink at the receptionist,
but she decided to ignore the implications.

The judge's office, hidden behind the third identical dark
wood door on the left side of a short hallway, was smaller
than Janice had imagined but every bit as 'legal regal' in its
decor: books, many of them apparently law books, lined the
bookshelves that ran the length of two walls; two overstuffed
black leather easy chairs and a massive dark wood desk sat on
what appeared to be an older Persian rug; behind the desk,
her black judge's robe hanging limply just behind and to her

right, sat Judge Dena Monahan - a stern but bright-eyed woman of about 60, her thick gray hair pulled back into a simple bun held in place by what appeared to be a pygmy poisoned dart, but might have been something less ominous.

"Detective Willard. I hadn't expected to see you in my chambers quite so soon." The voice was strong but soothing, the tone professionally playful. Janice guessed something had happened involving the two of them quite recently, but she neither knew nor wanted to know what it was.

"Your Honor. Officer Daniels got called away on a last-minute witness appearance."

"So you got stuck with me - is that it?"

"Something like that."

Janice couldn't figure out if they hated each other or just enjoyed the give-and-take.

"I guess we'll both have to live with it. So, what did you bring me?" For the first time the Judge looked over at Janice. "Someone giving you a hard time?"

"The man who raped me," Janice answered, her voice steadier and more controlled than she would have thought.

"Oh?" She turned back toward Willard. "Have you charged him?"

"Oh yeh. But some uptown Pro Bono jerk-off has already bailed him out."

"Somebody's brother or son?"

"Not anybody who could afford that guy's hourly rate - if he was charging."

The Judge returned her attention to Janice. "So, what's the story? How's this guy been causing you problems?"

Janice told the story of arriving at work to find Archer leering at her from the shadows of the warehouse. The Judge listened intently, showing no sign of emotion whatsoever.

"Did he do anything other than smile?" she asked when Janice had finished.

Janice could do nothing more than blink as if she'd been struck between the eyes with a 2x4. *What more did he need to do?'* she felt like shouting.

"No. That was enough," she said instead.

"It's blatant intimidation, Your Honor," Willard chimed-in. Janice had almost forgotten he was there. "The guy's trying to let her know he can get to her anywhere."

"Was that the message you got from his visit?" the Judge asked.

"Yes, that's exactly the message I got," Janice said, the anger in her voice poorly concealed. "The bastard want's me scared - and it's working!"

"Ok, ok - take a deep breath. I'm only asking because I don't want to give his attorney any cause to challenge the order."

"It's psychological abuse!" Willard spoke up again, this time with more energy and conviction than Janice had thought him capable of - at least working on *her* case. "He wants to shake her testimony, or maybe even get her to refuse to testify completely."

The Judge gave him a look that would peel paint. "Thank you for sharing that," she growled, then turned to Janice. "Ignore him. He's been watching too many cop shows... I can tell that you want this guy behind bars, and no amount of intimidation from some dirtbag is going to change that. Am I right?"

Janice spoke before she could think. "Of course that's right! He *raped* me! He should *rot* in jail!"

"Good. And to hopefully make that a little more likely, I'm hereby granting a restraining order, effective immediately and for the duration of the subsequent trial. If you even see the guy again, you call Willard - you understand?"

"Yes, thank you!" She almost felt like crying.

"Or Daniels," Willard added.

"Maybe Daniels first," the Judge said, her scowl not fully disguising a minimal smile. "But with any luck, you won't have to call either one of them. The guy's lawyer will point out the potential negative repercussions if he's caught stalking you. That should be enough."

Janice wasn't so sure. After all, he'd attacked her in her home, for God's sake, and in broad daylight! But she held her tongue. The Judge had been more than sympathetic. No need to ruin things by whining.

"We'll get out of your hair now, Your Honor," Detective Willard said, pushing himself to his feet. "I'm sure you must have *something* to do that's more important than chatting with us."

"I think I can find something," Judge Monahan answered straight-faced. She glanced over at Janice. "You just go about your business, Miss Greyson. Don't let that guy interfere in your daily life."

"Thank you, Your Honor. I'll try."

"Good. I'm sorry you have to go through this, but it'll be worth it if we get the guy off the streets. You're doing the right thing."

The Judge and Willard exchanged nods and the detective opened the door to show her out.

"While you're not letting the perp interfere with your life," he said as soon as the door closed and they were alone in the hallway, "just be sure you keep your eyes open and use your common sense."

He didn't have to explain what could happen if she didn't.

*****

She returned to her work feeling better, if not relieved. She tried to put that leering smile out of her mind, but from time to time it wormed its way back into her consciousness. She'd find herself staring at her computer screen, her hands frozen above the keyboard, her mind empty of everything but that smile. After the third time it happened, she got up and went to the break room to drink a cup of coffee. But the emptiness of the warehouse and the lack of something to redirect her focus to left her feeling more exposed, not less, so she brought the mug back to her desk and went back to the daily grind.

The day seemed to stretch interminably, perhaps because she peeked over at the clock every fifteen minutes or so to convince herself it was moving, and glanced even more frequently at the exterior surveillance monitor to make sure no one - that is, *him* - was sneaking around out there. She tried not to relive the attack, not to think of what had happened, but she found it was easier said than done. Sounds, smells, even completely unrelated images - all sent her back to that day. By late afternoon she was a complete wreck, unable to concentrate, heart pounding, mouth as dry as the stacks of paperwork she left unprocessed on her desk as she packed up and called it a day.

When she got to the door and set the alarm she paused, momentarily frozen in place. Only the increasingly irritating beeps it made eventually forced her to step out into the late afternoon sunlight and lock it all up.

'Wish I could lock up my thoughts as easily,' she fumed as she hurried to her car, her eyes glancing in every direction half-expecting to see *him.*

Only after she'd started the car and put it into gear did she realize she didn't want to go home, not yet, and found herself driving toward the only bar she knew in the neighborhood. It wasn't what you'd call a classy joint, more a dive, actually. But it was a place she'd known for years, and most of the people she saw there were from the neighborhood. Not that she visited often. Especially not since Jackie had been born. A few times during the divorce, maybe. Before that? Occasionally. Usually on a date night, or with the girls, or even a couple of times for karaoke.

Tonight, it was simply to get away - away from the police, away from the court case, away from anything to do with *him.* And maybe to prove to herself that nothing and no one could change how she felt about herself. Besides, it was only for an hour or so. She parked the car in the nearly-full lot, and after one quick look around to make sure no one (*him*) had followed her there, she went quickly and directly in through the front door.

The heady smell of stale beer and a swirling cloud of body odors engulfed her immediately, a stench so familiar, so welcome, she almost sighed with pleasure. The bartender - a woman not much younger than herself - waved a harried hello between customers.

'What was her name again?' Janice wondered as she pushed through the boisterous crowd to a table toward the back of the place where the noise was less than jet engine level. For several moments she just sat and looked around her, not so much to see if *he* was there but to see who *was* there and if anyone had watched her come in. It was an old habit - one that could instantly buoy a battered ego if an interested eye could be met. There were a couple of possibles... She smiled at both of them with her 'yes, I know you were looking and although I make no commitment I'm not opposed to a quick conversation' smile, knowing that even if they hadn't been eyeing her the proffered smile might generate enough interest to boost that battered self-image. One of the two, the younger - actually a few years too young, now that her eyes had adjusted to the dim lighting - smiled back shyly but then turned away and began talking rapid-fire to a guy friend at the same table. She secretly thanked her lucky stars and glanced none too surreptitiously at the older one. Now that she could actually see him, he wasn't half-bad. *'Not too old, not too young - a Goldilocks boy toy.'*

He held her eye without blinking, his smile more inquisitive than come-hither. She wasn't sure if he was checking her out or just curious why she was making eye contact. Janice decided to play it cool and looked around the room once more, feigning nonchalance. So she was honestly startled when her head swiveled back to its starting point and she found Goldilocks standing just a foot or two from her chair.

"Not drinking anything?" he asked. He had a nice voice. Well, not *nice*. That's a word old ladies use to describe cats. It was a rich, virile voice, low in timbre but strong and self-possessed.

"Haven't gotten around to it," she answered, trying not to sound too glib.

"Can I get you something?"

She debated answering with a straightforward "sure", but something prodded her to live dangerously. "Do you work here?" she asked.

He smiled, an *'are you kidding me?'* smile, but not ticked-off. "No. Do you?"

Her turn to smile. "I could use a beer."

"Draft okay?"

"Perfect. Thanks."

"Coming right up….uh…"

"Jan…et," she said after an instant's hesitation. She didn't know why she lied, or maybe she did. Maybe she wasn't going to trust quite so quickly, or make even the slightest commitment quite so easily.

"Okay, Jan…et. Be right back." He hadn't missed the hesitation, but was willing to accept it without comment. A good start. She watched him walk toward the bar. Nice ass. Graceful, self-confident stride.

She took a deep breath. *'What the hell am I doing?'* she thought, but not so vehemently that she changed her mind. She forced herself to look away from his swaying butt, trying to appear less nervous, confused and excited than she felt. No one was looking her way. No one cared that she'd been attacked, or that she was back out living her life once again. They were living their own lives, drinking and talking and flirting like people do.

"Hope Bud will do," that nice deep voice asked and she was yanked back from her reverie. He handed her a tall glass.

"What is this, a quart?"

"Probably a pint. Or maybe just 12 ounces. It's what they serve draft in."

Was he irritated at my little joke?' she wondered. *'Nah, just part of the game.'*

He sat down across from her and for the first time his sweet musky smell drifted in her direction. A good, clean smell.

"So, do you come here often?" he asked with a pointed grin.

She fought the urge to tell him about the rape, to let him know what an effort it was to sit there and smile, to avoid all the alarm bells ringing in the back of her head. "No, not really. Used to, maybe seven, eight years ago."

"Ah, a vet. What brings you back?"

She shrugged. "Just felt like a beer, I guess. How about you? You a regular?"

"Not really. Maybe a couple of times a month. Usually when there's a game on and I don't feel like watching it by myself."

'Was that a hint?' She glanced guiltily at one of the flat screens hanging on the wall. There was a baseball game in progress, but she had no idea who was playing or whether it was something special or not. She wasn't much of a sports fan. "I'm not keeping you from your game, am I?" she asked, half in earnest.

"Nope. It's pretty much of a pitchers' duel. I hate pitchers' duels."

"Yeh, me too," she said with a straight face, but then smiled.

"You're not a big baseball fan?"

"Not a big sports fan. Sorry."

"What *do* you like?"

Wow. This was going fast. Was she up for this? "Oh, I don't know, curling up with a good book, taking my son to see a movie..." She paused to see his reaction.

"How old is he?" He didn't seem nonplussed.

"Six. Going on 21."

He smiled. "My daughter's five. I know the feeling."

Her eyebrows shot up involuntarily. "You have a daughter?"

"Yeh, she's five," he said, the smile returning.

She felt the least bit foolish, but his smile cushioned the blow. "Ah, is that how it works?"

"I think so."

"Divorced?"

"Yep. You?"

"Same."

A lull. The dreaded lull. All the cheap easy lines had played themselves out. Now they had to fish or cut bait. "Does she live with you?"

"My daughter? Nah." His disappointment seemed genuine. "I get her on weekends and for a couple of weeks during the summer. Not long enough, but we have a great time while we can."

"Get along with your ex?"

"Whoa! You get right to it, don't you?"

She blushed and waved her hand. "Sorry! It's just a... subject very close to home. Ignore me if I get too pushy."

"I don't know about *ignoring* you, but how about changing the subject." He reached out his hand. "Mark, Ellington."

"Jan...et," she stumbled once again, drawing pink clouds of embarrassment to her cheeks.

"You'll have to practice that one a bit. Still a little rusty."

His grip was strong, the skin calloused but clean. She decided to ignore his jab. "A pleasure. Are you from around here?"

The conversation degenerated from there into the usual first meeting feeling-out, though with more detail and breadth than she would've initially expected. He worked as a construction foreman, mostly building homes but the occasional small business structure as well. He'd been divorced for three years after having been married for eight. He was originally from the northeast.

She felt an urge to tell him everything about her, including the attack, just to see his reaction. But good sense overcame her impulse and she told only a limited, somewhat edited version. She revealed that she worked as an administrator, but not where. She told the barebones story of her marriage, leaving out the identifiers. He listened. Showed appropriate interest. She was pleasantly surprised.

Pleasantly enough that when she glanced down at her cellphone she was shocked to see that it was nearly 8:30.

"Oh my!' she muttered, more to herself than anyone.

"Problem?"

"I didn't realize how late it'd gotten. I've got to get home to put my son to bed."

He nodded his understanding. "On my weekends with my daughter I'm usually home by 8."

"We're real party animals, aren't we?" she said, somewhat ruefully.

"*Parent* animals," he corrected. "You've got to have priorities."

It was the best thing he'd said all night. "I'm sorry. I've really enjoyed talking to you."

"Same here. Maybe we should do it again sometime." He tried to look nonchalant, but she could see the interest in his eyes. The sight sent a thrill through her body.

"I'd like that."

"Who calls who?" He pulled out his cellphone.

"Give me your number. I've got so much going on right now that I'm not exactly sure when I can get free, but when I do I'll give you a call."

She tapped it into the memory as he dictated. There was something so intimate about the act her hand trembled.

"Well then, until next time." She stood and held out her hand.

"I look forward to it." He held her hand just an instant longer than necessary for a polite goodbye, his eyes staring into hers. Her knees felt weak.

Before any other part of her body could succumb, she turned heel and hurried out through the crowded bar. She was tempted to look back over her shoulder, just to make sure he'd been real and not a figment of her tortured imagination, but she decided she'd rather go home with the fantasy intact, if that was what it was.

When she pushed open the bar door the cool night air and inky blackness injected a chilling dose of reality into her dream world, leaving her dazed and confused. *What was that?*

she wondered. *'Am I nuts giving him even a sliver of hope of something more than a beer and a chat?'*

She started walking toward her car, her mind awhirl. Suddenly she realized where she was, *who* she was, and stopped leadenly in the middle of the lot. Her eyes yanked her head around, peering into every shadow, every unseen space between and behind the parked cars. What was she doing?! He could be there, watching, waiting… She struggled to suck in a breath. As soon as she'd steadied herself, she hurried to her car. No one intercepted her. No one saw her leave.

At least no one she could see.

*****

When she got home she found that her mother had already gotten Jackie into his pajamas and somehow had managed to persuade him to brush his teeth.

"You're kidding me!" she said when informed about the teeth.

"Nope. He seemed to have a good time."

"You're gonna have to let me in on your secret. It's always been a battle."

"Let's talk when he's all tucked-in." It was clear her mother wanted to talk about more than just tooth brushing.

She found her son sitting on his bed, a pile of Legos dumped unceremoniously on the blanket.

"Uh oh, what happened?" she asked.

"Earthquake," he answered without missing a beat.

He barely looked up from what he was doing. She knew she was in the doghouse. She decided to try to ignore his pique.

"How you doin' tonight? All ready for bed?"

"I'm building."

"I think it's about your bedtime…"

"If you don't have to come home for dinner when *you're* supposed to, why do I have to go to bed when *I'm* supposed to?"

She didn't know whether to laugh or cry. "I had something I had to do," she said. It wasn't a lie, not really. She *had* to go someplace where none of the past week mattered.

"Work? He asked. His little face suddenly looked so sympathetic, so understanding, that a few tears actually leaked from the corners of her eyes. She gave him a big hug, both because he deserved it and because it gave her a second to wipe the tears away.

"Something like that," she said. "Now come on, let's get this mess cleaned up."

She began to toss pieces into the box. He started, then stopped.

"Mom - are you still sad?"

The question hit her hard, someplace very close to her heart. "What do you mean, honey?"

"You don't laugh like you used to. You seem… sad."

She forced a smile. "No, Jackie, I'm not sad. Just… sometimes things happen and you don't know how to handle them."

"I could help you."

Her eyes began to water again. "Thank you, honey. You help me every day just by being you." She kissed the top of his head.

"That's not much help."

She laughed out loud. "Of course it is! You have no idea how much I look forward to coming home each night and seeing your smiling face."

"But you didn't come home tonight..."

"No, no I didn't. But if I ever decide to do that again I'll let you know ahead of time so you don't worry. Okay?"

"Okay. But Mom?"

"Yes, sweetie?"

"Don't do it too often. Okay?"

"You've got a deal." Another hug. Another kiss. Some more tears.

*****

"Did he fight you?" Jennifer asked as her daughter came out into the living room and flopped down in an easy chair.

"Not exactly. Definitely let me know he wasn't happy with me missing dinner, though."

"That makes two of us. You couldn't call?"

A wave of guilt swept over her. "Sorry. There was something I had to do."

"Something requiring beer?"

Janice winced. Her mother had always had an incredible sense of smell. "I needed a drink. Away from home. Just needed to get away." She steeled herself for a lecture.

"And? Did it help?"

Janice smiled. "A little." Then she went on to tell how she'd met Mark.

"Mark, huh? Well it's about time."

"Not again, Mom."

"Well it's true. You've been divorced for over three years now, and from what little I know, this is the first *date* you've been on in all that time."

"It wasn't a date." She sounded petulant even to herself.

"Okay, a secret, unexpected meeting with a strange man in a bar involving beer and conversation. Is that specific enough?" Her look dared Janice to disagree.

"Something like that."

"You going to see him again?"

"Mom!"

"What? I can't ask my daughter if she's interested in a guy she just met?"

"Maybe."

"Maybe I can ask, or maybe you hope to see him again?"

"Both. Neither. I don't know!"

"Okay, all right," her mother calmed, "don't get all flustered. I'll just have to wait and see."

"Yes, you will."

An awkward silence lasted just a couple of seconds.

"Still, I'm happy to see you're open to meeting new people."

"You mean, despite *all that's happened to me*?" It was a bit below the belt, but she couldn't help herself.

"I didn't say that…"

"But that's what you meant."

"Look, honey, I'm your mother. It's my *job* to worry about you. I want you to be happy, and you haven't been for some time. Even before the… attack."

"I was happy."

"No, you were *not* unhappy. It's not the same thing. You hid yourself away at work and here at home, hardly ever interacting with anyone but Jackie."

"He's a child! He needs his mother to *interact* with him."

"Of course! But every grown-up needs to talk with other grown-ups now and then."

"I talked with you…"

"Oh, right. I almost forgot. Those two or three times a month, usually when I called you."

"I was busy."

"Doing what? Washing dishes? Helping Jackie build another Lego tower?" She cut her daughter off before she could interject. "Yeh, yeh, I know - he needs someone to help him build towers. But every day for three years? Come on."

"I… wasn't in the mood."

"You were afraid! Afraid you'd have another unsuccessful relationship."

"Mom, I don't need this right now."

"Then when *will* you need it? If anything good can come out of all this, maybe it's you getting back out there and restarting your life."

"I have a life."

"Really?" She didn't say anything else. She didn't have to - - Janice knew she was right. She'd been putting-off getting back into the dating scene for the exact reason her mother had suggested. Oh, she'd come up with a hundred excuses, but no one knew better than she did that they were all just that - excuses. She was afraid. Not just that she'd have another romantic disappointment. She'd survived the last one; she could survive another. What worried her most was that she wouldn't have *it* anymore, she wouldn't attract any interest from the kinds of guys she wanted to pay attention to her. That she'd be one of those pitiful women she saw hanging around clubs, often with other, more attractive women who let them tag along to make themselves look better in comparison.

Worse yet, would *any* show of interest bring on the same self-justified insanity as her attacker had displayed? Could she risk smiling at a stranger in a bar for fear he'd take it as an invitation... for what? To rape her?! The very idea made her furious. Do men worry about being attacked because they smile at a woman? Of course not!

She caught sight of her mother looking at her with an expression halfway between sympathy and concern.

"What?!" she snapped harder than she'd intended.

"Was just wondering what you were thinking."

Her Mom's calm understanding cut deeper than the usual overbearing spitefulness.

"Just thinking about what you said. How maybe some of it, maybe a lot, was true."

Her mother stood and came straight over to where she was sitting, throwing her arms around Janice's shoulders without saying a word. It took a few seconds for Janice to realize the tiny shakes she was feeling were from her mother sobbing.

"It's alright Mom, I'll get through this," she said despite no sense of confidence whatsoever.

"I know you will, honey," Jennifer sniffled. "I know you will."

They sat there for the longest time, each of them unthinkingly drawing on the physical presence of the other: the warmth, the tactile reassurance, the simple solidity of the other's body. It had been a long time since they'd hugged like that, like mother and daughter.

Finally, Janice felt whole enough to gently pull away from her mother's grasp.

She tried to think of how to thank her, and more than that how to explain all the anger and venom that had flowed from her own sad times over the years to the one person who'd never given up on her.

Her mother seemed to already know. "Have you eaten dinner?" she asked.

Janice grabbed her in one last crushing hug. "No, I haven't. Have you?"

"How about grilled cheese?"

"And tomato soup?"

Her mother smiled, a genuine spark of happiness in her eyes. "You sit here and rest. I'll go whip something up."

"Sure you couldn't use a helper?"

They walked arm in arm into the kitchen.

CHAPTER 11

Daniels hadn't slept much. Her dreams kept bringing her back to groping hands and a helpless feeling of being trapped. Yes, she was a cop, but she was a woman too and what those punks did to her shouldn't happen to any woman, cop or not. If anything, their attack had hardened her resolve to ensure that Archer got what was coming to him - maybe even more. If they thought they could scare her off, they were mistaken.

As she dressed, she stared into the full-length mirror that covered most of her bedroom door to examine the myriad bruises and scrapes that mottled her skin. The angry reds had already begun to darken, and she knew she'd have to wear her long-sleeve uniform until her arms healed up if she wanted to avoid unwanted questions and jeers. If anything, a woman cop had to be even tougher than her male colleagues. The guys were always looking for a weakness in a woman, a shortcoming they could gripe about to each other and to any poor soul cowered enough to listen. Oh, they'd mouth the required sympathies and occasionally even show anger at the perp, but the behind-your-back comments began almost immediately and the to-your-face variety weren't far behind.

Sometimes she wondered why she bothered to show up for roll call every morning. Rarely did a day pass without someone commenting on her "fine caboose" or wondering pointedly whether she'd put on a few pounds. It was usually the guys with the bulging guts, the guys who were more pounds overweight than she weighed who made the biggest fuss. It was as if they could only enhance their own pride by demeaning someone else, and who better than a woman cop?

By the time she got to headquarters, she'd worked her way into a bit of a tizzy and was spoiling for an opportunity to ream one of the many misogynistic assholes who shared her work-space. Her intensity must've shown on her face, because the Duty Sergeant - a 30-year vet who took it as a job requirement to rag on everyone, man or woman, who entered his domain - took one look at her and edited himself in mid-rag.

"How's it goin' Daniels?" he asked instead.

"Dandy," she muttered as she stomped passed without even a glance in his direction. The Sergeant looked over at one of the civilians waiting to be seen and raised his eyebrows.

"Must be that time of the month."

The civie shrugged but maintained absolute neutrality.

Meanwhile, Daniels continued back to her office, the thunderclouds resting on her brow a clear warning to everyone in her path. Well, nearly everyone. One of the less astute and most sarcastic of the younger generation didn't get the message.

"Officer Daniels: what's 'a matter, the batteries in your vibrator die again?" The schmuck looked over at Detective Willard expecting a shared guffaw, only to see the Detective look down quickly at his desk. He was about to question Willard's sense of humor, when the storm struck.

"McGraw," Daniels growled, "I'd take a vibrator with a dead battery any day over that limp little strand of spaghetti you keep tucked in your shorts. I've seen sparrows hung better than you." She swept past him without pause, a chorus of chuckles erupting from the adjoining cubicles and offices.

"Guess you told her, eh McGraw?" one of his contemporaries called out.

"Real smooth," another added.

Daniels didn't wait for the reactions but made her way directly to Willard's office, where she shut the door hard and flopped down into the lone chair that faced his desk.

"I don't need this crap," she said before Willard could brace for the onslaught. "It's getting harder and harder to tell which are the good guys and which are the creeps."

"Want a cup of coffee?" Willard asked, ignoring her diatribe as he'd learned to do over the 7 years they'd worked together.

She paused as if considering a comeback, but apparently thought better of it. "Brewed anytime this century?"

"Sometime." He was already out of his chair and on his way to the coffeemaker by the time she answered in the affirmative. As she watched him fetch the coffee she wondered why she would possibly need more caffeine. She was already amped up to the rafters. '*What the hell…*' she decided. '*In for a penny, in for a pound.*'

"Having a good day?" the hefty Detective asked as he slid the coffee cup in front of her.

"Not particularly. You?"

"Let me guess: it's that Archer schmuck again, right?"

"Partly." She didn't feel like spilling her guts so she took a sip of the coffee.

"And what's the other part? Car acting up again?"

"No, it's not the car." She flipped open a file on her desk, hoping he'd take the hint. He didn't.

"Look, if I'm gonna have to live with this dreary puss for the next 8 hours, at least you can let me know what's behind it."

She shut the file. "Yesterday, when I went out to check on Archer..."

Yeh..."

"A gang of punks jumped me in the stairwell."

His eyes widened. "Did you get... hurt?"

"Just some scrapes and bruises. No big deal. A local guy scared 'em off."

"You buy him lunch?"

"All he wanted was to get the hell outta there. It was bad enough he'd helped a cop - he didn't want to be seen hanging with one."

Willard nodded. "You gonna press charges?"

She hesitated, just long enough to suggest she'd been giving the idea some thought. "Nah. Too much paperwork. Chances are I'll run into those losers sooner or later anyway, and then we'll work it out."

"You know what the DA thinks about vigilantes..."

"Screw him."

Willard's eyebrows shot up. "So, you gonna be in a piss-poor mood all week?" He smiled to let her know it was a joke.

She wasn't in the mood. "I'll be in whatever mood I feel like being in. That okay with you?" She phrased it as a question, but nobody in their right mind would've answered any way other than how Willard did: "No problem."

"Good. Then can we get back to work, trying to find the perp before he goes after Greyson again?"

The Detective didn't speak for a long moment. He looked puzzled. "You know he's out on bail, right? We go after him, he's likely to start screaming 'police misconduct.'"

"Fuck 'em. I wanna know where that schmuck is every minute of the day until the DA gets him into court."

"And we're going to do that how, exactly?"

"APB." She knew she was bending the rules, but she couldn't shake the feeling that Archer had been behind the attack in the stairwell of that dump apartment building. And even if he wasn't, *he* should be the one locked up and worried, not his victim.

"You outta your mind? The Captain gets wind of this, your ass'll be in a sling."

"It's been worse places." She saw Willard smile ever so slightly. "Get your head outta the gutter."

"I just had this image come to me…"

"Don't want to hear about it. You with me on this?"

He frowned. "I suppose so. But we get caught, you're gonna step up and admit it was your idea, right?"

"You're a helluva guy, you know that?"

"Just don't get caught."

*****

It took all of Janice's will-power to keep from calling in sick. In a way, she *was* sick. Just thinking of that bastard stalking her, waiting in the shadows to… what? Attack her again? Threaten her? It made her guts ache. But she'd decided she wasn't going to let him get to her - not any more. She was going to live her life and hope the restraining order and the regular patrols that drove past the warehouse and through her neighborhood every few hours would force the asshole to think twice before coming after her again. Hope wasn't confidence, however, and so her guts ached like they might explode as she drove into work the next morning, the dark circles under her eyes reflecting the crappy night's sleep she'd endured. She kept thinking of *him*, of that taunting smile, the cocksure attitude that nothing was going to happen to him. Worst of all, she half-believed he was right.

She'd read all about rape and how it usually played-out in the court system. She knew his high-powered lawyers would try to break her down, try to paint her as some kind of slut who'd led him on, lured him into having sex with her. She didn't know how, but she didn't doubt they'd try. She couldn't remember ever having seen him before, but she'd been to a lot of places, met a lot of people. Maybe she *had* met him. Maybe she'd even talked to him. Although she doubted it. He wasn't her type, even without the attack. That wouldn't stop the accusations, the innuendos about her love life.

Huh! That was a joke. She hadn't been with a guy for months, maybe a year. When she broke-up with her ex-, the last thing she wanted to do was chance falling right back into another bad relationship. It made sex radioactive, the very thought of it making her feel uneasy. Not much different than she felt right then.

She slowed for a stoplight and was fuming about the unfairness of it all, when a car horn beeped close by. She glanced in her rear-view mirror but saw no one, and was about to ignore the irritating bleat when it sounded again, this time right next to her. She glanced over to find her attacker sitting in an expensive-looking sedan, his broad smile beaming out from the shadowed interior. It felt as if she'd been punched in the stomach. She realized how completely alone she really was, how no court order or even a police presence could keep this crazy person from invading her life and threatening her existence. She tore her eyes away from his smile and stared straight ahead, trying to force the stoplight to change by force of will. The red light seemed to drag on for minutes, and when it finally changed she had to restrain her foot from stomping on the gas pedal.

She pulled away slowly, hoping that Archer would zoom on ahead, leaving her to fume in peace. No such luck. He slid into the space right behind her and followed at the same snail's pace she was setting. She felt her palms begin to sweat as her heartbeat raced.

'*What now? What should I do?*' she agonized. If she pulled over and stopped, he could do the same. If she tried to speed away, he'd just follow. She struggled to slow her breathing and focus. In an instant her options became clear. She pulled out her cellphone and hit the speed-dial button she'd just recently programmed. The sound of Officer Daniel's voice brought instant hope.

"Officer Daniels, it's me - Janice Greyson."

"Yes, Janice, what can I do for you?"

The Officer sounded harried.

"It's my attacker - Archer. He's following right behind me in his car." Her voice sounded unnaturally high-pitched and shaky.

"What?! Where are you?"

She told the Officer her location.

"Just keep driving on Windwood," Daniels directed. "I'll be there in three minutes."

Three minutes! It sounded like an eternity. "What if he gets out of his car and comes after me?"

"Then run it if you can. Don't let him get into your car, no matter what you have to do."

"Okay." What else could she say?

"I'll be there! Stay calm and keep moving."

Janice was about to answer, more than anything to keep the conversation going, when the phone call disconnected. She kept holding the phone to her ear, hoping it would look like she was still talking. Up ahead, no more than three or four blocks, she saw a stoplight. It was green. If only she could make it through...

She stepped on the gas hard and the car lurched ahead, leaving Archer in the dust. She felt exhilarated as she saw his car grow smaller in the rear-view mirror, her sense of control over the situation soaring.

And then the light turned yellow.

She was still a good twenty feet from the intersection, and a glance in the mirror showed Archer was closing the gap - quickly. She had to make it through the light! Another minute or two and Daniels would be there. She stomped down hard and the engine whined as she barreled into the intersection just as the light changed. She was staring in the rear-view, feeling good about her chances, when she saw a car coming fast out of the corner of her eye. She swerved hard to avoid the collision and her car skidded up over the curb and onto a sidewalk. Her head slammed into the roof and then bounced off the steering wheel. Everything went black.

*****

"Janice, Ms Greyson, are you okay?"

The words seemed to be coming from far away. She struggled to force her eyes open.

"Wha...?" Her mouth didn't want to form words.

"Take it easy - don't talk. You've been in a car accident. Hit your head. An ambulance should be here in a few minutes."

Janice recognized that voice. It was... Daniels. The police officer.

"It was him. He was following me..." she muttered, not sure if her words were intelligible.

"I know, I know. Just take it easy for now. We can talk about Archer when you're in better shape."

Janice heard a siren approaching. Or was it? It seemed to waver in and out, like a train passing in the wind...

*****

The next time she opened her eyes she was lying in a hospital bed, a bandage wrapped around her head, an IV stuck in her right arm. She tried to sit up but instantly felt sick to her stomach, her head pounding.

"Hey, there you are!" a woman's voice said as a hand pushed gently against her shoulder. "Just lie back down. You've had a concussion." It took her a moment to realize it was her mother.

"Who's looking after Jackie?" Janice asked, her face contorted in pain.

"He's still in school - it's only around 11 in the morning. Don't you worry, I'll take good care of him while you're recuperating."

When Janice's eyes finally focused, she looked around the hospital room: bed, side-table, small TV up on the wall. Pretty typical. Her mother looked small, and old - worried. "What happened?"

"They say you ran a stoplight. Swerved to avoid hitting another car and jumped a curb. Must've hit your head."

"Yeh, that sounds right." She struggled to remember, but it was like trying to look back through a thick fog. Then an image came back to her. "It was him! The bastard who attacked me. He was following me!" Again she tried to sit up, and again she fell back in a dizzied swoon.

"I know, I know, honey. Officer Daniels told me all about it. Now you need to take it easy. They say the only way you're going to get better is to rest."

She closed her eyes. The light seemed too bright. "Maybe just shut my eyes for a few minutes…"

Her mother stood watch for another hour or so, until she had to leave to get home for Jackie's return from school. Another hour passed. And another. Janice slept fitfully, the image of *his* smile tormenting even her unconscious mind. Wherever she went, he followed. He stayed silent, but his smile never wavered. She heard footsteps and her eyes flew open.

"Who is it?!"

"Take it easy, Ms. Greyson. It's just me, Officer Daniels." She leaned over the bed to look into Janice's face. "How're you feeling?"

"Head hurts. A little dizzy."

"Yeh, that's about par for the course. I've had a couple concussions. Takes a few days, but it gets better."

"I hope so."

"Feel like talking? Wanna tell me what happened out there?"

She didn't feel like talking, but knew she had to. As soon as she began, the words poured out. "He was following me - Archer. Pulled up right next to me, and smiled at me like he didn't have a care in the world. I tried to pull away, but he pulled in right behind me and followed. So I slowed down, and he did the same thing. I was trying to get through a light when a car came at me from the left and I swerved."

"Up over the curb. Yeh, we know that part. Did he say anything?"

"I don't think so…" The details were still hazy.

"Anything else? Any threatening actions? Any weapon?"

"No! Not that I can remember."

Daniels looked like she wanted to ask more questions, but something stopped her.

"Okay, it doesn't really matter. He was much closer than 100 yards, so he broke the terms of the restraining order. We can pick him up, though I don't know how long we can hold him."

"What do you mean?" The dim color that had returned to her cheeks faded rapidly.

"Unless you got a video of him tailing you, it'll be 'he said, she said' and most judges rule a tie in favor of the accused."

"What?! Why?" A monitor began beeping, its cheerless electronic cry ignored by both of them.

Just then a nurse hustled into the room. She took one look at the vitals panel above the bed and turned to the Officer with obvious disdain. "You do realize this is a *hospital*, don't you?" the 50-something woman spit. "She needs rest, not a grilling."

"She needs to be safe, and as long as the person who helped put her here is running around loose, she isn't." Daniels looked down at Janice and noticed her wide-eyed stare. "We're putting a 24-hour guard on your room," she announced with unsupported confidence, hoping she would be able to convince her Captain it was a worthwhile expenditure of scarce funds.

"That may be," the nurse continued as if the cop hadn't said a word, "but for now I need you out of here. My patient needs some sleep."

Daniels looked as if she might respond, then turned to Janice.

"I'll post two of my men on the exits right now, and I'll ask the Captain to okay a corridor guard just outside your door. I'll let you know what he says."

"Thank you," Janice mumbled weakly. Her eyes were already closing.

The nurse cleared her throat.

"Get some rest," the Officer said toward Janice. "We'll go have a little talk with Archer."

With that, she glared at the nurse and left the room.

*****

Daniels called-in to Willard as soon as she got to her car. "Anything yet on Archer's APB?"

The Detective hesitated a second. Daniels could see him in her mind's eye scanning his emails, looking for any messages about the perp.

"Nope. Nothing yet. What're you up to?"

"I'm at the hospital. Janice was in a car accident." She went on to explain Archer's role.

"So now you've got the cover you need for the APB. Lucky."

"I don't think Janice sees it that way, but I'm pretty happy."

"As long as no one looks at the start-up date."

"I'm not particularly worried. I'm more focused on finding this asshole before he can do anything else to her."

"And how to you intend to do that?"

"I've got a description of the car he's driving and a partial on the plate - that I'll send right off to you - so it should make finding him a bit easier."

"Okay. I'll put it out on the network. And what are you gonna be doing in the meantime? We've got a stack of other cases sitting here, you know."

"I know. But until we can get Archer off the streets, Janice is in danger."

"Says who? Her?"

Daniels restrained herself. "Says me. This guy's already committed one rape we know of, and he doesn't seem particularly cowered by the restraining order. I get the feeling he's just waiting for the right moment."

"To do what? Up till now, he's only smiled at her a couple of times."

"He forced her off the road!'"

"Did he? From the way you described it, it sounds like she wasn't paying attention and drove off the road. You think a judge is going to throw him back into a cell for *happening* to drive near her?"

"I don't believe in coincidences. Maybe the judge won't either."

"Good luck with that."

She was about to lament the current lax attitude of judges toward perpetrators when Willard cut her off.

"Okay, looks like your luck is holding. A black and white just spotted the car parked on the East side." He gave her the address.

"I'm on my way," Daniels said. "Tell them to keep eyes-on until I get there."

"Daniels - remember, he's just a suspect. Take it easy."

"Like he took it easy on Greyson?" She hung up before he could answer.

She was only ten minutes or so from where the perp's car had been reported, but even so she needed to restrain herself from punching the siren to get there faster. She pushed past the speed limit and hit the flashing lights a time or two to clear the way, making it to the East side in seven minutes flat. She parked her car a half-block away, trying not to tip him off before she could ID him.

The car he'd been driving was planted conspicuously in front of a string of small shops and restaurants. Daniels tried to imagine which of them he might be visiting. A glance at her watch gave a strong hint: it was 12:35. Time for lunch. She hoped the boys in the B&W had seen something, but she wasn't counting on it when she walked up the block to where they were sitting, watching the shops.

"Boys," she greeted them in her best cop monotone. "See where he went?"

"What's up, Daniels? He owe you a couple of bucks?" the younger of the two cops said with a beaming smile. He glanced at his partner for a reassuring grin.

"Don't have time for your shit," she growled. "Where'd he go?"

The smiles faded. "Jesus, what's he got, outstanding parking tickets?"

Daniels had had enough. She reached through the open driver's-side window and grabbed the cop by his tie, hard. "Tell me where that motherfucker is or your next duty's gonna be a foot patrol in Spicville." The guy's face was gradually turning from bright red to a deepening purple.

"He went in Annie's," the other officer volunteered quickly, indicating a small lunch place near the far end of the strip mall.

"Get your lazy asses around back," Daniels said. "If he comes out, stop him. Violation of a restraining order. Suspect in a violent rape. Got it?"

The cop with bulging eyes nodded; his partner managed a guttural grunt.

Daniels didn't wait for clarification. She charged off toward the shop with a heavy step that made an impression on her two brothers in blue. "Wouldn't want to be that poor SOB," the younger cop said. His choking partner could only shake his head.

Daniels didn't stop to surveille the area, or linger at the entrance to surreptitiously scan the clientele. No, she barged straight in, stomped to a halt in the middle of the nine or ten tables, and quickly stared with bladder-emptying intensity at everyone having lunch. Most of the diners stopped in mid-mouthful, paralyzed. Two dropped their forks to the floor.

The only one who seemed largely unconcerned was one Daniel Lee Archer, who sat in the far back corner, smiling as if this was the funniest thing he'd seen all day. Daniels didn't return the smile. Instead, she marched straight to his table.

"Afternoon, Offic…" he began. Daniels didn't let him finish.

"Keep your hands where I can see them!" she barked, pulling her service pistol and leveling it in his direction. At that, three customers fled out the front door, their food left cooling on their plates.

"Having a bad day?" Archer asked with mock sincerity, keeping his hands right where they'd been when she'd come in. Had to hand it to him, he showed no concern whatsoever.

"Where were you about an hour ago?" Daniels asked.

"Let's see," Archer said, stroking his chin and staring at the ceiling as if he expected to see the answer up there. "I s'pose I was on my way over here."

"On West Ingram?"

"Let me think. Might've been."

"You come here regularly? If I ask the staff, will they recognize you?"

He hesitated. "Not so often. Now and then."

"What's your favorite dish?"

"Wha? What kind'a crap is this?"

"I asked, what's your favorite dish?"

He reached for the menu. She slapped her hand down on the table, hard.

"Why do you come all the way out here to eat?"

"I don' need this crap," he said, pushing back in his chair as if to stand.

She pulled cuffs from the back of her belt. "Down on the floor," she ordered, pointing with the barrel of her gun. "You're under arrest for violating a restraining order."

He looked utterly flummoxed. "How do you mean?" he asked, his expression as close to angelic as a lying POS could manage.

"I mean you purposely came within one hundred yards of Janice Greyson with the expressed intent of causing her mental or emotional distress."

"Oh no, not that crazy woman again! If I came within a hundred yards of her, it was by accident. I don't want nothing more to do with that nutcase."

"I don't believe you. Now are you getting down on the floor of your own choice, or do I need to help you?"

Archer looked out at the other diners and addressed them directly. "Can you believe this? Some crazy woman says I was driving *near* her, and this cop wants to arrest me!"

"Probably got a quota," one guy muttered.

"Damn cops think they *own* this city," another added.

The mood was turning bad fast, and Daniels realized she needed to act before things got out of hand. She pressed the transmit button on her vest walkie-talkie: "I've got him here in Annie's. Come on in and help me drag him out to the car."

"10-4" came the reply.

"What's a' matter Officer, need help to bring-in the big bad criminal?" Archer's grin was neither warm nor good-natured.

"What I need is for you to get down on the ground and put your hands behind your back. Now!" She yelled the last with such vehemence that several of the diners jumped. She realized she was close to losing it.

Archer was about to mouth-off again, when the cavalry came to the rescue.

"She said to get on the floor, asshole!" the younger B&W officer ordered as he came rushing in the back door. He grabbed the perp by his upper right arm and gave him a pretty good tug.

"All right, all right - take it easy!" Archer whined as he stumbled down on all fours. "This floor's dirty as sin'!"

"And it ain't getting any cleaner with you down there. So put your hands behind your back and let's get you outta here!" He nudged Archer in the back with his foot and the creep fell over as if shot.

"I said 'take it easy'!" He raised his head awkwardly. "You saw that!" he continued, addressing the other diners once more. "You all saw what he did. Police violence is what it was! You saw it!"

"Shut the fuck up before we show you what real police violence looks like!" Daniels exploded, snapping the cuffs shut on his wrists and then pulling him up by the chain. She turned to the stunned onlookers. "This asshole raped a woman in her own house!"

"I'm innocent!" Archer cried out as they shoved him toward the front door. He noticed a young woman following his every move with her cellphone. "Yeh, that's right! Record everythin'! Put it up on the Internet! Let people know what the cops do when no one can see 'em!"

With that, Daniels half-threw him out the door. "Now you can shout all you want," she told Archer. "No one gives a shit."

"You're gonna give a shit once my lawyer gets a hold of you."

"He'll have to try to get a hold of you first. Next stop, Central Jail."

Archer glared at her but didn't say another word as they hauled him to her car and shoved him into the back seat.

"I kind'a like this - me sittin' back here like some bigwig and you sittin' up there like my sho-fer," he taunted with his best inner-city impression once Daniels had closed her door. She ignored him. He stayed quiet for a few seconds before starting-up again. "What's 'a matter, you mad 'cause that crazy bitch got some of my sugar and you didn't?"

Daniels wanted to slam the brakes so hard his head smashed against the metal grate that separated the front and back seats, but she took a deep breath and kept driving. "Just keep running your mouth, Archer. Maybe your cellmate will have some sugar for you."

That did not go over well.

"You bitch! Once I beat this bullshit rape charge in court, you better be lookin' over your shoulder."

"Are you threatening me, you little weasel?"

"Threatening?" he said, his tone lightening. "I wouldn't say that. Maybe... advising. Yeh, I'm *advising* you."

"And I'm advising you: stay away from Ms. Greyson or else."

"Ooo, I'm scared now. Are you this tough when you're in bed? You like bein' on top?"

Daniels weighed a dozen comebacks, but decided in the end that silence was the best approach. Archer babbled-on with more threats and toothless jabs; Daniels turned up the radio.

*****

Officer Daniels barely had time to deposit Archer in a holding cell and start filling-out all the paperwork when her desk phone buzzed.

It was her Sargent. "Daniels, there's a lawyer out here wearing a $500 suit who says we need to release some suspect named Archer. Know what he's talkin' about?"

"Where is he?" she asked, none too politely.

"Here in Reception."

"I'll be out in a minute." She hung up before he could say anything else. *'Damn it!'* She'd been hoping it would take a few hours before his pro-bono bigshot lawyer got word the perp was back behind bars. Now she'd have to waste time with *another* asshole.

She signed-off the computer and made her way out to Reception. It didn't take long to guess who his lawyer was: tall, young, not bad looking, wearing the aforementioned five hundred buck suit. She had to admit, he looked the part.

"Mr. Allen?" she asked, stopping just in front of where he paced but not extending a hand of greeting.

"And you are?" the lawyer asked with more than a tad of attitude.

"Officer Daniels. I'm working the Greyson rape case."

"*Alleged* rape," he said without missing a beat. "I thought a… Detective Willard was in charge of this investigation."

"We're working it together. Anything I can help you with?"

He stared at her as if debating whether to tolerate her presence. "You can let Mr. Archer out. He's clearly being held without cause."

"Did you bother to request the booking report?" She wasn't going to be bullied by some two-bit Ivy League kid.

"I glanced at it. Sloppy. Incomplete. Certainly doesn't provide sufficient justification for returning Mr. Archer to a cell."

"He violated a restraining order."

"From the report it seems he did nothing more than find himself driving on the same street as Ms. Greyson. Hardly a violation."

"He followed her. Taunted her. Willful violation of the terms of the order."

"Not what he says. He says he didn't even know it was her until he pulled up next to her at a light and glanced over to see who was next to him. She raced off before he could apologize. Or explain."

"You expect me to believe that in this entire city, your client just *happened* to pull up next to his victim and just *happened* to look over at her and smile?"

"*Alleged* victim. And what would you have him do, frown? He was acting like any other driver would in similar circumstances."

"But he was under a restraining order. And so, he's back in his cell."

The lawyer's tone changed dramatically. "You're kidding, right? If we take this to the issuing judge, he'll have Archer out on the streets in two minutes flat."

"The Judge is a woman. Give it your best shot."

"At best you're going to look like a fool. At the worst, a rogue cop out to get my client."

"You don't think much of Judge Monahan, do you?"

"If you're hoping she'll back your play because she's a woman, don't get your hopes up. My experience suggests she'll go by the book."

'*What experience? You can't have been a lawyer for more than a few months,*' she thought. "That's exactly what I expect: she'll go by the book," she said instead. "And more than likely throw it at your *client.*"

The lawyer looked as if he might explode. "I can see I'm just wasting my time here. I thought you might listen to reason. I was wrong."

With no prelude or goodbyes, he pivoted and stormed out of Headquarters.

"That went well," the receiving Sergeant on duty said with arched eyebrows.

"Fuck 'im."

Daniels hurried back to her desk and dialed the DA's office. It took a few transfers and holds, but she finally got through to the boss-woman herself.

She explained the situation quickly, leaving nothing out other than her sarcastic interaction with the kid lawyer.

"You confident this Greyson will hold up under examination by his lawyer?" the DA asked.

"She's a tough woman. She'll hold up."

"You better be right. I'll give the judge a call." It was clear she wasn't enthusiastic. But she was going to do it.

"Thanks."

"Don't mention it. To anyone."

She hung up. Daniels wasn't sure whether to smile or sigh. So she did both.

*****

Jennifer went to meet Jackie's school bus at the corner. As she waited, she couldn't help wonder about the lasting impact of the attack on her daughter - and Jackie. She still couldn't bring herself to call it a rape. Somehow the word seemed... nastier, more life-altering than *attack*. She tried to convince herself that it would all be over soon, that the attacker would go to jail for a long, long time, and Janice would bounce back to her old self - and with her, Jackie.

She tried, but in her heart-of-hearts she had her doubts. Janice hadn't been in the best of places even before the attack, or so it seemed to Jennifer from the little personal information her daughter had shared during the period after her divorce. Maybe she had been too forceful in her insistence that Janice get rid of her ex-. Maybe she should have kept her own counsel and let events transpire as they would. Probably wouldn't have ended up much different than they did, but they might have.

She was so lost in her thoughts she didn't realize the school bus was arriving until it pulled to a stop right in front of her. A couple of groups of neighborhood mothers kept chatting non-stop even as their kids began to file off the little yellow mini-bus. When she'd first come to the city to help her daughter after the attack, Jennifer had thought about inserting herself into one of the waiting groups, for simple social interaction as much as anything. Janice was even more close-lipped than usual those first few days. It almost seemed she was afraid to open up even a crack, for fear everything she'd kept bottled-up inside would come flooding out. But Jennifer couldn't make herself do it. She'd eavesdropped enough to hear the mind-numbing mundanities many of the women

spouted when they weren't spreading petty gossip or
criticizing whichever mom wasn't present at the time. She
couldn't force herself to become one of them -- the idle,
bored, self-important stay-at-homers whose entire lives
revolved around their kids, their pets, their zumba or yoga
classes (what the heck was *zumba*, after all?), and above all the
glamorous lives of reality TV stars.

She'd worked nearly her entire adult life. She read, when
she had time. She watched political commentary, when she
could stomach it. She could certainly talk all day long about
Jackie, but she wasn't his mother, just a grandmother. A
second-class citizen. And reality TV? She'd rather clean her
oven. No, she couldn't bring herself to join their Mary Kay or
Tupperware parties.

She was lost in thought when Jackie's excited voice cut
through all the nonsense. "Grandma!" He was always eager to
see her, always free with his hugs and affection. Unlike her
own daughter. Of course, Janice hadn't always been that way.
When she was a child she'd been outgoing and loving as well.
But ever since the divorce, or perhaps ever since Jennifer had
inserted herself *into* the divorce, their relationship had
become more... complicated.

"Wanna see what I drew?" Jackie asked as he pulled the
crayon drawing on yellow lined paper out of his little
backpack.

"Of course!"

She knew better than to ask what it depicted, and instead
waited for him to tell her.

"That's our house, and this is Mommy, and this is you!"
he eventually said. She could see a resemblance to the real
thing; he had some artistic talent. But over in one corner of

the room there loomed a great dark creature. She was almost afraid to ask, but couldn't resist.

"What's this?" she said, pointing to the creature.

"That's the bad man," he explained, his attitude much subdued. "He made Mommy sad."

"You know there isn't a bad man anymore, don't you?" she tried to reassure. "He's gone forever."

"Then why is Mommy still sad sometimes?"

So he understood. At least in part. Probably as much as Jennifer did.

"Everyone gets sad sometimes," she recovered. "Even Mommies."

She was afraid he'd want to launch into a longer discussion, but just then one of his friends called over to him and the conversation flew in another direction. As she walked her grandson home, she couldn't help but wonder what effect his mother's trauma would have on him long-term, and whether she could do anything to minimize its impact.

'Maybe I should get him an appointment with a child psychologist,' she thought as he babbled-on about his day. *'Or would that just make it worse? Would Janice see my concern as help or hindrance?'*

There was no way to know.

CHAPTER 12

The ringing phone made Janice jump. Nowadays, everything made her jump.

"Hello?"

"Janice, it's Officer Daniels."

She was in no mood for niceties and cut straight to the chase. It had only been three days since the accident, and although she was at home and feeling better, her head still ached and her arm was in a sling.

"Did you find the bastard?"

"Found him, and put him back in his cell."

"That's wonderful news! Thank you, Officer!"

"But..."

The smile on Janice's face fell flat. "But?"

"His lawyer is petitioning the judge to let him out again. He's saying the *interaction* with you was pure coincidence."

"What?! Surely Judge Monahan won't buy that nonsense!"

"We're going to find out - this afternoon at 4, if you can make it down to the Courthouse."

"I don't understand."

"The Judge is going to hold an informal meeting with both parties to determine whether Archer violated the restraining order or not. It would be good if you could be there, to give your side of the story and all."

"Do I have to go?" Daniels could hear the fear in her voice.

"You don't have to, but if you're not there his testimony will carry more weight and the judge might just give them what they want."

Silence.

"You there?" Daniels asked after several seconds.

"Yeh, I'm here. Just trying to persuade myself that I can do this."

"You *can* do it! This won't be some big courtroom thing - just a little meeting in the Judge's chambers. Probably just you, me, Archer, and his lawyer - and Judge Monahan, of course. Probably won't last more than a half-hour."

"Can Detective Willard come too?" She said it before considering the consequences. She heard the change in Daniel's voice immediately.

"What? Oh, yeh, I suppose he could…"

"It's just that he seemed to know the Judge when we were there last time," she explained, attempting to undo any damage to Daniels' ego. "Besides, it'd give us one more body."

"And a big one at that."

She pushed out a laugh. "I don't think the Judge is someone who can be easily intimidated."

"No, probably not. But I suppose it can't hurt. I'll ask him."

"Thanks, Officer. And yes, the insurance company got me a rental car, so I'll be there at four."

"Good. See you there."

As the Officer hung up, Janice felt that queasy feeling growing in her gut once again.

*****

The Central Courthouse didn't seem as intimidating as it had the first time Janice visited. In fact, this time she saw the structure for what it was: an old, poorly maintained shadow of what it once had been. She shook her head sadly and went inside, ready - she thought - to confront her attacker, and his lawyer.

Detective Willard and Officer Daniels were waiting for her in the Reception Area.

"How're you doin'?" Willard asked even before saying hello.

"I'm fine, thanks."

"All you gotta' do is tell the Judge what happened," Daniels coached, apparently unconvinced.

"Ok."

"Any questions?" Willard finally asked.

"I think I've got a pretty good idea of what to expect."

"This could get a little rough, if his lawyer wants it to," Daniels warned.

"I'm ready for him."

Willard shot a quick glance at his partner, his look suggesting more than a little doubt. But he held his tongue.

"Now remember, this isn't a trial," Daniels said, "so no one will be sworn-in, but lying can cause you big problems."

"I don't have any reason to lie."

"Good. Then just listen carefully to what the Judge says, and answer as best you can. You'll do fine."

Her words echoed in Janice's mind as they made their way through familiar hallways to the door to the Judge's chambers. Janice took a deep breath in preparation for confronting her attacker, but the portly Detective led them to the next door where he knocked.

"This isn't where we went last time," Janice protested, but before either cop could answer the knock drew a response.

"Come in, come in!" Judge Monahan's muffled voice echoed in the hallway.

As soon as the door opened Janice could see Archer and his young, well-dressed lawyer turn to eye them from their seats on one side of a long table.

"It's the Conference Room," Daniels whispered.

"Sit, sit," the Judge directed from her place at the head of the table.

"Are we late?" Willard asked, glancing theatrically at his watch.

"Not at all. We're a little bit early. Can I get you something to drink: water, coffee?"

"Nothing for me," Willard said.

"Me either."

"Nothing, thanks," Janice said, even though her tongue felt like it had been welded to the roof of her mouth.

"I could use a beer," Archer suddenly offered, his smirk poorly disguised.

The judge looked over at him with undisguised disgust. "Counselor," she said, addressing the lawyer, "see if you can keep your client under control until this little meeting is completed. Think you can do that?"

The lawyer looked as if he'd stepped in a big juicy turd.

"I'm sorry, Your Honor. It won't happen again - right, Mr. Archer?"

"Yeh, sure, whatever you say, as long as you get me outta here."

"That's yet to be determined," the judge said brusquely. "So, Detective Willard, Officer Daniels, I see you want Mr. Archer's bond revoked for violating the restrictions in Ms. Greyson's restraining order. Why?"

Willard deferred to Daniels, who explained how Archer
had stalked Janice by car.

"Is that what happened?" the judge asked Janice as soon
as the Officer had finished.

"Yes, Your Honor," Janice answered, her voice clear and
strong.

"Your Honor, my client..." the lawyer began. Judge
Monahan shut him down immediately.

"We'll get to him when I'm ready. Understand,
Counselor?"

"Yes, Your Honor."

Janice could almost see his pout.

"So, you were minding your own business, driving along -
where exactly was that?"

"On Windwood," Janice said.

"It's on the East side," Willard volunteered.

"I know where Windwood is, Detective," the judge
growled.

"Just making sure," Willard mumbled in return.

"So you're driving along on Windwood - *on the east side*,"
she stressed, glancing at Willard, "when you see what?"

"Actually, it was what I heard - a car horn. I was stopped
at a light, and when I looked around, *Mr.* Archer was sitting
right next to me - in his car, I mean, and grinning at me."

"Ain't no law against grinnin'" Archer said.

A look from Monahan and his lawyer's hand on his arm
stopped further comments.

"'Grinning.' Did he say anything, or make any hand
gestures?"

"I don't know. As soon as I saw who it was, I turned
away to see if the light had changed."

"Okay. And then?"

"When the light did change I started out very slowly, hoping he'd pass me, but I saw him pull behind me and continue to follow me."

"For how long?"

"I don't know - a couple of minutes."

"And then?"

"Then I called Officer Daniels and she said she'd be on her way to meet me. But when I came to the next light I thought I could get through it..."

"And that's when you had your accident."

"Yes."

"Are you fully recovered?"

"Not really. My head still hurts and my wrist was badly sprained."

"My client had nothing to do with her accident!" the lawyer said, nearly jumping out of his seat.

"I told you, I'll get your side of the story when I'm ready for it. Another such interruption and we'll postpone this meeting for a week or two and your client can cool his heels in jail. Got it?"

The lawyer fumed but kept his cool. "Got it."

"Ms. Greyson, did you at any time share your driving plans with Mr. Archer?"

"No, of course not!"

"Then there was no way, to your knowledge, that he could've known ahead of time where you were going?"

"Unless he followed me."

"Did you see him following you?"

"No..."

"Okay, thank you. Officer Daniels, did Mr. Archer say anything to you when you apprehended him?"

"He claimed he was just driving to a restaurant."

"But you didn't accept that explanation?"

"Your Honor, Mr. Archer lives on the West Side. He could give me no reason for being on Windwood other than his desire to eat at the cafe where we grabbed him. Said it was a favorite of his. Problem was, he didn't seem very familiar with the place. Couldn't even tell me a favorite dish."

"Is that right, Mr. Archer?" the judge asked.

"You get a gun stuck in your face, you see how good *your* memory is."

Monahan turned back to Daniels. "You drew your service revolver?"

"Standard procedure, Your Honor. He wouldn't show his hands."

"Is that right?" she asked Archer. "Did you refuse to show your hands?"

"I was caught by surprise," he said. "Took me a second to realize what she was sayin'"

"A lot more than a second, Your Honor," Daniels corrected. "He ignored my order."

"Ok, so what happened then?"

"Then I ordered him to the floor, put the cuffs on him - standard procedure - and with the help of a couple of black and white guys got him into my cruiser."

"Is that how it happened, Mr. Archer?" the judge asked.

"Not nuthin' like that," he began. His lawyer whispered something in his ear. "Yeh, okay," Archer answered him before turning back to the judge. "I was just mindin' my own business, gettin' ready to order, when in comes this crazy cop, pulls a gun, and starts askin' me a bunch of wacked-out questions about why I'm eatin' at that place."

"And why were you eating there?"

"Because I like the food!" he insisted with an injured look. "Anythin' wrong with that?"

"Daniel…" his lawyer warned.

"Yeh, yeh," he said belligerently.

"No restaurants in your neighborhood you like?"

"Sure, there's a few. But I felt like eatin' on the East Side that day."

"And you'd been there before?"

"A few times."

"Like how many? Three, four? More?"

"I don' know. Maybe four."

"Okay, so you felt like driving a half hour across town to have breakfast. Did you know Ms Greyson was driving on the same street as you?"

"'Course not! How would I know?"

"And you just happened to pull up next to her at a traffic light."

"Stranger things have happened."

Judge Monahan looked down at some notes. "Ms. Greyson says you looked over and smiled at her. Why'd you do that?"

"What was I s'posed to do, give her the evil eye?"

"She has accused you of rape, Mr. Archer. One would think that alone would stop you from smiling at her."

"Well, it didn't."

"Obviously. So Ms Greyson says she drove very slowly when the light changed, and you pulled in right behind her and followed her for several minutes. Is that correct?"

"I hadn't been to the cafe for a few months and wasn't sure where the turn was, so I went slow."

"And when she accelerated, so did you."

"Got tired of crawlin' along."

"Uh huh. And when you saw another car hit Ms Greyson's, did you stop and offer help?"

"Didn't see it. Must've happened after I went through the intersection."

"You were behind her but went through the intersection *before* her?"

For the first time, Archer hesitated. "Must've passed her."

"Did Mr. Archer pass you, Ms Greyson?"

"I was looking at him in my rearview mirror when the other car hit me." Janice sounded *very* sure of herself.

"Your Honor, all this happened several days ago and my client's been through a lot since then," his lawyer interrupted. "It's not surprising that he can't remember every little detail."

"Not surprising to who?" the judge asked. "Never mind - just thinking out loud." She turned her attention to Archer. "Let's continue, Mr. Archer. So after you *accidentally* met Ms Greyson, you went straight to the cafe?"

"Was hungry."

"And what did you order?"

He stared at her for just an instant, but it was long enough for everyone in the room to know he was weighing his answer to try to determine whether it could harm his argument.

"Your Honor, what's the relevance?" his lawyer asked.

"As you are no doubt aware, this is not a trial," Judge Monahan answered. "I'm trying to decide whether your client goes back to jail or not. Interrupting me every few seconds doesn't help with that."

"Sorry."

She turned back to Archer. "So, as I was asking, what did you order for breakfast?"

The short delay had given him just enough time to decide how to answer. Or so he thought. "Ham and eggs, with whole wheat toast and a cup of coffee," he said with complete assurance.

"So, you drove all the way across town for ham and eggs. Is there something special about the ham and eggs at that cafe? If I went there, would I notice how special they are?"

The slightest of hesitations. Then a smile. "Not the ham and eggs, Judge. The *coffee*. I like the coffee."

"Ah, so it was the coffee. I see…" She looked down at her notes again. "Ms. Greyson - do you always travel that same road when you go to work?"

"Almost always. It's the most direct route."

"Okay." Now she turned to face the lawyer. "Do you have anything *substantive* to add, Counselor?"

He looked at Archer, who shook his head. "Only that this was not a deliberate act, Your Honor. I know it seems unlikely, but coincidences *do* happen." His look of self-satisfaction grated on Daniels.

"Not this much of a coincidence," she muttered.

"Enough," the judge warned. She read her notes for a long moment while all five of the others in the room held their collective breath. "All right, I think I've heard all I need to make my decision. Mr. Archer, my gut tells me that you followed Ms. Greyson over to Windwood with the expressed intent of shaking her determination to press charges against you. From what I've seen, that attempt failed."

"But Your Honor!" the lawyer tried to protest. The judge waved him off in no uncertain terms.

"However," she continued, "there is absolutely nothing that *proves* Mr. Archer was not simply driving all the way across town to have a *cup of coffee*." She said the last with dripping sarcasm. "So I cannot in good conscience remand you to jail. But if you ever have another similar *coincidence*," she said, her voice rising, "I can assure you that your backside will land on a jail cot so fast your head will swim. Do I make myself clear?"

Archer looked to his lawyer with consternation. "What's she sayin'?"

"You don't have to go back to jail. But if you happen to bump into Ms Greyson again, she'll throw your ass back in the slammer. Excuse my French, Your Honor."

"Now do you understand?" the judge asked Archer.

He nodded. "Got it. If I ever even see her again, I'll go runnin' in the other direction."

"That would be an excellent idea, Mr. Archer. Now, unless there's something else..?" She looked to Janice.

"He goes free?"

"I don't think he'll go anywhere near you again. And if he does, he knows what will happen."

"He knew what would happen last time. That didn't stop him."

"Perhaps. The fact that he didn't threaten or assault you was also a mitigating factor. I realize smiling at you can seem disturbing, but it's hardly a jailable offense in and of itself."

"So this piece of crap wins again, huh?" Willard said.

"I wouldn't call it a win, Detective. More like a stay of execution unless/until he messes up again."

Officer Daniels took Janice's hand and grasped it tightly. "You'll be okay, Ms Greyson. We'll get that 24/7 guard to make sure."

A look of fear morphed into tired resignation. "I guess that's all we can do at this point. Thank you."

"Then if there's nothing more, I've got a dozen other motions to consider today," Judge Monahan said as she rose. "Thank you all for coming." Everyone stood, even Archer after a nudge from his attorney.

The second the door to the Judge's chambers closed, Archer became instantly more animated.

"This was bullshit!" he announced to the room in general. Then, turning to Janice: "You got a screw loose!"

"Watch it, Archer. The judge may not be here, but we're still officers of the court," Willard said.

"Well woopdy-do! You keep that bitch away from me. I had enough of that nutcase."

"It's you that needs to keep away from her," Daniels said, stepping towards the animated suspect. "Next time you won't be this lucky."

"What's this? Couple'a dykes standin' up for each other?"

"Mr. Archer, I think we'd better just get out of here and let it lie," his lawyer cautioned.

"I ain't afraid of no cops!"

"Well maybe you should be," Daniels said, her voice cold enough to freeze even Archer's overheated rhetoric.

"Huh," he said, sneering. He nodded toward the lawyer. "Let's get outta here. Don't like the company."

He led the way out the door, but not before one last dismissive glare at Janice. She didn't know where she found the courage, but she stared right back at him.

"What an asshole," Willard said the moment they were gone.

"Make that two. His lawyer wasn't much better."

Janice sat back down in her chair in a slow-motion collapse. "I can't believe she let him go," she mumbled, shaking her head in disbelief.

"Don't let it bother you," Willard said. "Like Daniels said, we'll ask for a full-time detail. He won't get anywhere near you."

"That's what you said last time. He doesn't seem to care what the law says."

"He'll care if we take him in again for violating the order."

Janice didn't say what she was thinking, but from the look on her face both cops knew full-well she was scared.

*****

Janice walked through the Courthouse corridors in a fog. She had been so sure the judge would lock her attacker up again, she'd allowed herself to relax, just a bit, and now she felt the full weight of his release. Police detail or no police detail, Archer could get to her if he wanted. He'd made that perfectly clear.

Her footsteps echoed along with Daniels' and Willard's, but she felt as alone as if they hadn't been there.

"You're awful quiet," Willard said after an extended period of silence.

"I thought he'd go back to jail," Janice said, trying not to sound as fearful as she felt.

"We told you, you'll get a protective detail…"

Daniels interrupted her partner with a raised hand. "We get it - you're afraid he'll somehow manage to evade the detail and get to you."

"Or my family."

"Or your family. We understand. But everyone in our precinct already has a photo of Archer on their computer."

"Thanks to your APB," Willard said with a grin.

"Thanks to whatever. The point is, they all know what he looks like, and they all know there's a restraining order out there. That makes every cop in this sector of the City part of your security detail. They'll *all* be on the lookout for that asshole."

Janice felt a small rush of optimism. *'Maybe they **can** keep him away from us.'*

"But you still need to keep your eyes open as well," Willard chimed-in.

"Oh, don't worry. I'll be watching every shadow, every unexpected visitor - everything! The way things have been going I'll be lucky to get more than a few hours of sleep, knowing he's running around out there somewhere."

Daniels stopped her in mid-step. "Don't let him get inside your head," the cop said. "That's what creeps like him want. They get off on it. Think about something else - your job, your kid, whatever, but not that jerk."

Janice took a deep breath and nodded. "I'll try. I'm not sure if I can do it, but I'll try."

"And you too," Willard said softly to Daniels.

She glared at him a moment, but didn't deny the truth of his words.

The three of them walked out to the parking lot, the conversation once again lagging.

"You're gonna be ok, right?" Willard said when they'd escorted Janice to her car.

"I'll do my best."

"And we'll do ours. If you even *think* you see that guy, you call us. Right?"

"Will do. Thanks."

"Sorry it came to this," Daniels said.

"Yeh, me too."

Janice climbed into her car and drove off with a last wave goodbye.

"That was a real goat-hump," Willard said as her car pulled out of the lot.

"I can see where the Judge was coming from, though. The guy hasn't done anything other than smile at her, and we can't prove he wasn't just going for breakfast. Monahan had to give him the benefit of the doubt."

"I know, but it still stinks."

The two cops stood there for a few seconds, each weighing the vagaries of Janice's situation.

"And what was that about me not thinking about Archer?" Daniels asked out of the blue. "You really think I've got that asshole on my mind?!"

"I didn't mean Archer. I meant those punks - in the stairwell."

She was about to bite his head off, when she stopped and smiled. "What punks?" she asked.

"No idea."

He gave her a fist-bump and they went their separate ways.

CHAPTER 13

That night, Janice got Jackie to bed without problems, then begged-off having a heart-to-heart with her mother. She knew her Mom meant well, but after that circus in the Courthouse earlier in the day, she was in no mood. She poured herself a tall glass of wine, secreted herself in her bedroom (after locking the door), and prepared for some badly-needed r&r. But after only a few sips she changed her mind, deciding to take a nice hot shower to help wash away any lingering thoughts about her attacker, that afternoon - all of it. She stripped off her clothes and tossed them into the hamper like radioactive waste.

She hummed to herself as the water heated and an embracing cloud of steam began to envelop the stall. The warmth of the water and the thrumming spray from the shower started her in the right direction, had begun to carry her to a place where she could almost forget the past week, when a soft, nearly subliminal sound crept into her consciousness.

*'What is **that**?'* she wondered, straining to hear past the rushing water. Immediately her thoughts reverted to the same anxious nightmares that had been tormenting her ever since the attack. The sound was… indistinct. She couldn't get a good fix on it.

She turned off the water and stood utterly still in the middle of the shower stall, water dripping from her rapidly cooling body. She held her breath to try to identify the sound, but the pounding of her heart obscured anything less forceful than a timpani drum. She grabbed a towel and wrapped it around her shivering body, the cool of the tile floor competing with her own fears. Like some anxious cat-burglar she slowly inched her way toward the door, her mind now working overtime to generate every horrible eventuality possible.

There! There is was again!

She cracked the door open just far enough to peer out into the dimly-lit hallway. A single yellowed nightlight cast an eerie glow. She held her breath once again, this time unconsciously, and pushed the door open a bit further. What was she going to do if there *was* someone out there? What if it was Archer?

She had nearly steeled herself sufficiently to be able to push forward, when suddenly the sound of rushing water tore through the tiled hall. She flinched for an instant, until her conscious mind realized it was just a flushing toilet. Probably her mother.

She exhaled a breath she'd held much too long and half-crept, half-staggered back into her bedroom. She closed the door softly, sat down on the edge of her bed, and wept.

★★★★★

The next few days were muddied waters flowing slowly. Janice forced herself to go to work each morning despite feeling as if someone was watching her every time she left the house. She never actually saw anyone, but several times she got the sensation of something - or someone - just disappearing out of the corner of her eye before she could turn and catch them in the act.

But catch them doing what? *Smiling* at her?

The unending pressure of those days, combined with little or no sleep, created a kind of cocoon of desperation that seemed to surround her at all times. Only when she was talking with customers or co-workers, or sometimes with Jackie or her Mom, did she have the strength to feign normalcy, to smile and nod and speak in a clear, unwavering voice that sounded like a real person, not the ghost she had become. She'd even considered calling that guy she'd met at the bar. *Ellington,* wasn't it? She knew it was, but couldn't see bringing all her troubles to someone she barely knew. Maybe later. After it was all over, if there ever was such a time.

So it was with a sense of relief that she took a phone call late one afternoon while she was sitting staring mindlessly at her desk in the big, echoing warehouse.

"Hello?"

"Janice? Officer Daniels here. Has anyone from the DA's office contacted you yet?"

She felt her stomach fall to the floor. "No. Should they have?"

"Maybe not yet. We just got the word ourselves. The DA's asking for a court date."

"What does that mean, exactly?"

"It means she thinks she's got enough evidence to bring your case to trial."

'My case.' Is that what all this was? Her *case?* To Janice it seemed a lot more like her *life,* though she could understand how a cop could see life as a series of cases.

"Any idea when?" She wanted to know more, but the timing was crucial. It would give her some sense of whether she'd be able to hang on to her sanity until her attacker was found guilty - *if* he was found guilty - or whether she could expect a descent into nightly wine and junk food orgies designed to allow her to sleep, if not to sleep well.

"Hard to say. But it might be as soon as next month."

"That seems pretty quick, doesn't it?" Actually, she knew very little about court cases. Pretty much just what she'd read in check-out-line mags or seen on TV.

"A little," the officer admitted. "But it seems like the DA and Judge Monahan want this to move through the system sooner rather than later. No grass's gonna grow on this case."

"What if the defense isn't ready? Can they stall it?" She didn't know where that question came from, only that it seemed inordinately important.

"Don't know. Maybe. The judicial system usually gives the benefit of the doubt to the defendant."

"Why is that? Why would they want to favor the perps?!"

Daniels heard the frustration bubbling over. "Because they're *suspected* perps, not proven," she explained, as she had a thousand times before. "You know, *innocent until proven guilty* and all that."

She did. Know. But it all looked a lot different from her side of the equation.

"I was *there!* I *know* he's guilty."

"But the judge doesn't. Or the jury if he chooses to go that route."

"He can ask for a *jury* trial? What a waste of time and money." Sometimes it seemed like the whole system was rigged in favor of the crooks.

Janice could almost feel the Officer shrug on the other end of the line. "A lot of the time, I'm sure it is. But every once in a while, we get the wrong person and the judge assigned to the case is impatient, or has an undisclosed bias, and in those cases a jury can save the day."

She shook her head. "So for that one in a thousand, the other 999 get screwed?" She knew she didn't sound at all like the liberal defender of the downtrodden she'd always prided herself for being. Of course, nothing like this had ever happened to her before. Maybe liberals were just people that nothing bad had ever happened to.

"That's easy to say until you're the one," Daniels explained patiently.

Of course. She knew that, even if she didn't feel it right at that moment.

"I don't know. It all seemed a whole lot clearer two weeks ago."

"Don't give up. Just because he can ask for a jury, doesn't mean he won't be found guilty and sent to prison."

"As he should."

"And as he probably will. The DA's office should be in touch with you any time now. Just hang in there. I know it's tough, and sometimes it seems like it's all stacked against you, but most of the time it works like it's supposed to."

Janice didn't know what to say. A feeling of helplessness hung over her so heavy it sometimes felt as if it might crush her into nothingness.

"I guess we'll just have to wait and see," she mouthed without conviction.

"You'll see. It'll all work out."

"Yeh. Thanks."

Daniels held the phone in her hand even after Janice hung up. She only wished she was as confident as her words. What would happen to that poor woman if the asshole got off? She dropped the phone into its cradle. She didn't want to think about it.

*****

Janice had blown-off two scheduled appointments with Dr. Thurman - once because she had to go downtown to meet with Judge Monahan, and once… well, because she just couldn't get motivated to drag herself to the medical office building and spend an hour whining about things she couldn't change.

So why was she going today?

Good question. Perhaps because Archer's release had brought her worst fears to life. Perhaps because she needed to find sufficient peace of mind to get a decent night's sleep or she was going to collapse. Physically or mentally, she didn't know, but either would be disastrous. Whenever she thought about what her life - and Jackie's - would be like if her mother was forced to assume control of their world, she nearly shook with apoplexy. Oh, Jennifer would try to do the best for both of them, she had no doubt about that. At heart her Mom was a good, caring person. The problem was, her Mom's idea of a good life was so alien to her own that her good intentions would be doomed to failure, the kind of painful, public, all-encompassing failure that would not only leave Janice and her son permanently scarred, but would pretty much end what little mother-daughter relationship still existed between them. And that, truth be told, was not something she wanted to experience.

At the door to Dr. Thurman's office, Janice took a deep breath, tried a few tenuous meditative *'Ommm's,* and stepped into the prototypical modern medical waiting room: off-white paint, stark, nearly maintenance-free plants, quasi- but not too-comfortable chairs lining the perimeter, and the ever-present bank-teller window behind which sat a harried middle-aged woman with an 'Oh Jesus, not another one' smile plastered to her face like a Halloween mask that had fused to her skin.

"Do you have an appointment?" the office administrator asked without prelude. Apparently neither "Good morning" nor "Welcome" were required greetings in this age of unknown online *friends* and *sayin' it like it is*, not even in a shrink's office.

"Janice Greyson," she said. "Ten o'clock."

The woman scanned her online schedule with such exactitude that Janice wondered if she looked like the kind of person who would fake an appointment with a psychologist.

"Ah yes, Ms. Greyson. Have you filled out our forms?" she asked, holding up a clipboard with a half-dozen two-sided forms that demanded way too much personal information and gave away way too much personal control.

"Last time I was here."

Perhaps she'd sounded a bit snippy, because the woman's phony smile slipped a bit.

"All right then. Have a seat. The doctor will be with you shortly."

Before Janice could even nod, the receptionist was looking down at her desk. Janice tried to see what was so interesting that she couldn't meet her eyes, but she saw nothing that might qualify. She chose one of the peripheral seats in the waiting room, flipped through a pile of old, pristine-looking copies of Psychology Today and The

American Journal of Psychiatry, and older, dog-eared copies of People and Sports Illustrated, before deciding she was too wound-up to read anything. So she sat and tried to focus her thoughts instead.

She was successful enough that she didn't quite hear the receptionist call her name the first time. She heard something - just enough to rouse her from her reverie.

"Ms. Greyson?" the woman called again, this time with a stronger hint of attitude.

"Yes?"

"The doctor is ready for you now. You can go in."

She almost said thank you, but caught herself. She was tired of self-important nobodies imposing themselves on her world. She marched through the door without even a nod to the woman, who'd already resumed her pose of staring at her desktop.

"Janice!" Dr. Thurman said, getting up from her desk and moving gracefully toward her as she entered. "How are you?"

All Janice's stored-up frustration and indignation flickered like the proverbial candle in the wind; with a brief hug from the good doctor, it was snuffed-out completely.

"I'm... okay," she lied. Or dissembled. Lying was much more calculated.

The psychologist looked askance at her. She'd caught the dissembling. "Are you? You sound a bit... uncertain."

Janice debated lying, again, but thought better of it. What was the point of visiting a psychologist if you were going to lie to her?

"My attacker is free on bond, and he just violated a restraining order that was supposed to keep him away from me but didn't!" She spit it all out so quickly she had to take a deep breath.

The doctor controlled her facial expressions admirably, but not completely. "And how does that make you feel?"

"Threatened." There was no other word, really. She felt threatened. Not just for herself, but for Jackie, and even her Mom. Daniels and Willard might be in harm's way as well. Who knew with a crazy person like Archer?

Dr. Thurman gave a sympathetic smile. "Why don't we both sit down and talk about it."

The desire to unburden herself battled with the cynical sense that any discussion would be useless. This time, her desire overcame her fear. She sat.

"So, tell me, what's been going on?"

Janice told her everything, slowly and methodically, all the while staring at an abstract painting that seemed quite disturbing, given her current mental and emotional state.

"I'm so sorry," the doctor emoted. "How do you feel about it?"

Janice closed her eyes, trying to summon the courage to be frank and open. "I feel… alone, unprotected. I feel like the asshole who attacked me is getting all the breaks from our judicial system, and I'm being ignored, as if I'm the one who did something wrong. It doesn't seem fair." She struggled to keep tears from her eyes, but failed. For a long moment no one spoke, as if Dr. Thurman was waiting for her to say more. But she wasn't ready. She wanted something from the Doctor. Some give and take.

"You're not alone in that feeling," the doctor finally said. "Many of my patients have experienced the same frustration, the same sense of unfairness."

"What did they do about it?" It was all well and good that other people saw the system the same way she did, but it didn't help her any. She wanted to get past those feelings - somehow.

"Well, for the most part they learned to trust the system, to give it a chance. Many of them were pleasantly surprised." Her smiling face seemed to beg for acceptance.

Janice wasn't in the mood. "And what about the people who weren't pleasantly surprised? What about the ones who got jerked around and saw their lives ruined by the very people the system is supposed to protect us from? What about them?" She hadn't meant to raise her voice; it just happened.

"It makes you angry."

It wasn't a question so much as a simple declaration of fact. "Of course it makes me angry!' Again, over-modulated.

"What are you thinking right now?"

She tried to bring her heart rate down by breathing slowly and deeply. Gradually, she felt the adrenaline leak from her system. "I'm thinking that I didn't do anything to deserve all this. It's not my fault!"

The dam broke and tears streamed down her face. Doctor Thurman jumped up, grabbed a Kleenex and put her arm around Janice's shoulders. At first Janice flinched, drawing away in embarrassment and pain, but in moments the simple human contact broke down the barriers and she leaned into it with childlike abandon.

"It's okay, Janice. Let it out. Let it all out."

She didn't know how long she cried. Seemed like several minute, maybe more. During that time the doctor didn't say anything further, just consoled her with gentle pats and her strong, unwavering presence. Eventually, Janice caught her breath, choked off the sobs, and dabbed away the lingering tears.

"I'm sorry," she said, her voice still tremulous. "I don't know what came over me."

"You have every right to be angry, to be frustrated with the legal system. It *isn't* fair." The doctor stepped slowly away from her, settling back in her chair with a pained look. "But life often isn't fair. I'm sure you know that."

She nodded.

"But knowing it doesn't make it hurt any less. Is that right?"

That was *exactly* right. "It's like you're a number, a case, not a person. You become a victim a second time, and in some ways that hurts even worse."

"I'm sorry."

Janice didn't know why, but she was sick and tired of people who had nothing to do with causing her problems telling her they were *sorry*. What did that mean, anyway? Was it going to help her get past all the thoughts, the emotions? Not likely. It was little more than a politeness mantra, a knee-jerk reaction that probably made the speaker feel better than it did her. She was so lost in her thoughts that she didn't realize the doctor was talking to her until the question was repeated.

"Janice - are you with me?"

"Oh, sorry. I guess I wandered off a little bit."

Dr. Thurman eyed her more closely. "What were you thinking about?"

She hesitated. "I was just thinking how everyone says they're sorry except the guy who actually did it," she began, "and none of it helps. None of it makes it any better."

Now it was the shrink's turn to sigh. "It takes time," she explained softly. "Sometimes a few minutes of trauma can take years to overcome."

"Reassuring." She did not even try to keep the sarcasm from her voice.

Her doctor's smile was bittersweet. "We need to tell each other the truth. Otherwise, we might never get to the point where the attack no longer affects you so strongly."

"Now you're scaring me."

"I don't mean to. I've talked to a great many women who've had similar experiences, and the vast majority of them return to their lives happier and much more in control."

"But not all."

"No, not all. Some won't face their trauma, and so it lingers."

She felt her lips squeeze tight. "That's not for me," she said. "Let's go after it."

||*|*|*|*

Jackie knew something was wrong. He could feel it. His Mom was mad a lot of the time, and even worse - sad. She tried to act like nothing was wrong, but she couldn't fool him.

And it made *him* sad.

He wished he knew what he could do to make her happy again. He made his bed every morning, Didn't leave his dirty clothes in the middle of the room. But she hardly noticed. And she hugged him a lot. Even more than before she got sad. He didn't really like so much hugging, but if it helped make her feel better, then he was willing to put up with it.

That night she had come home from wherever she'd gone and seemed sadder than usual. He could see that her eyes were red. He thought maybe she'd been crying.

"What's wrong, Mommy?" he asked as soon as she came through the door. "Does your arm hurt?"

She still had that cloth tied around her neck to hold her arm in one place. She'd hurt it in the car accident.

"Not too much," she said, but her voice was deep and raspy. "It's feeling a little better every day."

"Then why do you look so sad?"

She smiled, but it wasn't her usual smile. He thought she was making believe.

"Oh, sometimes things happen to grown-ups that make them unhappy."

Jackie had heard that kind of explanation too many times. It was what adults said when they thought kids wouldn't understand.

"It's about the bad man, isn't it?" he asked.

He saw a look pass over his Mom's eyes. It hurt her to even think of that man. "Yeh, it was. But everything's going to be okay. It's just going to take longer than I had hoped."

"How long?"

Her face twisted. "I don't know. Maybe a month or two. Maybe more. Depends."

"On what?"

"Oh, on the police, and the court, and... I don't know, on a lot of things. But enough about that. How are you and Grandma doing?"

He knew she was changing the subject, but maybe that was what she needed to feel better. "We're great!" he said, exaggerating a little. They *were* doing ok, but it was hard to do great when your Mom was sad.

"I'm so glad!" his Mom said, bending down and giving him another big hug and kiss. He held still for it, even though it went on a little too long. He wanted her to feel better.

Just then his Grandma came into the room. She looked worried.

"How'd it go?"

"Okay…" He saw her glance down at him quickly, something he thought he wasn't supposed to see. That meant she didn't want to say something in front of him.

"The judge believed him?"

"Uh huh." Mom took off her hat and sweater, hardly looking at Grandma at all.

Grandma didn't say anything for a while as Mommy fussed here and there in the kitchen.

"What are they going to do about it?" Grandma eventually asked.

Mom looked at her with a sort of frown. I could tell she wasn't happy with the question.

"Station some officers," she said. "Not much else they can do."

"Do about what?" Jackie asked. He felt that they were talking about the bad man, but he wasn't sure exactly what they meant.

"Nothing to worry your sweet little head about," his Mom said. "What should we have for dinner?"

She was changing the subject again.

"Pizza!" he said. He could always eat pizza.

"Mom? Pizza okay with you?"

Grandma looked a little sad, but then she sort of smiled. "Yeh, sure. Pizza is fine."

Maybe the pizza would make Mommy happier.

CHAPTER 14

For the next three weeks, life returned to a semblance of normalcy. The damage to her shoulder healed enough to forego the sling, and although the assortment of green and black bruises dotting her body still brought back vivid memories whenever she saw them in the mirror, at least she was up and about. She had contacted both Officer Daniels and the District Attorney's office several times to ask when the trial would take place, but had received only standard evasions suggesting no one really knew. To be fair, Daniels had told her that the wheels of justice sometimes turned ever so slowly under the best of conditions, yet still held out hope that it would begin in less than a month, unless the *perp* accepted a plea deal, in which case the only court appearance would be that public acceptance. But given his previous smug denials, Janice thought it unlikely he'd go for a deal. So... What did it all mean? Could the case remain in legal limbo indefinitely?

She was beginning to wonder whether justice would ever be served, when early one evening, as she was helping her mother prepare dinner, the doorbell sounded.

"I'll get it!" Jackie called out. He found answering the doorbell somehow exciting, which was fortuitous since at that moment Janice had her arms floured nearly to the elbows as she rolled out pizza dough.

She heard the door open and an unintelligible woman's voice speaking to him. Moments later, he came running into the kitchen.

"Mommy, it's for you! Some woman."

"Did she tell you her name?" she asked, beginning to brush off some of the flour as she prepared to go see who was there.

"Uh... I forgot."

"Okay. Let's go see." She took off her apron and walked into the living room, Jackie close behind. She found the door wide open - as her son had no doubt left it - and a young woman of no more than 25 or so, thin, with short light brown hair, silhouetted against the pinkish-orange twilight.

"Hi. May I help you?" she asked, her antennae sensing some sort of salesperson or donation hustler.

"Mrs. Greyson? Janice Greyson?" the woman asked.

"Ms.," Janice corrected. "And you are?"

She held out a business card. "My name's Barbara Reynolds. I'm a reporter with the Herald."

A reporter? What did a reporter want with her? "Okay," she said measuredly.

"We just learned that the trial of the man who attacked you..." she looked down at a small notebook. "... Daniel Lee Archer, has been set for the 15th of next month. We were hoping you might talk to us about that day..."

How did she know about the attack? Or more accurately, how did she know it was Janice who'd been attacked? The DA's office had told her that rape victim's names are protected. This shouldn't be happening...

"Ms. Greyson?" the woman said. Apparently she'd drifted off again. "How do you know my name?" she asked.

"When we contacted Mr. Archer and asked for a comment, he told us," she said matter-of-factly. "Said you were a crazy woman. We wanted to give you a chance to tell your side of the story."

She found her hand gripping the doorknob very tightly. "I'm sorry. I have nothing to say until the trial."

"Don't you want people to know what really happened?"

The reporter seemed so sincere Janice almost relented - but not quite. "No, I'm sorry. Please go."

She didn't wait for any further discussion. She closed the door, threw the deadbolt, and leaned back against the thin barrier of wood that separated her from the nightmare outside.

"What's wrong Mommy?" a little voice asked.

"Nothing, honey. Just someone Mommy didn't want to talk to."

He seemed to ponder her answer for a while. "What's a reporter?" he finally asked.

He had been listening. "It's someone who writes for a newspaper."

"Why don't you want to talk to her?"

"She wants to talk about something I don't want to talk about. So I asked her to leave."

"Is it about the bad man?"

She looked down at him, more shocked than angry. How could he possibly know? "Yes, she wanted to talk about that man. And I don't."

Another moment of reflection. "Would it make you sad?"

How could she explain that reliving that day was almost like experiencing the attack all over again? How could she make him - or anyone else - understand the thin, brittle shell she'd encircled her spirit with, a shell still too tenuous to risk shattering by exposing it to the past? She did not know how. She would not try.

"It might," she said. "But I don't want to find out. Better to talk about other things, like what a smart little boy I know learned in class this week!" She grabbed him around the waist and tickled, hoping he wouldn't notice the tears pooling in the corners of her eyes. He laughed with such gleeful abandon that she felt some of the weight lift off her heart. By the time she abandoned her attack, she'd regained control over her emotions.

"Who wants hot chocolate?!" she asked before her son could pummel her again with questions she didn't want to think about.

"Me!" he cried.

"Then let's go!"

She led the way into the kitchen, her mind a hundred miles away.

*****

Sure enough, the next day the DA's office called her at work and informed her of the trial date.

"How come my attacker knew the date before I did?" she asked, not caring whether she sounded like an unthankful victim.

"Excuse me?" the woman on the other end of the call asked. It seemed to Janice that she was not accustomed to people questioning *The System*.

"The jerk who attacked me knew the date of the trial before I did. Why is that?"

"We have to call *one* of the parties first," the woman began, but Janice shut her right down.

"He knew yesterday. Maybe even earlier."

"Well, I wouldn't know about that." The woman sounded offended.

"You should. A victim should know everything about the trial before her attacker."

"I'm not arguing with you, ma'am. But it doesn't always work out that way."

"No. So I see. Maybe you could suggest it to your boss."

"I'll do that." She sounded like she was playing Janice, hoping to get her off the phone without further conflict.

"Good. I'll mention your helpfulness to the DA when I see her. Have a *nice* day."

She slammed the phone down with more vehemence than the situation deserved. She didn't doubt that the woman was just doing her job, probably exactly as she'd been taught. But that didn't make it right. And it didn't make her feel any better about it. She decided to call Officer Daniels while she still felt the fire of her indignation.

"Daniels," the familiar voice answered after only one ring.

"Did you know the trial date has been set?" she asked without prelude.

"Janice?"

"You want to know how I know? A *reporter* stopped by my house last night to ask me questions about the attack, and she says she found out about it from Archer."

"I'm so sorry about that," the officer said, and Janice was willing to believe she really was. "We were only notified today. I was going to give you a call, but I got caught up with another case."

Her apology quelched Janice's indignation. "Yeh, well the DA should have let me know at the same time she notified that asshole. No, earlier!"

"I agree. It was a screw-up. I wish I could say it never happens, but it does."

With the fire gone, Janice could only fume. "So now what? I get to see my name all over the media? Can I do anything about it?"

"You're probably okay. I mean, most of the local press are pretty good about keeping the names of victims out of the public eye."

"But…?" She heard something in Daniel's voice.

"But… if one releases it, all bets are off. Then they're like sharks in a feeding frenzy."

"Nice image."

"Sorry. With any luck it won't come to that."

"Anything I can do to help make sure it doesn't?"

"Well, I suppose you could call the DA's office and tell them you're worried about unauthorized release. Ask them to make it clear to any reporters who contact them that their office will hold them responsible for keeping a victim's name protected."

"Does that generally work?"

A pause. "I don't really know anyone who's tried it. It should."

With that encouragement, Janice hung up and called the DA. She was transferred to an assistant, who listened politely.

"So what exactly do you want us to do?" the young man asked when she'd finished explaining the situation.

"I want you to tell the press people not to release my name! I'm a victim. The world doesn't need to know all about it."

"Okay. I understand. But you must realize, we have certain first amendment constraints."

"I've heard of Freedom of the Press, yes. But the public interest should be in the criminal, not his victim."

"Yes, of course. I'll be sure to tell the District Attorney about your dilemma."

"Can I speak to her?" She'd always believed face-to-face was much more effective than second-hand.

"The DA?" The assistant sounded horrified. "I don't think so. She's pretty busy."

"Can you *ask*?" She tried not to lose her temper. Why didn't anyone understand what she was going through?

The assistant put her on hold for all of fifteen seconds. "Sorry, she's not available," he said when he came back on the line.

What a surprise,' she thought. "All right, thanks for checking. Please be sure to pass her my message."

"I will."

And with that, he was gone. Janice hung up and closed her eyes. It was so *unfair*. The frustration nearly overcame her self-control. But nothing was going to make her surrender.

Nothing.

*****

When she got back home she was so preoccupied with the day's events she didn't notice the small scrum of reporters until she'd already parked her car. Two burly men with video cameras book-ended two women with the coiffed hair and heavy makeup of local TV reporters, and three others with recorders and still cameras. She hoped they might not see her, but before she could turn off the engine they were already swarming.

"Ms. Greyson! Ms. Greyson!" the reporters called out, the video guys in stumbling pursuit.

She debated whether to run, to flee that entire circus and seek refuge in her home. But she was afraid they might follow her up to her door and Jackie and her Mom might have to experience the feeding frenzy. So she turned to face them.

"Look - I did *not* consent to the release of my personal information, and I don't appreciate your outlets smearing my name all over the pages and airwaves just so you can sell ads. You should be ashamed of yourselves!"

For just an instant, the pack froze. They looked startled, unsure, but not in the least apologetic. In that instant Janice thought she might avoid their interrogation. But the moment passed as quickly as it arrived and the journalists resumed their shouted assault with even more gusto. Janice swallowed her anger and her anxiety and shut her eyes to their increasingly demanding cries.

"We're just doing our jobs!"

"Don't you want people to know your side of the story?"

"You're a celebrity - enjoy it!"

The last nearly solicited a fist to the face. She maintained her tattered poise, however, and managed to step past them and up the front walk before they could cut her off from her escape route. They were still shouting and gesturing when her mother threw open the front door from inside, yanked her by the arm, and slammed the door behind her, throwing both locks in a panic.

"They're like animals!" Jennifer said, her face pale and wide-eyed. "Don't they have any decency?!"

Jackie was staring out the kitchen window, a big smile on his face.

"Are you famous, Mommy?"

She almost snapped at him, catching herself at the last moment. "No, not famous, Jackie. They just want to make a big deal out of our court case."

"Why?"

Why indeed. She wasn't sure herself, but she felt she owed him an explanation. "They make money by selling ads, and they get people to see the ads by doing stories like this one," she explained. "People like to hear about other people having more problems than they do. Makes them feel superior, or something."

Her son nodded his head sagely. "So people will feel good because you feel sad?"

She couldn't help but smile. "Yeh, I guess you could put it that way. But now we're all here, out of their reach, so let's just relax and enjoy each other's company."

Easier said than done. Jackie was bouncing off the walls with the TV cameras and all the people just outside, her mother was caught between fury and concern, and she... Well, she was lost. There were times in the days since the attack when she'd felt almost normal, almost able to banish the memories from her mind. But those days were very few. Most of the time, any little thing - or nothing at all - could trigger a thought, an image, something that dragged her back to that day, to those terrible moments when a stranger had stolen her dignity, her independence, her courage. Now she jumped at shadows, dreaded opening the front door, and trusted no one. No way to live a life.

"A penny for your thoughts," her mother said, pulling her back to a reality she'd rather avoid.

"Save your money. My thoughts aren't worth that much," Janice said.

"Oh, come on now. Don't let those vultures get to you! They'll get tired of taking pictures of nothing and go on to the next big thing, probably before you know it."

Janice would've loved to believe that, but the way things had been going she couldn't bring herself to embrace such optimism.

"I hope you're right," she told her mom. "I'd love to get my privacy back."

"It'll happen, honey. Don't you worry." Jennifer put her arms around her daughter in an awkward hug. The distance of years apart still intervened, as did the frequent and painful unsolicited advice. Jennifer's attempts at mothering over the past few weeks had mollified the painful memories a little, but old memories die hard. She felt Janice flinch and almost stepped away.

"It'll all work out. You'll see."

She wanted to believe. Maybe *needed* was the right word. She didn't know how much longer she could go on like that, always on edge, always expecting to see *that* smile again.

As soon as she could politely extricate herself from her mother's embrace, she went straight to the cupboard to get herself a glass of wine. These past few weeks she'd come to rely on the medicinal effect of a glass - or two. It eased her anxiety, allowed her to sleep more easily, even brightened her mood. For a while. She freely admitted that the initial benefits of the buzz faded (and in some cases turned around 180 degrees) after an hour or two. But for that short period, it was as if no one and nothing could hurt her, or her family.

That night, after the shock of running the gauntlet of all those reporters lying in wait, she felt as if she could down an entire *bottle* - or two. Her mother tried to dislodge her dark mood while Jackie playfully ignored it.

"Can anyone get some of that, or is it reserved for just the select few?" Jennifer asked as Janice poured herself a full glass of red.

"Oh, of course!" Janice said, reaching unthinkingly for another wineglass.

"Want to talk about it?"

She paused in mid-pour. She did, and she didn't. On the one hand she dreaded trying to fall asleep with all the thoughts and emotions of the past few days swirling around in her head. On the other, she couldn't see any solution to her troubles in the near future. So what was the use?

Her mother didn't wait for an answer. She grabbed both glasses and carried them out to the living room. Jackie was already fully engaged in Lego-building in his bedroom, so there was no easy out for Janice. She followed her mother meekly, trying to formulate a way to describe her emotions without sounding like a whiner. Luckily, her Mom had already come up with a strategy of her own.

"Look, Jan, you've got a lot on your plate right now: the court case, the reporters, your job... let alone the repercussions from the attack itself. It's perfectly understandable for you to feel... stressed, worried, whatever you want to call it. But I just wanted to repeat what I've already told you several times: I'm here for you, to help you around the house, run any errands you can't get to, or just to sit and talk."

Janice felt a rush of guilt for not having taken her mother
up on her repeated offers of help. It wasn't that they weren't
appreciated, but rather that the many years and many events
that had come between the two of them had left her unsure
of how far she could trust her mother. How much she could
say without having it flung back in her face during some
future argument. Her defensive shell tottered, but still stood.
Maybe she could risk just a little more intimacy...

"I..." she began, but before she could say another word
the tears streamed again and she struggled to catch her
breath. Her Mom jumped up out of her chair and ran to
where she sat, kneeling to hold her as she had when she'd
been a little girl.

They talked well into the night.

*****

Jennifer lay awake for quite a while.

She'd known her daughter was having a tough time of it.
A blind man could see that. But not until that very night had
she understood the depth of her pain. It hurt her to think
about it. She couldn't imagine how Janice kept going, kept up
the tough facade. Jennifer would have crumbled long ago.

She worried that the upcoming trial would reopen all the
old wounds, leave her battered and unprotected from the
assault of a world that saw rape as entertainment, a reality
show unlike any other. How could people be so uncaring?
How could they put their own curiosity before the needs of
the victim? Before the needs of her *daughter*.

She felt her chest tighten until she fought to take a full
breath. *'No!'*, she wouldn't let her heart fail, or do anything

else to make her daughter's burden heavier. She forced herself to breathe slowly, to calm her pounding pulse. With one last deep breath she turned out the bedside light and snuggled down into her covers.

No one could hear her strangled sobs.

CHAPTER 15

The weeks had passed agonizingly slowly, yet now that the date of the trial was upon her, Janice felt utterly unprepared. She'd met with the DA's office several times, going over her testimony, preparing for the grilling she'd been told to expect from her attacker's big-shot pro bono lawyer. She'd talked to both Daniels and Willard, more to hear a familiar voice than anything. She'd met twice more with Dr. Thurman, attempting to master coping techniques to allow her to concentrate and sleep without flashbacks from the attack disrupting both. All had gone well. But there she was, on the morning of the opening day of the trial, having slept no more than four hours, shaky, stomach in knots, head abuzz.

"You look nice, Mommy," Jackie said as she hurried into the kitchen. She'd changed her outfit three times, arriving back at the one she'd agreed to wear with the advice of the DA's office. Everything seemed to be moving so fast.

"Well thank you, Jackie," she managed to say with a smile. It was good to hear an encouraging word, even if it was from her six-year-old son. "What do you have there for breakfast?"

"Grandma made me a hard boil egg," he said, holding the peeled object of his affection up for her to see.

"Didn't want you to have to concentrate on anything but today," her mother said from the stove where she was stirring something in a small pan. "Feel like some oatmeal?"

If she was honest, she didn't feel like eating. But her mother had already made it...

"Yeh, sure. Thanks," she said, pouring herself a cup of coffee and sliding into a chair across from Jackie.

"Why are you so dressed-up?" her son asked between bites of egg.

"Mommy has a big meeting today," she said. She'd decided, with her mom's agreement, that it would be better to keep the fact and significance of the trial from Jackie. He was too young to grasp the specifics and too old to keep entirely in the dark. *Big meeting* seemed a good middle ground.

"At work?"

Why was it that young kids were so inquisitive about the very things they shouldn't have to listen to? "Sort of," she hedged.

"Here. Put something in your stomach. It'll help you settle down," Jennifer said as she handed a bowl of steaming oatmeal to her daughter. "How'd you sleep last night?"

If kids always asked the hardest questions, parents always saw through even the most determined facades.

"Not too well, really. Kept waking up."

Jackie was alerted. "Did you have to go pee? A lot of times I have to pee when I wake up."

For the first time that morning, she smiled without forcing it.

"Once or twice."

"It'll be fine," her mom joined in, sitting to her left. "You're not the one who needs to be nervous."

"Somehow I don't think he's anywhere near as nervous as I am this morning."

"Who?" Jackie was listening *much* too closely.

"Oh, nobody you need to know about," she evaded. She tried to short-circuit the conversation by taking a spoonful of the oatmeal. It tasted like lumpy wallpaper glue in her current state. She forced herself to swallow.

"You'll be great."

She shrugged. "I'll give it my best shot."

She tried to force herself to down another spoonful of the oatmeal, but finally settled for two cups of coffee - black. Buzzing from the caffeine as well as adrenaline, she excused herself, kissed Jackie, and patted her Mom on the shoulder.

"Thanks for the pep talk."

"It's what moms are for," Jennifer said with a sly grin.

"Yeh. I guess it is."

The front door closed behind her with a finality that sent a shiver up her spine. She marched to her car like a prisoner to a firing squad, each step both a physical and emotional effort.

*****

She arrived at the Courthouse more than thirty minutes early. Even then, she'd had to kill some time at home before leaving. She'd been up at 4:30, made one try at going back to sleep, and then got out of bed at 5:30. The spoonful of oatmeal and couple of cups of coffee for breakfast - she couldn't even think of eating anything more – had left her guts in turmoil. She'd watched a bit of the news on TV, until a reporter mentioned that the trial of an alleged rapist was about to begin today. She turned it off before she heard her name, as if it were some talisman that would protect her and bring her luck. Breakfast and a chat with her Mom killed some of the remaining time, but not all.

The parking lot at the Courthouse was mostly empty - only three other cars. She considered sitting there in her car until it got closer to the time she'd promised to meet with the DA, but after only a few minutes the closeness of the space chased her outside. She tried to focus on her testimony, to believe in the system, but something in the cool morning air, or perhaps it was the blueness of the sky, pushed her to consider making a break for it, hopping back into her car and driving without direction or destination. It was tempting. So tempting.

"Hey Janice!" a familiar voice called out, shattering her dreams of escape. She looked up to see Officer Daniels, in full dress uniform, climbing out of her black and white.

Part of her wanted to run to the officer, grab her in a bear hug and never let go. The other half wanted to scream and run the other way.

"Good morning, officer," she said as she walked resolutely to the parked cop car. "I see you're up and at 'em a bit early as well."

"Court appearances always get me stirred up. How about you? How you doin'?"

What to say? The whole truth and nothing but the truth? She decided to save that for the witness stand.

"Oh, not too bad. Could've used a little more sleep."

"I know that one. I was up before 5. Kind of silly, after all these years and all the court appearances. But I guess there's no telling your subconscious anything."

They chatted amiably as they walked to the Courthouse entrance, neither willing to poke the anthill of the trial itself. Janice admitted to spending way too much time deciding which dress to wear, Daniels laughing it off.

"Luckily, for us it's either blue, or blue."

Just inside the door a uniformed marshal kept watch over the metal detector, a stark reminder of the alien world they were about to enter. A few neutral words, the all-too-familiar empty pockets and jettisoned purse, and she was through.

"I've got to go see the DA," Janice explained.

"That makes two of us. Come on. I know the way. Been there a few times before."

The officer was doing her best to keep it light, but somehow that very effort made Janice feel less secure. Why did Daniels feel the need to handle her with kid gloves? Did she think Janice was at risk of cracking under the pressure? The thought made her stomach jump.

The walk through the tiled hallways probably took no more than three minutes, but it felt like an endless procession. The click-clack of her heels on the shiny white tiles reminded her how little time remained before 'the big show' as Willard had described it. Was she ready? Could she ever be ready to face that grin again, to relive that horror?

"Here we are," Daniels suddenly announced, pulling open one of the many nearly identical dark wood doors. "After you."

She walked into a reception room that was small, but orderly and officious. Photos of the President, the Vice-President and the Governor sat high on one wall looking down on the middle-aged receptionist like some political Holy Trinity.

Daniels introduced both of them. "I'll let the District Attorney know right away," she announced, and proceeded to do just that. In seconds a young woman in a very professional business suit and four-inch heels came out to usher them into the inner sanctorum.

The DA sat behind her desk studying files. She stood as they entered.

"Ms. Greyson, Officer Daniels, thank you for coming in so early this morning!" She sounded chipper and upbeat. Janice wondered if it was all an act for her benefit. "Can we get you anything?"

Janice shook her head no. "A cup of coffee - black?" Daniels said.

While an assistant got the coffee, the DA got down to business. "Look, we've got all the evidence we need to put this guy away. But as I've come to learn in my 23 years in this business, evidence alone sometimes isn't enough."

Janice's stomach fell off a cliff. "What do you mean?" she squeaked, her throat suddenly constricted.

"I mean, the defense is going to come up with their own version of what happened, with *alternative evidence*, to try to cast doubt on everything we present."

"But you've got the DNA!"

"I'm virtually certain they're going to claim the sex was consensual."

"I've already told you, that's ridiculous! I didn't even know the guy!"

"He says you did."

The silence stretched painfully.

"Look, Janice, the guy can say anything he wants. It all comes down to who the jury believes," Daniels cut in. "And if it was me making the decision, I know who I'd believe."

"But…"

"But, this guy's a compulsive liar. He lies as easy as he breathes. I don't think he even thinks about it. He just lies."

"So you think the jury will believe him?" She couldn't believe she was hearing this now, just minutes before the trial was supposed to start.

"I think they *could* believe him. But if all of us do our job, including you, Janice, then I'm confident Mr. Archer will spend the next 25 years or so behind bars. But we can't take anything for granted."

Who did she think was taking it for granted? Her?

"Nobody's saying the perp's gonna walk," Daniels added. "But let's just all stay on our toes."

'*I couldn't be more on my toes if I was doing a pirouette,*' Janice thought. "I understand," was all she said.

The DA did a quick run-through of the basic lines of questioning she would ask Janice, and then reiterated the cross examination she thought the defense team would counter with. They were the same questions she'd heard a half-dozen times before at practice sessions right there in the same room, and down the hall in large, empty conference rooms. It all came down to telling the truth. It would be hard. It would hurt. But she would do it. She *had* to do it. That bastard was not getting away with it.

*****

By the time Officer Daniels shepherded Janice into the courtroom, it was full of people. The many unfamiliar staring faces and the buzz of conversation set Janice aback.

"Who *are* all these folks?" she whispered to the Officer as they walked to their reserved seats up front.

"Reporters, trial freaks, busy-bodies - it's a mixture," Daniels said dismissively. "You always get 'em. Just ignore it."

Easier said than done. Janice tried to glance at the people on either side of the center aisle without letting them know she was looking. Not very productive. All she saw was a blur of unfriendly faces. It was a great relief when they arrived at their seats, just behind the Prosecutor's desk. DA Winters was already reviewing documents.

"They must think they've got a pretty good chance of nailing the asshole," Daniels said sotto voce. "Otherwise the DA would've farmed it out to one of her underlings. Politics being what they are."

Janice knew the officer was referring to the fact that DAs were elected in their city, and could not afford to lose too many high-profile cases. Hers probably met the profile, especially when an election was coming up in less than six months. She wasn't certain if the knowledge made her feel more or less optimistic about the likelihood of her attacker's conviction, but at least she knew it wouldn't be the 'B' Team handling the case.

Officer Daniels tried to engage in small talk as they waited for the trial to begin, but Janice wasn't in the mood. After a few failed attempts, the officer sat quietly and nodded to the occasional acquaintance who wandered into view. Janice, on the other hand, tried her best to ignore the row after row of spectators seated behind her, focusing all her attention on the empty high-backed chair behind the raised dais. In fact she was so focused on the judge's perch, it wasn't until the courtroom buzz rose to a crescendo that she realized her attacker had entered by a side door, flanked by armed marshals. She glanced once in his direction, but then locked

her stare back on the tall black chair. No way she was going
to give him an opportunity to get into her head, especially so
near to trial time. Moments later, twelve very average looking
people - seven women, five men, four black, two seemingly
Latino, the rest white - filed silently into the jurors' box. They
looked almost as tense as she felt.

Minutes passed, though it felt much longer. She was so
lost in thought that when a bailiff announced, "Please rise!"
in a loud, commanding voice, she nearly jumped out of her
skin.

Officer Daniels put a hand on her arm. "Take it easy
now. No need to get worked-up."

She tried to smile at the officer, but feared it came across
as a lopsided grimace.

Judge Monahan settled into her chair, looking much
sterner and maybe a little older than she seemed in her
chambers. The bailiff read the case number and the charges,
and the trial got underway. Janice tried to listen closely to the
opening arguments, but after the DA's crisp, concise
reiteration of the charges and circumstances, the Defense
Attorney went on and on about trivial details, mixing in an
assortment of outrageous opinions and plain old lies.

"How can he say that? It's not true!" Janice whispered to
Officer Daniels when the slick defense lawyer – wearing what
appeared to be a very expensive pale blue tailored suit, $500
shoes and a brilliant yellow tie that screamed *look at me!* -
claimed that Janice was a spurned girlfriend who filed rape
charges only after being dumped by *Mr. Archer.*

"Lawyers are paid liars," Daniels whispered back. "Most
of them deserve to be in prison as much as their clients do."
Clear where her sentiments lay.

The day dragged on hour after hour, witness after witness. Detective Willard was one of the first. He gave a clear, unhurried timeline and explained how he and Daniels had taken Archer into custody. The Defense attorney seemed determined to undermine everything the detective said.

One exchange: "Did the defendant express surprise when you appeared at the Eastside Café?" he asked.

"He *acted* as though he was surprised," Willard answered.

"Your Honor, could the Detective please refrain from coloring his testimony with directed inflection?"

Directed inflection? What the heck was that? But the Judge seemed to know.

"Detective, please keep your answers neutral in tone and inflection," the judge directed.

"Yes, Your Honor," Willard said. "Sorry."

The defense lawyer went straight back to it. "So, then, what did Mr. Archer say when you suddenly appeared at the Café?"

"He didn't *say* anything. He ran."

"He ran? Just like that. You walked up to him with a big smile, and he ran." The sarcasm was overpowering.

"I didn't walk up to him. Officer Daniels did." Janice had to hand it to Willard, he was tough.

"So there was nothing that might have made Mr. Archer fear for his safety?"

The hulking Detective looked confused. "How do you mean?"

"I mean, did you, say, reach for your gun, or anything like that?"

"Of course I reached for my gun! It's Department policy when confronting a possible perpetrator."

Judge Monahan looked down at Willard over her glasses. "Just a yes or no is sufficient, Detective."

"Yes, Your Honor."

"So you walked up to Mr. Archer and without saying a word pulled out your pistol…"

"No. I did not take my gun out of its holster until Archer ran. And I addressed him by his full name."

"Did you reach for your gun?"

"I reached behind me. My gun was not visible to Archer."

"But you reached behind your back."

"Yes."

"Detective, were you wearing a uniform?"

"Officer Daniels…"

"I asked you if *you* were wearing a uniform. It was you who confronted Mr. Archer, wasn't it?"

Willard looked as if he would spit. "It was. I was wearing a plaid sports jacket and black trousers."

"So let me reiterate: a person who Mr. Archer doesn't know, wearing a *plaid* sports jacket, appears at the Eastside Cafe´ in the middle of his breakfast, and reaches behind his back for *something* as he loudly calls out his name. Can you see how he might not react well to such a provocation?"

"Objection, Your Honor!" the DA yelled, jumping to her feet. "Calls for an opinion."

"Withdrawn," the defense attorney said, strutting back to his desk.

"Re-cross?" the DA asked the judge. She nodded her approval.

"Could Mr. Archer clearly see Officer Daniels before you called out his name?"

"She was standing no more than fifteen feet right in front of him."

"And she *was* wearing a uniform?"

"Bright blue. Couldn't miss it."

"Detective…" the Judge warned.

"No further questions," the DA said.

And so it went. Officer Daniels took the stand immediately after Willard and confirmed everything he'd said. But once again the defense attorney stressed that Detective Willard was not wearing a uniform and so Archer could hardly be expected to know Willard was a police officer. It seemed pointless to Janice: obviously the guy knew Officer Daniels was a cop, and since Willard was there with her, it didn't take a genius to figure out he was a cop as well. But the attorney kept harping on it as if it was an important point. It made her feel a bit queasy.

It was nearly lunchtime, after more than three hours of proceedings, when the DA's assistant turned and handed Janice a note.

'Feel up to testifying now, or after lunch?' it read.

Janice felt so jumpy she wasn't sure she could eat, but she wasn't thrilled with the thought of facing that sleazy lawyer either.

'After lunch,' she mouthed to the assistant. The DA requested a recess nearly immediately, and the Judge agreed.

As Janie expected, lunch was a tangle of nerves washed down with a cup of coffee.

"Not what I'd call a balanced diet," opined Officer Daniels, who'd sat with her in the Courtroom cafeteria without invitation. Not that she wasn't wanted, exactly. It was true that part of Janice longed to be alone to run through her testimony in her mind for the fiftieth time, while another part welcomed the company.

"I'm not all that hungry," Janice admitted.

"Butterflies?"

"Pterodactyls."

"Impressive." The officer took a few bites. "I still remember the first time I had to testify. Thought I might upchuck right there in the witness booth. But I didn't. Turned out it wasn't all that big 'a deal. Now, I hardly notice it."

Janice knew she was trying to soothe her nerves and appreciated the effort. But it didn't help.

"I'm dreading having to see that taunting smile again."

"Archer? Don't look in his direction. Keep your eyes on the DA, or on me."

Easier said than done. "I'll try. But just knowing he's over there..."

"Don't make him out to be something he's not," Daniels said, suddenly brusque to the point of rudeness. "He's just a perv loser, nothing more. And after all this is over, he'll be inmate number 4267912. He has no power over you, and pretty soon, he won't have any power over anyone. Probably just the opposite."

Even knowing the words were meant to bolster her courage, Janice took some comfort from the mental image of her attacker behind bars. Some; not much.

"What if he only gets a few years? What if he gets out?" There. She'd said it. The nightmare that kept recurring.

Officer Daniels shrugged. "Not likely. Rapists don't get coddled in this neck of the woods."

"But it's possible." She wanted to be contradicted, wanted the reassurance of an officer of the law.

She didn't get it. "I suppose. Every now and then the system misfires. But not this time. Not in your case. We've got the DNA, we've got the evidence, and we've got *you.*"

Her smile dared contradiction. "Well, I guess we'll find out," Janice managed to mumble. She glanced up at the large clock on the wall above the snack machines.

They'd find out real soon.

*****

As Janice joined the flood of people returning to the Courtroom, she felt as if that cup of coffee she'd just choked down was burning a hole in her guts. Not for the first time she regretted not sticking to water, or maybe some mashed potatoes. *'Too late now.'*

One of the DA's assistants corralled her just before she sat down, inquiring solicitously if she was ready. What could she say?

Sitting there in the front row, her mind drifted back to a junior high presentation she'd had to give on the earth's crust. She still remembered the nausea, the trembling hands, the sweat dripping down her forehead…

Just then the Judge returned to the courtroom. Everyone stood and sat back down at the Bailiff's urgings. Sound bounced around the high-ceilinged room like some crazy pinball.

Everything seemed to move in slow motion: the DA got up out of her chair, glanced back at her with a knowing smile, then announced "We call our next witness, Janice Greyson."

The Bailiff echoed her announcement, sans smile. She stood, feeling a bit light-headed, but managed to walk to the witness stand without assistance or obvious distress. Or so she hoped. The Bailiff droned on about telling the truth and she said yes. Or she thought she did. She moved her lips and sound came out, but it was so soft she could barely hear it herself. Seemed to satisfy the Judge, however.

The DA was sympathetic, careful with the questions and reassuring with her tone. She asked Janice to describe what had happened to her on *that* date, and - just as she'd practiced a few dozen times, both with and without the DA or one of her assistants making suggestions and editing her answers - she gave a brief but thorough description of the attack. She knew from her previous efforts that the complete story took just over four minutes, but there on the stand it seemed to take much longer. All those eyes watching her. All those spectators making decisions about her based on their own experiences and foibles.

And above all, *he* was there. She didn't look in his direction, not once. But she could *feel* him, feel the anger, the superiority, the arrogance. From time to time she could almost make herself believe she could hear his thoughts echo in her head.

'You think they're gonna believe you? No way. Not once I get up there on the stand. Not once I start tellin' 'em my story. You're just another victim, another woman complaining about a guy doin' what guys do. You're not the sort of person that jury wants to believe. They want to believe me! The underdog. The one falsely accused! Look at 'em - once I start talkin' they'll be eatin' outta my hand!'

She heard it so clearly, was so horrified by the monologue, at one point the DA had to repeat a question.

Janice had been so wrapped-up in her internal musings she'd missed the question entirely. She knew she blushed. Probably looked like a skittish fool in front of the jury members.

The questioning went on and on. She thought it might have lasted more than an hour, but when the DA at long last thanked her "for your bravery" and returned to her desk, she was stunned to see from her watch that it'd only been a little over 40 minutes. And now came the worst part.

The arrogant, self-important defense lawyer (*'a perfect match with his client'*), stood when invited by the Judge and sidled up next to the witness stand like a used car dealer closing in on his prey.

"Ms. Greyson. Are you feeling up to continuing, or would you like to take a short break?" he asked, his eyes all the while looking as dead as grey marbles.

Janice stared at him, her mind whirling. *Did she look that bad, that she needed a break?* She looked over at the DA, who was busy making notes, and then to Officer Daniels, who gave her a very subtle thumbs-up.

She took a deep breath. "No, thank you. I think I can go on."

He smiled at her. She thought of a shark about to attack. "Ok, fine. Ms. Greyson, had you met my client, Mr. Archer, before April 19th?"

"No. I'd never seen him before!"

"Never? Not even once?"

"Asked and answered!" the DA objected.

"Sustained," Judge Monahan intoned, not deigning to look at the offending attorney.

"My apologies, Your Honor." He turned back to Janice. "So, if I told you I have in my possession a video that shows you chatting away quite *chummily* with Mr. Archer, you'd say... what?"

Janice's mind went blank. *A video? Of what? When? It must be a fake!*

"I'd say it was impossible."

"Your Honor, the Defense would like to submit this video," he held up a thumbdrive, "which only just came into our possession this morning."

"Still enough time to share it with my office!" the DA argued.

"Both of you - approach the bench."

The two lawyers stood a few feet from where Judge Monahan sat, glaring. Although they whispered, Janice was close enough to hear the entire exchange.

"Explain yourself, Counselor," she began.

"As I said, Your Honor, we only learned of the existence of the video this morning. I only got this thumbdrive during the lunch recess."

"He should have informed us!" the DA fumed.

"Is there a good reason why you didn't?" the Judge asked.

"I needed to be sure it showed what we thought it showed. It does." The lawyer smiled sweetly.

"The State moves to exclude it."

"Whoa, whoa there Madame DA," Judge Monahan interjected. "We haven't even seen it. I'd like to take a look at that video. I'm going to call a recess - care to join me in chambers?" she asked both of them. It really wasn't an invitation they could refuse.

The three of them disappeared back into the bowels of the building while Janice stumbled numbly down from the witness box and out into the buzzing mass of humanity that filled the Courtroom. Officer Daniels took it upon herself to grab her by the hand and lead her out of the chaos, away from the yapping bystanders and the inquiring press.

"What the hell's on that drive?" the officer asked softly as she led Janice to relative safety.

"I don't know! I have no idea what it could be."

"From the way the lawyer played it, he seems to think it's a game-changer. Are you sure you never met that asshole Archer?"

"Not that I can remember! I mean, after my marriage broke up I admit I spent some time in a club or two having a good time, but I don't remember that guy, no!"

"Did *having a good time* include getting a little bombed?"

Janice winced. "A couple of times, maybe. Divorce hurts."

"That's one reason I never got married." Daniels dragged her over to a waiting room off the main corridor.

"What else could it be?" Janice asked as soon as the door closed.

"You tell me."

"I don't know! I swear. The only time I remember seeing him was on the day it happened."

Daniels didn't ask what *it* was. "Well I have a feeling we'll all know soon enough. No need to get too worried, not yet."

Janice wondered when *would* be a good time, because she was already battling heart palpitations. The officer tried to assuage her fears until a Court official announced that the trial was back in session.

"Showtime," Daniels said.

Janice tried to smile, but couldn't quite pull it off.

The courtroom was abuzz when they got back to their seats, as all the observers and reporters tried to guess what the Defense team had in their possession that required the session in chambers. Janice tried to catch the DA's attention, to get some hint as to whether she'd been successful in her efforts to block the newly-discovered video evidence, but for whatever reason, the DA didn't take so much as a peek in her direction.

After a few awkward minutes of silence between them, Daniels asked Janice about her son and mother. Janice recognized the ploy as an ill-disguised attempt to divert her attention from the judicial blade poised just above her heart. As poorly concealed as it was, she appreciated the intent. She played along, reciting a rambling synopsis of her recent family life, editing out only the most personal, depressing elements to shield the officer from the full impact of the attack upon her everyday existence. Judge Monahan's return interrupted her monologue, much to her relief.

After some administrative formalities, the Judge announced her decision on the motions the two sides had made just before the recess.

"Although it is extremely unusual to accept evidence that has not been shared with the opposing counsel," she began, "in this case the need to confirm the legitimacy and relevance of the evidence outweighs the timely sharing. I will allow it."

Janice didn't need to ask what impact the decision might have on the trial. Archer's horrid smile, flashed toward the gallery for just an instant, told it all. Daniels' attempts at downplaying the impact only reaffirmed it.

"Don't worry, it's just procedural," the officer said. "Happens all the time."

'*Not to me,*' Janice thought.

A choreographed duel between the Defense attorney and the DA followed, as the DA raised seemingly every objection within reason. His attorney objected to the objections. At the end of all the back and forth the video was cued and ready to be shown. The date, time and place were all verified by an employee of the bar. Then Janice was recalled to the stand.

All that was left was to watch the video.

The quality wasn't particularly good. The dim lighting in the bar carried over into the video, making it grainy and a little hard to make out. But it was clear, even to Janice, that she was the young, slightly provocatively dressed woman sitting at the bar as the video began. She was by herself, sipping her drink, looking up at the mirror behind the bar every now and then to track what was happening out on the main floor of the place. It was a place she'd been to many times back then. She didn't recognize anything distinctive about this particular night.

A man came up to her, said a few words, and left, apparently rebuffed. The guy looked nothing like Archer. The video continued.

After a minute or two, (which seemed like an hour to Janice), a familiar form approached. Janice cringed as she recognized her attacker. Dressed fashionably, Archer looked nothing like the creep who'd ruined her life. He looked like… just a guy.

He stopped, zeroed in on Janice, and approached. She had the eerie feeling of being stalked. He said something and she looked over at him, her head cocked inquiringly. Janice could tell at a glance that she'd had a good deal to drink.

Probably too much. He said his piece, which was more than a
simple hello, and she saw herself laugh.

'*Is that really me?*' she wondered. It seemed like… a movie.

He sat down. Chatted with her. She chatted back.
According to a time clock running in the upper left hand
corner of the video, he sat there for roughly 30 mins. Finally,
he asks her something, and she writes something on a
matchbook cover and gives it to him.

'*Oh my god!*' It was something she'd done more than once
during those grim days during and just after the divorce: give
a guy she had no interest in a fake name and fake phone
number. But on the screen it looked like… trouble. An
audible gasp hissed through the courtroom. She couldn't help
it: she blushed. She glanced up at Officer Daniels, who
looked stricken. Her heart sunk.

"Lights please," the Defense attorney said. Suddenly the
courtroom became much too bright. "So, Miss Greyson," he
went on, his tone something between a gloat and an
accusation, "do you still maintain you never met my client,
Mr. Archer?"

Janice swallowed. She took a deep breath to calm herself.

"I was going through a bad divorce," she said, her voice
impossibly calm, more controlled than she would have
thought possible. "I gave a false name and phone number to
any guy I didn't have interest in."

"And all that laughing and conversation?"

"Objection!" the DA bellowed. "Is there a question
there?"

Judge Monahan shot an irritated glance the DA's way, but
agreed with her point anyway. "You can do better than that,
can't you Counselor?" she asked the defense lawyer.

"Of course, Your Honor. Ms. Greyson, if you didn't have any interest in Mr Archer, why did you sit there and talk to him for 26 minutes and then give him your phone number?" She wanted to wipe that self-satisfied grin off his face with a 12-gauge.

"I was probably a little drunk, and bored. Like I said, it'd been a bad few months and I needed an escape. And as for the phone number, if he still has the matchbook you'll see that it isn't my number at all - not even close."

She sat back against the cool wooden chair, feeling marginally vindicated.

Archer's attorney was not convinced.

"So all that laughter, and all that conversation - all that was just... boredom?" He turned to the jury as if playing to the front row in a theater. She couldn't see his expression from her vantage point, but she'd bet he raised his eyebrows and probably scrinched up his mouth in a silent mocking of her claim.

"That's exactly what I mean," she said, without hesitation but not without a healthy dose of attitude. "I talked to him until I didn't want to talk to him anymore."

"And did you tell Mr. Archer that - that you didn't want to talk to him anymore?"

"I... I don't remember. Like I said, I'd been drinking."

"So you might *not* have said anything?"

"I suppose it's possible."

"So, if you didn't tell him you were bored with his conversation, and you spent nearly a half-hour chatting with him and laughing at his jokes, and then gave him something that he thought was your phone number, can you see why he might think you were interested in him - more than just as a drinking buddy?"

"Objection!" the DA screamed. "Ms Greyson is not privy to Mr. Archer's thoughts!"

"Sustained," the Judge intoned. "Do you think you can rephrase the question?"

His lawyer bowed his head slightly in imitation of a chastened soul - a pose Janice was pretty sure no one in the courtroom would buy. "Let me ask it a different way," he went on. "Did Mr. Archer apologize to you or seem embarrassed to have wasted your valuable time?"

Janice hesitated. The trap was obvious, the way to avoid it not so clear. "I don't think he apologized, no." She was going to say she didn't really remember, but he cut her off.

"Did he tell you he'd call you?"

"I... I don't think so, but I really don't remember."

"So he might have?"

"Your Honor..." the DA said, getting to her feet.

"Counselor, *please* ask about facts and actions, *not* opinions."

"My apologies. Ms. Greyson, can you say unequivocally that Mr. Archer did *not* say he'd call you?"

"No, no I can't." She thought she heard a gentle gasp from the spectators.

The attorney smiled that same arrogant grin. "Thank you. No further questions."

"Re-direct," the DA said before the Judge could say anything further.

"Go on."

The DA walked slowly but confidently to a spot directly in front of the witness stand. "Ms Greyson, did Mr. Archer ever call you after that night in the bar?"

"No! He didn't have my real name or number."

"Are you sure?"

"Of course I'm sure. There was no way he *could* call me." A pause for dramatic effect. "Did you ever call *him*?

"Are you kidding? No!"

She walked back to the Prosecution's table and grabbed a handful of papers. "I have here Exhibit 8b," she announced, holding the papers up to the Judge. "Archer's phone records." She brought the records over to the witness stand. "Ms. Greyson, would you please look through these phone numbers for the month in which Mr. Archer spoke to you and the following month as well and tell me if you see your phone number listed anywhere?"

Janice knew full-well she wouldn't find any such calls, but did as she was asked for the theatrical effect she hoped it would have on the jury. "No, no calls from *him*." She stressed the last.

"Not a single call?"

"Nope. Not one."

"So even though Mr. Archer claims he got your phone number from you, and had some kind of relationship with you, he never called you. Is that right?"

"It is. But there was no relationship."

"I think that's becoming quite clear," the DA said as she pivoted to return to her table.

"Objection!" the Defense Attorney insisted. "The District Attorney's opinions are no more valuable than anyone else's."

"Sustained." The Judge sounded weary. Perhaps she was growing as tired of the interplay between the DA and the Defense as Janice was. "Do you have anything for re-direct?"

"Your Honor, the Defense requests an adjournment so that we may consider all the implications of this new evidence."

'You mean you want to try to figure out how to spin it so it doesn't look so bad for your client,' Janice thought. She caught a small smile from Officer Daniels that seemed to suggest she was thinking along the same lines.

"Any objection?" the judge asked the DA.

"Your Honor, the evidence in question was introduced by the Defense."

"But we just got it today!"

"I'm fairly certain they didn't see it for the first time here in the courtroom, Your Honor."

"We didn't have sufficient time to analyze its implications fully!"

"Then why did they introduce it today?" The DA sounded triumphant. Janice wondered if they'd arrived at a turning point in the proceedings.

"Yes, why *did* you introduce it today?" Judge Monahan asked, leaning over the edge of the dais to peer down at the harried Defense Attorney.

"We had a duty to make the video available to the DA, and we didn't want to be accused of keeping it under cover."

"My office is open and fully-staffed all day," the DA answered, staring at the attorney

"Okay, okay, that's enough," Judge Monahan snapped. "Given the serious nature of the charges against Mr. Archer,

I'm willing to give him the benefit of the doubt. You have until tomorrow to figure out your strategy. Understood?"

The defense attorney looked as if he wanted to say something further, but decided against it. "Thank you, Your Honor."

"We will adjourn until 9 a.m. tomorrow morning. Does that work for you, Ms. Winters?

"I suppose it will have to."

"I suppose it will. Court adjourned."

And just like that, it was over for the day. The Judge stood and quickly retreated back to her chambers while the spectators rose en masse to dash for the exits. Janice was left sitting in the witness chair, staring shell-shocked at the turn of events. It wasn't until Officer Daniels walked into her field of view that she regained her poise.

"Looks like the DA handled that pretty well," Daniels said.

"But now they have another day to come up with more lies," Janice answered. "I wish she'd just told them 'no'."

"Maybe she gave them more rope to hang themselves. If they can't come up with something pretty strong, I think it makes Archer look really bad."

"I hope so," Janice said, but she didn't sound very hopeful.

*****

As she drove back home Janice was tempted to stop at one of her old haunts, a small neighborhood bar not two miles from her house. The urge to drown her doubts in a small torrent of Black Label beckoned. But she thought of

Jackie waiting at home, and her mother, and she drove by
with only a passing glance. As she walked up to her front
door, she took a deep breath and replaced the pensive frown
that had graced her lips ever since she'd left the courthouse
with a forced but possibly believable off-kilter grin.

"Hello there, Stranger!" her mother called out much too
cheerily as soon as she stepped through the door.

"Hi. How's everyone doing?"

Jackie came running, a sheet of crayon-scrawled paper
clutched in one hand. "Mommy, come see! I drew you a
picture!"

She bent down and grabbed him with both hands around
the waist, pulling him up to eye-level for a well-deserved kiss.
She wasn't sure if she didn't need the contact more than him.

"Look, Mommy, LOOK!" he insisted, shrugging off the
kiss like the six-year-old boy he was.

She took the paper from his hand and examined it closely.
A pretty decent caricature of herself - wearing a Supergirl
costume - brought just a hint of moisture to her eyes.

"It's wonderful!" she said, adding a second kiss to the
squirming young artist's cheek.

"You're Supergirl!" he exclaimed proudly, pointing to the
red and yellow logo.

"It was all his idea, not mine," Jennifer said in response to
a narrow-eyed glance in her direction from her daughter.
"He's very proud of his Mommy."

"I don't feel all that super," she said putting Jackie down
and depositing her jacket and purse in the hall closet.

"Was it bad?"

"Awful. They came up with a video from three years ago
showing him talking to me in a bar."

The look on her mother's face said it all. "What? I thought you never met the guy?"

"I need a glass of wine," she said, stepping past her stricken mom and her oblivious son with an urgency that surprised even her.

"That bad?"

She shrugged. "Not good. Turns out he hit on me when I'd had a few at Chase's not long after I broke up with Ed. I still don't remember it, even after seeing the video."

"How does that effect the prosecution?"

"What's *prosecution?*" Jackie suddenly asked, reminding both adults that little ears were taking everything in.

"It's when the police try to send a bad person to jail," his mom explained, leaving the finer points to a later discussion.

"Honey, why don't you take your drawing to your room and find a good place to put it up?" his grandmother suggested.

"Okay! I'll find a place!" He ran off without another word.

"So?" Jennifer pressed.

Janice held up the wine bottle. "Want a glass?"

"Yeh, thanks."

Jennifer refrained from further cross-examination until the two of them had settled-in to their respective favorite chairs. Janice took a big swig of red; Jennifer's intuition flashed black. But still she kept silent.

"It was a nightmare," Janice finally began, "an absolute nightmare." For nearly an hour she related the ups and downs of the courtroom drama. Her mother listened closely, trying to maintain a facial expression that neither gave nor took too much from the telling. During one of her daughter's frequent

stops for wine-sipping, Jennifer mustered enough courage to
pose the one question she'd been aching to ask: "Why didn't
you remember meeting the guy?"

Janice shook her head in stunned disbelief. "Like I said,
it was three years ago at Chase's over on 20th. Three *years* ago.
You remember how I was during the divorce and right
after?"

Jennifer remembered all too well. She'd made the
unforgiveable mistake of siding with her daughter's soon-to-
be ex during a particularly heated exchange on why the
marriage had gone straight to hell, and that turned out to be
an on-ramp to the Highway to Oblivion so far as her
relationship with Janice was concerned.

"Yes, I remember."

"Well, I was there, sitting at the bar, sipping a drink. Not
the first one, from the look of it."

Jennifer thought back to that period, to the weeks before
Janice had told her to go home and never come back. More
than once her daughter had arrived home so blurry-eyed, so
wasted, it was a miracle she'd been able to drive herself. She'd
made her opinions perfectly clear back then; today, she
refrained from commenting.

"Then *he* comes up to me and starts chatting. I laughed
at a few things he said." She looked over at Jennifer. "If
you're drunk enough, almost anything sounds funny." The
explanation drew a somber nod. She continued. "So he talks
to me for a while, nearly a half-hour, and finally he takes the
hint and decides to leave."

"That's it?"

"I wish it was. He asked if he could call me, so I gave him the fake phone number I always used on that type so I wouldn't have to lie if he actually did call."

"You never talked to him again?"

"I don't think so. This video's got me doubting my memory. But I don't think so."

"Doesn't sound so bad. What did the District Attorney say?"

"Nothing. She left the courtroom as soon as the Judge did, and I was so upset I didn't think to chase after her."

"Officer Daniels?"

"She always tries to put a good face on everything. I don't know if she'd tell me even if she thought it was terrible for the case."

Jennifer sipped her wine. "How did the jury react?"

"I don't know. I'm probably reading too much into it, but when that creep attorney first announced they had the video, I thought most of the jury members looked shocked. Some looked almost offended, like I'd done something to them personally. But after the DA gave me a chance to explain? Not so much. Maybe a few even looked sympathetic."

"Good. So maybe it wasn't so terrible after all."

Janice wobbled her head back and forth as if evaluating. "Maybe. Maybe I've just had enough wine to see things differently."

Her mother laughed. "Then more wine it is! Give me a little more while you're at it."

The smile she got in return was reassuring.

CHAPTER 16

The next morning Janice drove to the Courthouse with the radio blaring. Something about the auditory assault on her eardrums made everything outside seem less urgent, less weighty. Not that the music was able to completely erase the worrying thoughts that swirled through her head, a carry-over from the dreams she'd had the night before. In one, every time she opened a door – at home, at work, in a restaurant, and yes, in a bar – there was that man, his taunting grin as big as the Cheshire Cat's in Alice in Wonderland. Everywhere she turned, everywhere she ran, there he was. She'd awakened repeatedly, a couple of times drenched in sweat. The alarm had rung much too early and much too loudly, but she was determined to keep the good thoughts front and center, no matter how many contrary notions crowded the scene.

She'd received a couple of texts from Officer Daniels, but had purposely delayed responding. She needed to confront the whole trial circus herself, without anyone to lean on. For better or worse, soon the legal proceedings would be over. And then? Then she'd be on her own. Better to prepare now than to arrive on the last day of the trial and find herself bereft of crutches. No, today she'd confront her demons head-on.

She pushed open the door from the parking lot with a little more attitude than the day before and strode down the hallway with her new-found confidence glowing in her face and eyes.

Until she turned into the corridor where the entrance to the Courtroom was located.

No sooner had she turned the corner then *he* crossed just ten feet or so in front of her, a Sherriff on each handcuffed arm, his lawyer and a few hangers-on bobbing in his wake. He turned his head, and when he saw her surprised look the disconcerting grin shone full-force.

She tried not to react, to starve him of the induced fear he seemed to thrive on. But it had happened too quickly. She quashed the wide-mouthed/wide-eyed expression of shock she knew he craved, but a half-second too late. His smile grew even broader, if that was possible. And his eyes glowed. No, really, they *glowed!*

Just then a familiar voice pulled her from the self-ensnared web of his dark aura.

"Janice! I've been trying to get a hold of you!" DA Winters was walking so quickly her high heels echoed like the staccato rhythm of a sewing machine needle on the tile floor. She was on Janice so quickly she could barely brace for impact.

"Have you had your phone on?" Ms. Winters pressed, taking Janice firmly by the elbow and steering her into a nearby empty office.

"I… I don't know," Janice stuttered.

"Well it should be. We need to go over the possible scenarios we might see from the Defense. Do you have ten minutes?"

It seemed a rhetorical question. "Yeh, sure."

The DA hopped on her cellphone and called three of her young assistants to bring stacks of files, all of which she organized on a gray collapsible table as she carried on a non-stop monologue directed at Janice. Step by step she ran through scenarios, offering suggested responses and even

specific phrasing. Janice's head whirled. The energizing sense
of optimism that had carried her to the courthouse unraveled
in a barrage of what-ifs. But when the DA asked if she was
ready, what choice did she have but to say 'yes'?

The Courtroom didn't seem as intimidating the second
day, but the frenzy of press and onlookers was, if anything,
even greater. It's as if everyone within a hundred miles had
heard of the new video and everyone wanted to see how the
Defense would make use of it. Including Janice.

By the time she settled-in next to Officer Daniels, her
heart was racing.

"Here we go again," Daniels said with a welcoming grin.
"How you doin'?"

"Okay," she said, her attempt at a smile falling well short.
She glanced around. "I thought it might be calmer today. Is it
always this crazy?"

"Nah. Sometimes it's crazier!" Daniels seemed to actually
enjoy the insanity.

Judge Monahan made her entrance without fanfare. She
looked tired to Janice, or was it concerned? Everyone stood,
sat, and waited.

"Are you ready to begin?" she asked the Defense team.

"We are, Your Honor," the lead attorney said. He was
dressed in a basic gray suit, a checked gray and white tie, and
everything about him seemed more understated than the day
before. "The Defense would like to re-call Ms. Janice
Greyson to the stand."

Janice swallowed.

"Please take the stand, Ms. Greyson," the Judge
instructed.

The bailiff reminded her that she was still under oath.

"So, Ms. Greyson, you stated yesterday that you never saw or spoke to Mr. Archer again after the meeting captured by the security video we played to the Court – is that right?"

"Yes. That is right."

"What if I were to tell you we have evidence that you did indeed meet with him again. Some months later."

"Your Honor!" the DA leapt to her feet. "Again?!"

"I warned you yesterday…" the Judge began, but the lawyer cut her off.

"We don't have any such evidence, Your Honor. Yet. But my client has given us a time and place so we hope to have it in our possession shortly."

"Then why did you ask Ms. Greyson that question?" an exasperated DA shot back.

"I was hoping to jog her memory. Give her a chance to change her testimony."

Janice felt sick. She hadn't met with that man again – she was sure of it! But she'd been sure she'd never met him in the first place as well.

"You may continue, but watch yourself," Judge Monahan said.

"Thank you, Your Honor. So, Ms. Greyson, do you remember meeting Mr. Archer again, *after* your chat in the bar?"

"No."

"Are you certain?"

"Asked and answered!" DA Winters objected.

"Do you have any other questions?" the judge asked.

"Not at this time. But we reserve our right to re-examine when new evidence becomes available."

"*If* new evidence shows up, we'll consider it then."

"Excellent. Then we have no new questions at this time."

"Thank you. Ms. Greyson, you may step down."

If anything, Janice's legs shook harder this time than last. She wobbled her way back to her seat, where Officer Daniels held out her hand to guide her to a controlled landing.

"You okay?"

"Not really. But at least that's over with. For now."

"You did okay. And they looked like fools. Don't worry about it."

But she did.

*****

The trial continued at its own pace, sometimes faster, more often painfully slowly. Expert witnesses testified for both sides, each side attempted to discredit the other, and Janice sat through it all just wanting it to be over. But there was one more witness she wanted to see and hear, the one person she could not leave without confronting, if only from a distance – *him*. So she stuck it out, hour after stultifying hour, her jaw beginning to ache from grinding her teeth in nervous frustration.

And finally, after what seemed like forever, the bailiff called him to the stand.

"Mr. Daniel Lee Archer!"

His lawyer whispered something to him just as he left the safe confines of the Defense table, and he nodded with an assured smile. He glanced over at Janice, his eyes lingering too long for comfort. Then he walked slowly to the witness stand. He wore a black sports coat over khaki pants, his hair cut so short she wasn't absolutely sure it was the right guy –

until he smiled. His attorney sidled up next to him, the two of them looking like a pair of stock brokers out for a mid-afternoon lunch. After the usual identifying niceties, the lawyer got down to business. He strolled to his desk, glanced at some notes, then paused with an affected look of pained sincerity more suited to a Broadway stage.

"Mr. Archer, the District Attorney would have us believe that you raped Janice Greyson on May 14th of this year. Did you commit this heinous crime?"

Archer looked stricken. "No way! Not then, or any other time."

Janice wanted to cry out, to challenge the sheer dishonesty of his words, but she held herself in check. It took an effort.

"But you did have consensual sex with her, is that right?"

"Several times."

A muscle twitched in her jaw. How could he sit there and lie like that!

"Can you tell me when and where?"

"Firs' time must've been in early March. After we hooked up again."

"Hooked up again?"

"Yeh. I tried to call her a few times after I talked to her at Chase's, but I always got a disconnect number. Then I ran into her at McSorty's one night – a bar not far from there."

"Did she remember you?"

The DA objected. His lawyer didn't wait for a ruling.

"Let me rephrase: did she call you by name?"

"Oh yeh, called me *Danny*." He looked over at her with a look an outsider might interpret as intimacy. She knew it as pure evil.

"Did you have sex with her that day?"

"Went straight from the bar to her place."

The lawyer read her address from his notes.

"Yeh, that's it," Archer confirmed. He settled back in his chair, looking pleased with himself. Janice's face burned, whether from anger or embarrassment she wasn't sure.

"And that wasn't the only time?"

"Hell no! We got it on a three or four more times. Later that same month and first part of April too. She couldn't get enough."

"Always at her home?"

"Yep. Said she felt more comfortable there."

"And on May 14th – were you invited to her home?"

"Yup."

"But the DA said you never called her."

"Didn't have to. Made the date the last time we did the dirty."

"So you and Ms. Greyson had already decided on a date for your next... assignation the previous time you got together?"

"If you mean our next time in bed, yeh, that's right."

The lawyer turned to the jury with a triumphant glance and then started back to his desk. "Your witness," he called out to the DA over his shoulder, without so much as a look in her direction. As if she didn't warrant the slightest peek.

Ms. Winters did not hesitate, did not seem beleaguered or bested as she approached the witness. 'So, Mr. Archer, you went to Ms. Greyson's home at her invitation – is that right?"

"That's right."

"How did you get there – to her house? I mean, you didn't own a car at that time, did you? We certainly couldn't find one registered in your name."

He narrowed his eyes. "No, didn't have a car."

"So how'd you get there?"

"I… borrowed a car."

"Ahh. From whom did you borrow it?"

"From my friend."

"That must've been a pretty good friend, letting you use his car. What was that friend's name and address? We'd like to get in touch with him to confirm your account."

The pause this time was longer and more thoughtful.

"He moved. I don' have his new address."

"How about his name? Or did he change his name as well?"

"Your Honor…" the Defense attorney began.

"Just ask your questions, Ms. Winters," Judge Monahan cautioned. "The commentary isn't necessary."

She nodded respectfully before returning to her questioning. "Do you remember his name?"

"Antoine."

"Antoine what? What's his last name?"

"Elliston. Or somethin' like that. I ain't sure."

"You borrowed his car, but you don't even know his name?"

"Like I told you, his name's Antoine. Didn't need to know any other name."

"Okay, so you drove to her house. Was she home alone?"

"Nah. Kid was there."

"What kid was that?"

"The little boy. Jamie or Jimmy or sumthin' like that."

"Jackie?"

"Yeh, that sounds right. Jackie."

"And what was Jackie doing while you were there?"

"I don' know!" Archer exploded. "I wasn't there to babysit. I jus' came to do my business."

"Is that what it was, *business*?"

The defense attorney was having none of that. "Objection, Your Honor. Mr. Archer was obviously using a colloquialism. The District Attorney is being argumentative."

Judge Monahan leaned over the bench and looked down at the DA. "Can we get on to the facts of the case?"

"Of course, Your Honor."

Ms. Winters went on to grill Archer about all aspects of his testimony, not the least of which was his assertion that the sexual activity between him and Janice had been consensual.

"Mr. Archer, you heard Ms. Greyson testify that she asked you repeatedly to stop your sexual advances and that you ignored her. That doesn't sound consensual to me."

"Is there a question there?" the lawyer asked in a weary, supercilious tone.

The DA didn't wait for a ruling. "Did Ms. Greyson ask you to stop?"

"No way. She was hot for me!" The grin reappeared.

"Then how is it the medical report on Ms. Greyson suggests bruising and internal injuries consistent with force?"

"She likes it rough."

The DA spun toward Archer like a trap snapping shut. "And who decided that, Mr. Archer, you?" She turned back to her desk. "No further questions, Your Honor."

The defense lawyer got to his feet. "She asked Mr. Archer a question, Your Honor. We'd like the opportunity to answer."

The judge waved in Archer's direction. "Go ahead, Mr. Archer. Answer the question."

Archer looked to his lawyer for nodded permission. "It wasn't me who decided all that. It was her!" (He pointed at Janice.) "She's the one who wanted it rough. She's the one who told me come over to her place. She's the one who started all this, and now she's tryin' to make it sound like she's some kind of nun or sumthin'!" He turned to the Judge. "She looks pretty calm and all now, but get a few drinks in her, and BAM! She's like a tiger!"

The buzz from the spectators filled the courtroom to bursting.

"Any further questions?" the judge asked Archer's attorney.

"Not at this time. The Defense rests, Your Honor."

"Madame District Attorney?"

The DA glanced back at Janice as if weighing her options. "The State would like to re-call Ms. Janice Greyson." The buzz grew louder.

Janice moved as if in a daze, walking unsteadily back to the witness stand. The bailiff reminded her she was already under oath.

Ms. Winters approached her with a small smile, meant, no doubt, to relax her clearly tense witness.

"Ms. Greyson, you just heard Mr. Archer's testimony. Was it accurate?"

Like a bubble bursting inside her, all the frustrations that had been building over the past months exploded in an instant

"He's lying!" she said, directing her words, and her angry glare, directly at Archer. "I *never* invited him to my house, or anywhere else! He's a disgusting, lying animal and he raped me in my own bedroom with my son just feet away!" The tears poured forth, all her barriers finally breached. Winters walked to her side and patted her lightly on the shoulder. Her sobs echoed loudly in the suddenly silent courtroom.

"It's okay, Janice. It'll all be okay."

"Would you like a few minutes…?" Judge Monahan asked. For a few seconds, there was no answer.

"No, no," Janice finally said between sniffles. "I'm sorry, Your Honor. It's just…" She took a deep breath. "I'll be okay in a minute." She wiped her eyes with a Kleenex and forced herself to sit stiffly upright.

"Can you continue?"

Janice nodded to the judge.

"Do you have any further questions?" Judge Monahan asked the DA.

"None, Your Honor."

The judge looked to the defense attorney. "Re-cross?"

The dilemma facing the lawyer was evident on his face. If he badgered the distraught witness, he risked alienating some members of the jury. But if he let her emotional outburst stand unchallenged, it might well be enough to win over any jurists who until then had believed his client. After several long moments, he shook his head. "We do not, Your Honor."

"Then the witness is dismissed."

Officer Daniels took a few steps toward the witness box to help Janice make her way back to her seat.

"You okay?"

"Yeh, yeh, I'm fine," Janice lied. "It's just that I get so mad sometimes…"

"I know, I know," Daniels soothed as she eased Janice into her seat. "You just have to take everything he says – or his lawyer – with a grain of salt."

"More like a grain of arsenic."

The officer smiled even as she shook her head disapprovingly.

Just then Judge Monahan addressed the two attorneys.

"Ms. Winters – are you ready for your closing statement?"

"We are, Your Honor."

"And the Defense?"

"We are, Your Honor!" The defense attorney nearly shouted his reply. Janice wondered if that indicated extreme confidence or nervousness.

"All right then. Madame District Attorney, please begin."

Winters whispered to one of her assistants and received a whispered response in return. Then she tabled the stack of papers she'd been holding and walked over to where the jury sat.

"Ladies and gentlemen of the jury, I know rape cases are often referred to as 'he said, she said' cases," she began, looking into the eyes of each juror in turn. "To some people, this suggests that the testimony of the accused and the victim carry equal weight, and that you have to make a difficult decision based largely on your *hunch* of who's telling the truth and who's lying. I personally don't think that's ever the case, but in this instance, I know it isn't. In this instance, you have the physical evidence from the doctor who treated Ms. Greyson the day after the attack, indicating extreme force was used in the committal of this crime. This was not 'rough sex.' This, ladies and gentlemen, was rape. Pure and simple. The defense introduced a security video that showed the defendant, Mr. Archer talking to Ms. Greyson in a bar. She did not approach *him*. She did not instigate the conversation. And at the end of Mr. Archer's long monologue, Ms. Greyson purposely gave him a wrong phone number. Does that look or seem like she had any interest whatsoever in the defendant? Of course not. Mr. Archer was stalking his victim, finding out as much about her as he could so that he could later track her to her home and perpetrate the heinous crime he committed." She paused and shook her head sadly before continuing.

"Mr. Archer claims he 'ran into' Ms. Greyson at another bar some months after that first meeting between them. Isn't it a coincidence that the bar he mentions has no internal security cameras and so no proof exists to verify his story – which, by the way, Ms. Greyson denies. And as Mr. Archer corroborates, Ms. Greyson's young son was at home at the time of his attack. Do you really think a professional woman such as Ms. Greyson would invite a man she'd met only once before to her home and then not send her young son to a friend or relative's house during that visit? It is absurd.

"No, ladies and gentlemen, this is not a 'he said, she said' situation. This is a 'he did, he lies' situation, in which Daniel Lee Archer came to the home of Janice Greyson, threatened her son to secure her passive acquiescence, and raped her in her own bedroom. This is a situation in which Mr. Archer wanted something from Ms. Greyson, and when he couldn't get it by sweet-talking her at a bar, he decided to take it from her at her home. This is not 'date rape.' This is not consensual sex. This is a brutal, heartless, violent attack on a woman in her own home, with her small child sleeping just feet away.

"You must find the defendant guilty of first-degree rape, to ensure that he can *never* do this again to any woman in our community. It is not only your duty, it is your responsibility. You should be proud to do what is right, not only for Ms. Greyson, but for every woman in this city."

The District Attorney caught the eyes of several woman jurors before she turned and strode confidently back to her desk.

"Thank you. Is the Defense ready?" Judge Monahan asked.

Archer's lawyer stood slowly, shaking his head in mock dismay.

"My, my. I don't know what trial the District Attorney has been watching, but it sure doesn't seem to be this one." He walked to the jurors' box and put both hands on the bannister. "To convict anyone of a felony, the State must prove *beyond reasonable doubt* that the charges filed against that person are true. Which means, they need to have overwhelming, conclusive evidence that the person charged with the crime actually committed it.

"With that as the standard, let's take a closer look at the State's evidence. Let's start with their allegation that Mr. Archer wasn't invited to Ms. Greyson's home. Now the only person making that assertion is Ms. Greyson. But wasn't it Ms. Greyson who initially claimed she'd never even met Mr. Archer, and certainly had never spoken with him? The

security video you all saw certainly showed that to be a lie.
Mr. Archer claims he *was* invited. And that that wasn't the
first time. Has anything Mr. Archer said on the witness stand
been shown to be false? Not that I remember.

"The District Attorney would have us believe that a
professional woman such as Ms. Greyson would *never* invite a
man to her home when her son was there. But wasn't Ms.
Greyson the same woman who admits to trolling bars and
getting drunk, looking for... what? Men? I submit that Mr.
Archer was not the first man she invited to her house after
her divorce, and probably not the first with her son at home.

"Ms. Greyson was depressed. That's understandable. Her
marriage had gone bad. She went to a number of bars looking
to drown her sorrows and perhaps find someone to keep her
warm at night. Also understandable. But Ms. Greyson was
also angry, and frustrated, and maybe, maybe just a little bit
crazy. And so maybe one night, after inviting a guy she'd
picked-up in a bar to her home for an evening of casual sex,
maybe she decided the relationship wasn't taking the course
she'd hoped, or maybe she had a change of heart after the
fact and the guilt of what she had done made her flip out. We
don't know. We'll never know. But what we do know is that
she decided to accuse Mr. Archer of rape. Was she getting
back at men, all men, by accusing him of this crime? Was Mr.
Archer just at the wrong place at the wrong time? It's
certainly a very real possibility.

"And because it *is* such a real possibility, I suggest that
you cannot *know beyond a reasonable doubt* that Mr. Archer did
anything to Ms. Greyson that she didn't want him to do. That
she didn't invite him to her house specifically *to* do. And
because you can't know, I would ask you to do the one thing

the law *demands* you do in such a situation: that you find my client, Daniel Lee Archer, innocent of all charges. Thank you."

The courtroom buzzed. Janice felt sick to her stomach. Archer turned toward her and flashed a brief, contemptuous grin.

"That bastard," she muttered.

"Don't give up just yet," Officer Daniels said. "Jurors aren't fools. They just might see right through that lying asshole."

'And they might not,' she thought.

The Judge took care of some legal housekeeping, instructing the jurors how they should deliberate, what evidence they could and could not consider, and reminding them not to speak to anyone except each other about the details of the case. Janice heard the words, but they barely penetrated the haze that surrounded her. It was as if someone had wrapped her entire chair – with her in it – in bubble wrap. Sounds were muted, visuals dim and distorted. Was she having a stroke?

A hand grabbed her elbow and pulled her to her feet. She only realized then that the Judge and the jury were leaving the courtroom.

"Let's get the hell outta here," Daniels said, leading her by the arm. She followed docilely, unwilling – perhaps unable - to protest.

As soon as they stepped out the Courtroom door, a swarm of reporters rushed to confront her with their questions, their cameras, their professional enthusiasm.

"Do you think they'll convict him?"

"What do you think of how the DA handled the case?"

"What sentence would you like to see him get?

Daniels held up her hand in front of Janice's face, partially shielding her from the prying lenses. "No comment!" she said repeatedly, even as she realized she might get some grief from the higher-ups in the Department over her protective stance. She didn't care. She tugged Janice through the crowd and into a corridor guarded by a uniformed officer. Daniels nodded to him, and he nodded back. No journalists would be allowed to pass.

Janice half-sat, half-collapsed into the first chair she came upon.

"You, okay?" Daniels asked.

"I don't know..." she mumbled. "No, no I'm not okay! Did you hear that SOB lie right to our faces! He *belongs* in prison!"

"And that's where he's headed. Don't get yourself all spun-up about it." Daniels looked as frustrated as she felt. "Can I get you anything?"

Janice shook her head. "No, thanks… Maybe some water?"

The Officer left without comment, leaving Janice to stew over the unfairness of it all in the bright white, sterile conference room.

'What if he gets off?' she wondered. *'What if all this is for nothing, just theater to make it seem like someone gives a damn that he raped me? What then?'*

She had no answer. There was no answer. All her actions, all her energies had been focused on his conviction, on the system working to punish the guilty. Now, for the first time, she not only recognized the possibility of a miscarriage of justice, but she felt it, deep inside her. It was like a cold dagger, twisting inside her chest. She struggled to take a full breath.

"Here you go!" Daniels announced with unnatural cheerfulness as she came back into the room carrying a plastic cup of water and a can of Sprite. "Not very cold…"

"No problem. Thank you." She drained the cup in one long gulp, her mind locked on Archer and the twelve men and women who were even then deciding his future. But not just his. Hers as well. She wondered if they understood that – how their decision would impact upon her world, as well as upon her son, her Mom, and everyone who knew her. Did they know that?

"Ran into the DA," Daniels said matter-of-factly, lending no emotional color to the comment.

"Yeh? Was she optimistic?" She felt foolish even asking the question. But she couldn't help herself…

"She seemed… pretty confident, yeh. I'd say so. She said we shouldn't expect a quick decision."

"And is that good for us?"

"Could be. Hard to say. Predicting juries is kind of like picking horse races, but even harder."

"That's reassuring." Janice took a deep breath and tried to bring her nerves under control. But no matter how she tried, the image of that smile - that horrible, taunting, self-important smile - remained tattooed on her brain. "Think we should stay here - in the Courthouse?"

"Nah. Unlikely they'll come back today. Maybe not for a few days. Go home. The DA's office will get ahold of you when the jury reaches a verdict."

Home. Did she really want to bring all this… *crap* back to Jackie and her mother? Hadn't they suffered enough, put up with enough of her torment? No, that wouldn't work.

"I think maybe I'll get a hotel room," she announced, surprising even herself.

"Why? Don't you want to be around your kid and mom while you're waiting this out?"

"It's not what I want, it's what's best for them. And I don't think me being there right now will be very positive for them."

"Ah, right." Janice could see the realization dawn on Daniels. "Hey, I've got a pull-out couch in the living room and I'm hardly ever home – wanna come stay with me?"

"Oh, I couldn't," she said and she meant it. But Daniels was having no part of it.

"Don't be ridiculous. No sense you spending big money on a hotel room when I have an apartment just sitting there. Come on. Let's go. We can pick up some toothpaste and all that on the way." She grabbed Janice by the arm and literally lifted her out of her chair. Before she fully understood what was happening she found herself walking out the Courthouse door, relieved and uncomfortable in equal measure.

*****

Janice hadn't really thought about Daniels' living arrangements. It hadn't come up. Now as they pulled up in front of a very modern high-rise condo complex with a spectacular curved glass façade, she found herself surprised - and slightly embarrassed for feeling that way.

"It's… nice," she stammered.

The policewoman smiled. "Surprised? Probably thought cops live in old run-down duplexes, huh?"

Janice knew Daniels was kidding her, but it still stung. "No, of course not. It's just…"

"…That it's nicer than you expected. I know. You're not my first visitor to react that way. And it's all legit, I promise you. No favors, no under-the-table deals. I probably pay too much, but after the work days I have, I need a place like this to come home to."

"It's beautiful."

If anything, it was even more impressive inside. The lobby was all white marble with a reception/guard desk manned by a thirty-something GQ guy wearing a $400 suit, looking like a retired NFL linebacker on a job interview. The elevators swooshed shut with that solid, understated sound that gives you confidence the construction is top-notch. They climbed 16 floors without so much as a squeak; Janice could barely tell they were moving.

They stepped out into a smaller version of the lobby, complete with real artwork (no print copies or mass-produced schlock here) and a white leather loveseat fronted by an eye-catching glass and steel coffee table. The hallways followed the curve of the front of the building, always arcing away so that the next apartment door was just out of sight. Daniels chatted away without any self-consciousness.

"Here we are," she announced when they reached her door. "Get a load of this." She swiped her finger on a tiny reader pad just to the left of the doorknob. The pad emitted a series of electronic beeps and the lock slid open with scarcely a sound.

"Wow. This place is like Fort Knox."

"Security gives you peace of mind. Come on in."

Even then Janice half-expected to find a sparsely furnished living room, or perhaps a truckload of the ubiquitous rental furniture that graced many of her friends' places. Instead, she stepped into a large, high-ceilinged room tastefully decorated in much the same tone as the building itself, with huge floor-to-ceiling windows looking out over the cityscape in the distance.

"My God!" Janice said without realizing she'd spoken.

"Not bad, huh?" Daniels said, finally revealing a little of the pride she clearly felt.

"Not bad? It's gorgeous!" She walked over to the windows in a daze, staring out at a panorama she'd only seen before in photographs. The inky black of the river set a hard edge boundary to the foreground, giving way gradually to bustling streets and low-rise apartment blocks, all crowned by a jagged skyline that spoke of lives so very different than her own.

"Can I get you something to drink?" Daniels asked, tossing her blue uniform jacket on an easy chair as she made her way toward the kitchen.

"Uh, sure. You have any wine?" She really needed something to take the edge off.

"Red or white?"

"Yes."

"I'll bring a bottle of each."

Janice debated whether she should go to the kitchen and keep Daniels company as she opened the wine, but in the end she stood transfixed at the windows, hypnotized by the dark beauty of the city she'd known most of her life. The thought of all those people, living separate but interconnected lives, sharing not only a place but a spirit, a sense of purpose, a commonality of outlook - somehow it all made her feel better. Sure, there were a few bad players – who knew better than she? – but from this distance, this lofty perch, she could see the bigger picture and she could glory in it. She swallowed down a lump in her throat.

"Here we go," the officer said as she came back with the two bottles, some crackers and two wine glasses on a silver tray. After one look at Janice, however, her upbeat attitude shifted immediately to concern. "What? What happened?"

"Nothing," Janice said, wiping at her eyes with the back of her hand. "I was just thinking how great it is living in this city."

"Oh? Yeh, sure, why not? Ready for your wine?"

The two women sat on the couch, and for a few moments neither said a word. Sipping wine, munching on crackers – for each of them the quiet moment was too perfect to disturb. But Daniels felt the responsibility of hosting as well as her professional obligations, and so it was she who broke the silence.

"You're gonna be okay after all this, no matter how it turns out. You know that, right?"

Janice lowered her glass and smiled. "You're a good person, Officer Daniels, you know that?"

"Patrice," Daniels said. "I'm only *Officer* when I'm on the clock."

"Okay. Then you're a good person, *Patrice*.

"I try," she said, slumping back into the welcoming cushions of the sofa. "Lord knows I try."

The conversation stretched until the first bottle was empty, the second well on its way, and outside the evening shadows engulfed the city streets in their irresistible embrace. The women didn't talk about the trial so much as about their lives. More feeling than fact. Janice listened as much as she spoke, welcoming the chance to focus on something besides *him*. For the first time in months she felt completely safe and at ease.

"I'm getting hungry, how about you?" Daniels suddenly announced when the wine-lubricated conversation lagged for a moment.

Janice glanced down at her watch.

"Oh my God, look at the time! I've got a kid and mother waiting for me at home."

"Call them."

She considered it for an instant, but a mixture of guilt and want made her reject the offer. She finally felt calm enough to go home without dragging the trial along with her. More importantly, she wanted to be with them.

"Maybe another time?"

Daniels nodded. "No problem. I eat most every day."

Janice pushed herself to her feet. "Maybe you'd like to come over to our place sometime? I've told Jackie and my Mom so much about you they're probably dying to meet you."

Daniels laughed. "Somehow I doubt that! But thanks for the invitation. Maybe one of these days."

The Officer walked Janice to the door, conversation suddenly hard to come by.

"Thank you, Patrice," Janice said, pausing with her hand on the doorknob. "You don't know how much I appreciate everything you've done for me. For my family."

Daniels waved it off. "All in a day's work. You good to drive?"

"Yeh, I'm fine."

They stood there, neither knowing quite what else to say, until Janice spontaneously wrapped the officer in a heartfelt embrace. At first Daniels froze, but then returned the hug with the same emotion as had been offered.

"Take care of yourself," the Officer said.

"Yeh, you too," Janice said, stepping back awkwardly. "Always."

With a smile and a quick nod Janice went on her way, Daniels watching from the doorway until the elevator door closed silently.

CHAPTER 17

Janice half-expected a quick decision, and half-feared it. Some of the people she spoke with told her 'quick is good for the prosecution,' while others said the exact opposite. For her, it was almost to the point that any decision was better than the frustration of waiting... and waiting... Almost, but not quite. She wanted him behind bars, wanted it so much she dreamed about it. Which scared her.

When she received a call from the DA's office telling her the jury had reached a decision, she drove downtown with a mixture of elation and trepidation. She kept trying to convince herself that it didn't really matter, that however the jury decided it would be okay. She kept trying, and failing.

When she got to the Courtroom she immediately scanned the waiting crowd for Officer Daniels, who was nowhere to be found. She quickly dismissed the disappointment she felt. *'I'm an adult, independent woman. I don't need anyone to hold my hand.'* Then she craned her neck in the hopes Daniels had been standing behind someone, or maybe was running late. Nope. No sign of her. She tried to dampen the wave of dark feelings that swept over her.

An assistant from the DA's office – a young woman she'd met once or twice before – came scurrying over to her.

"Ms. Greyson! We're so glad you got our message. We thought you'd want to be here for the verdict." She smiled, bubbly and enthusiastic. Janice noted the use of the plural pronoun.

"Yes, thank you," she muttered, her mind bouncing in a hundred directions at once. Did the enthusiasm mean the

DA was confident of a conviction? Or did it mean nothing more than a young, energetic assistant?

"The District Attorney wanted me to let you know the Judge will take care of some odds and ends before getting to the verdict – just so you don't get confused."

"Oh? Well, that's good to know. Thank you." *What kind of odds and ends?'* she wondered. *What could be more important than ending this seemingly endless torment?'*

The assistant glanced around restlessly. Janice could see the wait weighed on her, despite the veneer of optimism.

She decided to let her get back to whatever she'd be doing if she weren't cheerleading for Janice.

"I think I'll take a seat. Shouldn't be long now."

"No, it shouldn't be long at all!" the woman chirped before scurrying off in a cloud of barely repressed energy.

Janice navigated her way through the knot of waiting spectators, ignoring their pointed stares and ill-controlled stage-whispers. Of course they knew who she was. Everyone knew who she was by now. 'That poor girl who got raped in her own house.' 'I think she's just a tease who got more than she bargained-for.' 'Women these days…'

She tried not to listen. Who were they, after all? Just people from the street who had nothing better to do than spend day after day watching the gears of justice grind her life into an inanimate powder. They knew *nothing* of what it had been like. Of what that man had done to her, had done to her life. No one knew but her.

The bailiff interrupted her musings: "All rise for the Honorable Judge Monahan."

The whispers slowly died away as the Judge settled into her seat. As the DA's assistant had warned Janice, the Judge called the DA and the Defense lawyer up to the bench for an extended discussion; she paid little attention. After having spent all the trial avoiding her attacker's swaggering stare, for some reason she now sought it out. To her surprise, the man she'd previously thought to be cocky, tough and downright terrifying appeared to her as a skinny little frightened loser who wouldn't – or couldn't – meet her gaze. He stared down at clasped hands, his lips moving in what appeared to be an internal dialogue.

"Bailiff, please call in the jury," the Judge announced, tugging Janice's attention back to the courtroom.

The twelve men and women slowly filed into their seats. Janice watched them closely, trying to read into their body language any hint as to what they may have decided. She could discern nothing.

"Has the jury reached a verdict?" the judge asked, even though everyone in the room knew they had.

A middle-aged man, balding, with glasses that distorted the eyes behind them, stood at his seat. "We have, Your Honor," he said with a much more sonorous voice than his appearance would suggest.

"Please give the written decision to the Bailiff."

The bullish man in a police uniform took a piece of paper from the foreman of the jury and carried it slowly to the Judge.

'Get on with it!' Janice wanted to shout. She didn't appreciate the legal theater at all.

Judge Monahan unfolded the paper and skimmed it quickly. Her face showed no reaction whatsoever.

"On the first count, rape in the first degree, the jury finds the defendant, Daniel Lee Archer…"

The judge paused, just for an instant, but in that instant Janice's heart stopped completely – or so it felt to her.

"…Not guilty," the judge continued, and all hell broke loose in the courtroom. Many people gasped, a few shouted their outrage, one or two even applauded. A sizeable number of people – Janice thought they might be reporters – rushed out the door. The judge was having none of it.

"Order! Quiet in the courtroom!" she shouted, pounding her gavel with a vehemence that brought color to her cheeks. "I will have order or I will clear this courtroom!"

Slowly, painfully, the ruckus settled. The judge waited impatiently until quiet returned. Or at least Janice thought it had. A loud whine echoed in her head. She wasn't sure it wasn't coming from her.

The judge continued on, but Janice didn't hear a word. She shook her head, as if by doing so she could shake the high-pitched scream from her mind. It didn't work. She glanced over at the Defense table, where her attacker looked more stunned than pleased. His lawyer, however, made no attempt to disguise a cat-ate-the-canary smile that nearly launched Janice into a head-on attack.

In just a few seconds, it was all over. The judge thanked the jury for their service. Janice scanned their faces as they stood to leave; not one of them could look her in the eye. They scurried from the jury box like the proverbial rats from a sinking ship. Janice felt rather than saw the people all around her make for the exits. No one said a word to her. In what might have been pity, or was it guilt?, most didn't even look in her direction.

Suddenly she felt a hand drop leadenly on her shoulder.

"You okay?" a voice asked. She looked up to see Detective Willard standing beside her, his expression a mixture of anger and concern. He seemed… blurry, and it was only then she realized she was crying. A camera appeared out of thin air, a flash blinding her before she could shield her eyes.

"Get the fuck out of here!" the Detective roared as he shoved the camera out of her field of vision. There was a scuffle, or was it something more? Her thoughts dissolved before they could take form. "Come on, let's get you out of here." A strong hand helped her to her feet and half-guided, half-pulled her from the courtroom. Her feet seemed far too heavy; she could barely put one in front of the other. But Detective Willard was nothing if not determined and his unrelenting tug dragged her out into the hallway and then back to an empty office. "Let's wait it out in here for a little while," he announced, lowering her gently into a plastic office seat as if she might shatter from the effort.

She wanted to answer, to thank him, but the words would not form. They seemed just beyond the tip of her tongue, just beyond coalescing.

"Can you believe that shit?!" Willard asked as he began pacing in the small room. "What the hell were those jurors listening to?! 'Not guilty'?! My ass!" He continued on as if she weren't there in the room, venting from more than just this disappointment, Janice thought.

Slowly, painfully, awareness seeped back into her world, a trickle at first and then a torrent of too-bright colors and sounds that grated. After a few minutes of Willard's ranting, she held up a hand.

"Stop. Please – stop."

Willard looked at her as if surprised she could speak. "What? Oh, yeh, sorry. You feelin' any better?"

Is feeling more the same as feeling better? Is hurt superior to nothingness?

"I suppose," she said.

He eyed her for a long moment. "Aren't you pissed?" he finally asked.

She took time to think. "Yeh. I'm pissed. I'm disappointed, I'm shocked, but above all, I'm scared, Detective. You guys won't be able to protect me and my family from that animal forever."

"He's not dumb enough to go anywhere near you again. Not after all this."

She sighed. "After all what? Unless I missed something, he just walked out of that courtroom a free man. He got away with it. He won."

Willard's mouth twitched as if he wanted to say something, but thought better of it. "He'll screw-up again, and when he does, we'll get him."

Janice fought the urge to tell him how naïve he sounded, how over-confident. "I hope so," she said. "I really do."

*****

When she opened the door to her house, a big part of Janice was relieved to be back in her own space with her own people – away from the bright lights and intrusive gawkers – while another dreaded having to tell her mother the outcome of the trial. As it turned out, she didn't need to say a word.

"Oh, you poor thing!" her mother said, hurrying over to give her a hug. "I saw it on the news. Those idiots!"

The recent displays of affection from her Mom still felt slightly alien, but she did not resist. In fact, she melted into the embrace without a second thought. But when tears began to form under her lashes, she fought with all the spirit she could muster to keep them from falling down her cheeks. Sympathy she could accept from her mother. Pity she could not.

She tried to order her thoughts, to respond with cogent statements that would show she had not been broken, had not been defeated. But before she could utter a sound, her mother stepped back and held her at arm's length.

"Are you hungry?"

She almost burst out laughing, but was afraid that any emotion would lead inevitably to a complete breakdown.

"No, thanks Mom. I think I just need to sit down."

"Glass of wine?"

She didn't have the strength to argue. And a little wine wouldn't be so bad after all.

Whether her mother felt the distress she was experiencing or just didn't know how to begin the conversation, she busied herself in the kitchen uncorking and pouring two full glasses of Cabernet in silence, leaving Janice to catch her breath - and attempting to organize her thoughts.

The latter was the more difficult. *'How bad is it? What if he **does** come after me – after **us**? Should I change jobs? Move?'* All of it ran through her thoughts like a whirlwind through dry leaves, tossing the possibilities up in the air and scattering them to the four corners of her personal universe.

"Jan?" She looked up to see her mother standing next to her chair, holding out a glass with a perplexed expression and inquiring eyes. Janice hadn't realized she was standing there.

"Oh, thanks Mom." She took the glass and gulped down nearly half its contents in one shaky inhalation.

"That bad?"

She forced a smile. "Better now."

"Ready to talk?"

She was, and she wasn't. But she could see that her mother wasn't going to let it go without a fight. And she was in no mood for a fight. She took another small sip of the wine and began her story.

It was quite a while later, in the wee hours of early morning, when the sound of shuffling feet interrupted their conversation. Both of them looked into the hallway to see Jackie, his eyes half-closed, dragging his favorite blanket, making his way to where they sat surrounded by two empty wine bottles, a crumpled chip bag, a box of crackers (or actually, a box of cracker crumbs), and an assortment of dips and spreads in various states of consumption.

"Honey, what are you doing up?" Janice said, struggling to her feet and nearly toppling over an unseen footrest.

"I couldn't sleep," he said, eying the remnants of their night-in with disbelief. "Did you have a party?"

Janice glanced back at the leavings as if seeing them for the first time. "What? Oh no, honey. Grandma and I were just talking."

"You drank wine."

Nothing got past him. "Just a little. So we can sleep better."

"Would I sleep better if I have some?"

"Wine is for adults," Jennifer said, sounding sage and a bit tipsy. "It can make little children sick."

Jackie made a face. "Can I have some hot milk then?"

"Of course you can."

While her mother heated the milk, Janice collected her son in her arms and pulled him down into her easy chair to cuddle in her lap. At that moment she felt more acutely than ever how much she loved him, and how integral he was to her sense of self. He was part of her, a very important part. All the activity of the past few months had taken that from her, hidden it behind legal briefs and court appearances and her own fear and trepidation. No more.

She hugged him tighter.

From now on all that would be behind her. Her son would come first, last and always. But even as she committed to focusing all her love and attention on Jackie, she felt the nagging worry that *he* would not go away, in her memories if not in reality. And the thought made her sad.

*****

There were a few documents and signatures still to be dealt with, but for all intents and purposes the legal part of her ordeal was over. The constant barrage of press calls and photographer ambushes gradually faded away as well, until the entire ordeal seemed almost like a bad dream, or a scab that refused to heal entirely. Janice continued to lose weight, not due to any effort on her part but simply because she rarely felt like eating, at least not like she had *before*. That was it, actually: everything came down to *before* and *after* – Pre-Attack and Post.

For the first two weeks after the trial, she'd spoken with Officer Daniels by phone nearly every day. At first it had been the policewoman who'd instigated the daily 8 p.m. call.

But after three or four days Janice had felt a need, almost a compulsion to talk with someone who really understood what she'd gone through, a woman who'd been there through every ugly step, even having experienced the horror of an attack – well, *attempted* attack. So when Daniels' call hadn't come by 8:15 one night, she took the initiative. She was greatly relieved when Patrice made no comment, offered no excuse, but instead took her call and chatted for over an hour. It was exactly the kind of therapy Janice craved.

Not that she'd ignored her shrink. Dr. Thurman wasn't quite so accessible as Daniels, but less than a week after the end of the trial Janice found herself in the familiar waiting room, eying two other *crazies* who were awaiting their sessions as well. She wondered why they were there, then wondered if they were wondering the same thing about her. Or maybe they *recognized* her. How horrible would that be?

The Doctor was her usual evasively supportive self, making all the right mewing sounds while dancing just out of reach of a conclusive diagnosis let alone a prognosis, which was what Janice especially craved. She knew what the problem was. What she needed to learn was how she was going to solve it. How she could banish the nightmares – and even worse, the daytime flashbacks and crippling fear that kept her constantly looking over her shoulder, literally.

"The only cure to a psychological prison is a break-out," Theresa said, the closest thing to useful advice she was willing, or able, to give.

"And how would I go about doing that?" she'd asked.

"Get out of your normal routine. Go to a bar – not to drink yourself senseless, but to be around people, to inculcate trust through group association. Join a club. Take up a hobby that puts you in contact with similar-minded individuals. Break down the barriers this trauma has erected."

Break down the barriers? Janice was skeptical she had the energy, or the courage. Heck, she jumped when the screen door slammed too loudly. She carried pepper spray in her pocketbook. She parked so close to the warehouse where she worked that some of her fellow employees joked about getting her a parking space *inside* the building. She feigned amusement.

But the idea stuck with her, challenging her perception of herself as a strong woman, someone who would not be defined by a madman's senseless act. And as the days dragged by, her excuses sounded increasingly hollow. Eventually, she could no longer justify inaction. So she acted.

The phone ran three times before he answered.

"Mark?" she asked, his voice no longer so well-etched in her memory.

"Yes?"

"This is Janice, Janice Greyson – we met at Harvey's a couple of months ago?"

"Janice! How nice to hear from you!" His reaction seemed genuine, the warmth in his greeting bringing a rare smile to her face. Despite rehearsing this conversation in her mind a dozen times, she froze trying to think what to say next.

"I…I'm sorry it's been so long since we talked…"

"No worries. I'm sure you've been as busy as I have."

Did he know? Or was she just being paranoid?

"Yes, I've been quite busy myself." Long pause. Should she wait or make the first move?

"I want you to know I was very disappointed by the verdict in your court case. I don't know what those jurors were thinking about. How are you holding up?"

He knew! My god, what now? She almost hung up the phone but fought-off the knee-jerk reaction.

"I'm… doing okay. It was quite a shock."

"I bet."

"Took me a few days to work it through, but I think I'm back on the right path."

"Good! Does that path include dinner, or drinks?"

It was the question she'd hoped to hear, but now that she had she wasn't sure how to respond. "Well, yes, I guess it does."

"Good! How about this coming Friday, 7:30?"

A sudden flush of insecurity nearly derailed the conversation. She took a deep breath. "Great. That would be great. Where did you have in mind?"

"How about I pick you up at your place – if that'd be okay."

She wanted to say yes, but the thought brought too many memories too close to the surface.

"My Mom will be putting my son to bed around that time. Better if I meet you at the restaurant." In reality, Jackie rarely responded badly to her going out at night. Not that it happened all that often.

"Oh, yeh, sure." He mentioned a fancy place less than a mile from her house.

"Okay, good. See you at 7:30 then."

When he hung up she listened to the dial tone for several seconds before she could put the phone down. She'd planned the call expecting to feel either elated or crest-fallen by his reaction. What she hadn't expected was to feel utterly, and completely, confused.

******

The days leading up to their dinner seemed to pass ever-so-slowly, but she took comfort in thinking about something other than *him* for the first time in what seemed like a very long while. It was a tremendous relief. It was a tremendous burden.

What should I wear? Is my hair too shaggy? What should I say if he brings up the trial?' Despite her best efforts to *normalize* her life, as Dr. Thurman had suggested, she couldn't help but focus on the Friday date. If it even was a date. *It's just a dinner, for cryin' out loud.* Am I ready for this? *If not now, when? If not Mark, who?*

The thoughts spun round and round; she found herself caught between a real-world Scylla and Charybdis – hope and fear. What if she was making too much of a simple dinner? What if even a dinner was too much, too soon? People at work began to notice her distraction. Most thought it was due to the outcome of the trial. They would speak to her, and she wouldn't hear. She'd confirm information and times, and then forget.

"Are you okay?" a solicitous co-worker would ask. She'd smile, put on her best show of unforced normalcy, and respond: "I'm doing great! Thanks so much for asking."

Two minutes later, she'd barely remember who had asked.

Even her mother and Jackie noticed the change.

"What's up with you lately?" her Mom asked one evening after a particularly unresponsive dinner. "It's like your head's in the clouds."

"Me? Just thinking."

"About what? Something at work?"

Janice smiled. "No, work's good." She knew that wouldn't be enough to put-off her mother. They didn't call her The Doberman for nothing. Actually, *they* didn't call her that at all; only she described her Mom that way, and not to her face.

"Not that awful trial still."

"No, not really. A thought or two from time to time, but not often."

Jennifer studied her daughter closely. Janice ignored the prolonged stare.

"You know," her mother began after an exhaustive examination, "if I didn't know better, I'd think you had a man in your life…"

Janice tried to maintain her poker face. Unfortunately, she was never very good at poker.

"You do?! When? How? Come on, spill the beans."

Janice feigned disinterest, made a show of not wanting to *spill the beans*, but in her heart she was glad her secret had come out. It made it seem more real when she spoke the words, and her mother was nothing if not judgmental. A second opinion, even hers, was welcome.

She gave the Twitter version of the budding relationship, if that's even what it could be called. As predicted, it wasn't enough.

"Who is this man? Do you know anyone who knows him? Did you run him through an online background check?"

"Mom?!"

"I'm only saying, you just met the guy."

Janice made some plaintive squeaks about privacy and trust, but beneath all that she was kicking herself for not thinking of checking him out on the Internet herself. *Will you never learn?'* one thought thread went. *'Don't shut yourself off,'* another countered.

But as probing as her mother's questioning had been, it was Jackie who made her most aware of her growing distraction.

"Mom," he said during a breakfast at which she'd only said about ten words to him, "are you feeling okay?"

She'd been startled. "Of course, honey! Why do you ask?"

"Well, 'cause you've been walkin' around the house with this dopey look on your face most of the time, and you didn't even yell at me for putting three spoons of cocoa in my chocolate milk."

Janice blinked and noticed the open can of cocoa and the trail of brown powder leading to her son's glass for the first time.

"That *is* a lot of cocoa," she ventured.

Jackie got up out of his chair and walked to where she sat, throwing his arms around her waist and giving her a big hug.

"It'll be okay, Mom," he soothed. "Grandma and I will take care of things until you 'cuperate."

Janice promised herself to try to stay in the moment, if only with Jackie. Only problem was, it was darn difficult to do that.

*****

She'd spent an inordinate amount of time getting ready. Normally she didn't have trouble picking an outfit, slapping on some makeup, arranging her hair. Friday night, everything seemed to be working against her. She even broke a long-standing rule and had a sip of wine to calm her nerves. Well, maybe a half-glass.

Jackie and her Mom played their parts by reacting with appreciative astonishment when she finally emerged from her bathroom.

"Mom, you look *pretty*!" her son shouted gleefully. "Like a movie star!"

"I have to agree – you clean up well," her mother added, keeping the enthusiasm down to a believable level. "This guy must be quite something."

She shrugged. "I'm tired of hiding. Time to take my life back."

"You go, girl," Jennifer joked. "When do you think you'll be home?"

"Depends," she answered with a sly smile, "how well it goes."

"Ooo la-la!"

Everyone laughed, and she stepped out her front door with just the right mix of excitement and hopefulness.

That's not to say there wasn't a healthy dollop of nervousness tossed into the mix. Her heart was racing as she settled into the driver's seat. She flipped down the visor to take a peek in the mirror. Damn, she *was* looking good!

She drove to the restaurant on auto-pilot as her focus stayed fixed on this relative stranger she was about to eat dinner with. He seemed like a great guy. Smart, funny, good-looking – check, check and check. She had run a quick online

records search to ease her flaring paranoia, and to her great
relief nothing worrisome had come up. Truth was, he seemed
like a normal, happy, successful guy. But did he know what
he was getting into?

She banished such thoughts from her mind by singing
along with the radio, a trick she'd learned back during her
divorce. It was difficult to remain despondent while singing
"Yellow Submarine." The drive took no more than ten
minutes; it seemed even less. She gave the keys to the valet
attendant – she wasn't sure she could park safely the way the
butterflies fluttered.

She was ten minutes early. It didn't so much matter if she
arrived first or last, but she didn't want to be late. The inside
of the place was so dark it took several minutes for her eyes
to adjust. The music was low-key and jazzy. No Yellow
Submarine there. When she could eventually see beyond the
greeting podium in the entranceway, she quickly scanned the
diners to determine if Mark had arrived before her. No
familiar faces. Not even... She shook her head in irritation.
There was no way she could ever set herself free from the
nightmare of the past few months if she couldn't even block
him from her thoughts. She tried a meditation trick Dr.
Thurman had taught her, but before she could judge its
effectiveness a familiar voice broke her concentration.

"Masterful synchronization," Mark said from just behind
her.

She tried to react with utmost sophistication, turning
gracefully with no show of surprise. She wasn't sure how
successful she appeared from his point of view, but to her it
felt like the first time a boy had asked her to dance back in
seventh grade: awkward and yet thrilling.

"Mark! I didn't see you there…"

The first moment of internal conflict: kiss on the cheek, extend hand? She went for the cheek. He responded without missing a beat.

"My, my – aren't we looking gorgeous tonight."

She couldn't help herself – this time her smile showed plenty of teeth. "As do you."

"*Gorgeous?* Not a word that's often used to describe me. But I'll take the sentiment. Ready to go in?"

She was, and they did. As he put his hand lightly on the small of her back, shivers ran through her body.

"Been here long?" he asked as the black-suited host walked them to their table.

"No, just a couple of minutes. Your timing was excellent."

Before the maître de could pull out Janice's chair, Mark was there doing it for her.

"Ah. A gentleman," she said. Her words wobbled a little in her ears, though whether it was her nerves or simply perception she wasn't sure.

"So," he began as soon as he'd sat down across from her, "with this place being right around the corner from where you live I suppose you've been here a million times."

"Actually, I've never been here," she answered with complete honesty. "A bit too rich for a single mom."

He smiled. "Then I'm glad we could get you here." Just then the sommelier appeared with a wine list so extensive she despaired of making a choice. "Are you a wine drinker?" Mark asked.

"I've been known to sip a glass or two." *'More like a bottle or two lately,'* she thought, but she kept that personal info to herself.

She wondered if he'd just plow ahead and order without any input from her. He didn't.

"White or red?" When she chose red, he ran through an exhaustive list of varietals. She didn't know half of them, but she knew she liked "Cab." He ordered a bottle from Napa.

The lingering presence of the 'wine guy' stifled any real conversation. Mark asked if it was too cold in the restaurant, she demurred. As the sommelier walked away, however, Mark leaned forward to initiate what Janice could only imagine would be an intimate conversation. She felt queasy.

"You know, after all that time went by, I was afraid I'd never hear from you again."

Afraid? "I… wasn't in the right space," she said, wincing internally. *'Too hip.'*

"I understand completely." A moment of silence raised her blood pressure. He continued just as she was about to utter some nonsense syllables to fill the dead space. "So what changed your mind?"

'Wow. How to explain?' "These past few months have been… hell. First the…attack," *just a light stutter, keep going,* "and then all the demands of the investigation and the trial. It was very difficult to give so much energy to that and still have any left for my *real* life – job, family, friends…"

"Wine?"

She giggled nervously. "What, do you have a camera hidden in my living room?"

"Whenever I feel the pressure building, a glass or two takes the edge off."

"What pressures can penetrate that cool, controlled exterior of yours?"

He looked surprised. "Moi? You should try getting screamed at by contractors, suppliers, government inspectors, and customers – sometimes all at the same time. Some days I start dreaming about that first glass at lunchtime." He suddenly realized he might be giving the wrong impression. "Not that I actually drink during the day. Heavy machinery, big crews – all that."

She smiled. It was a relief to hear that even normal people needed an outlet. She considered opening up about the pressures she'd been feeling, but now that he'd started providing some insight into his own psyche, she wanted him to continue. "What is it you *do*, exactly?" she prompted, and he was off and running.

*****

The food was good, the company even better. But Janice couldn't dispel the feeling that something was going to sour, something was going to spoil her night. It wasn't anything she could identify with any specificity – just a sense of disquiet, unease. "Give yourself a chance!" Dr. Thurman had suggested, but it was easier said than done. Even while she tried to focus on Mark's captivating and occasionally funny biography, her mind wandered to much darker and threatening vistas. *How can I permit anyone to share my life when they have no clue about the demons I'm facing? Am I just being selfish, allowing him to believe I'm the smiling, well-adjusted woman he sees in front of him? How forthcoming should I be?*

She smiled, laughed where it seemed appropriate, maintained eye-contact. But from time-to-time she could see from his expression that she'd reacted badly, or failed to react when expected. In some ways it was more nerve-wracking than everyday life, with all its predictably unpredictable distractions and possibilities for unexpected disaster.

"Have you ever been there?" he was asking when her conscious mind returned to the table.

She barely missed a beat. "Which one?"

"St. John?" She could see from his quizzical look she'd missed key information.

"No, no I haven't. Never been to the Caribbean, actually."

"Never been to the Caribbean?!" he roared in genuine surprise. "We'll have to get you down there!"

And off he went again. This time she tried doubly-hard to follow every word, throwing up meditative roadblocks to every stray thought. It was like swatting mosquitoes at an evening campfire. No matter how many she slapped down, dozens more swarmed every exposed centimeter of her person. But these bites didn't just itch, they burned.

*****

For the first two hours, time truly flew. When she glanced at her watch she was shocked to see the hour. But as dessert morphed into coffee and liqueurs (she didn't partake – of either), time slowed as her heartbeat raced. Dinner was predictable, public, *safe*. Whatever came next was… none of those.

"Sure I can't help with the bill?" she'd offered, trying to appear ever the well-adjusted modern woman.

His smile was disdainful. "I think I can handle it. After all, I invited you. Besides, I took a loan to make sure I'd have enough money."

She'd drifted, just for a moment, and didn't realize he was expecting a response until his eyebrows made it clear.

"Oh, I hope that wasn't necessary!" she fumbled with an embarrassed smile.

"It was worth it," he said, leaning forward as if to ensure the intimacy of his words.

Her smile was unforced, though utterly unreflective of the turmoil that raged within her.

He hurried to her side of the table to help pull out her chair. Suddenly words were scarce. They walked through the gauntlet of tightly-packed tables without a word.

"I hope you enjoyed yourselves!" the maître de said cheerfully as they approached the door.

"Very much!' he responded in kind. She could barely force a tight-lipped smile. It wasn't that she hadn't enjoyed the evening. She had. It was just… She didn't trust her voice. If it shook as badly as her heartbeat, her disquiet would be clear for all to see.

As each step took her further and further from the cozy embrace of the restaurant, her knees seemed increasingly unwilling to obey her. She wondered if it was as obvious to him as it was to her, which added embarrassment to the potent mix of emotions that swelled through her veins. Finally, after what she would later characterize as the Death March to the Parking Lot, they arrived at her car.

"Well," she began, turning to face him, hoping the dim lighting would disguise the fear in her eyes.

"I had a wonderful night," he jumped in, his sincerity a balm to her nerves. "Maybe we can do it again sometime? Sometime soon?"

His teeth shone under the muted security lights.

"Yes!" Her assuredness surprised even herself. She recalibrated her reply before continuing in a less exuberant but still receptive tone. "I'd like that."

Before she could think, or even flinch, he leaned in and gave her a quick peck on the cheek.

"It's a date. Should I give you a call, or...?"

The thoughts arrived unbidden but too fast to censor: *'Give him my number? He seems nice, but...'*

"No!" It took a moment for her to realize she'd said the word out loud. Mark was looking stricken. She felt like an idiot.

"No?" he asked.

"I meant... of course. Have you got a pen?"

"No need." He held up his cellphone.

"Oh, right." Her cheeks turned an even darker shade of pink. "Twenty-first century. I forgot."

"Happens to me all the time. Pretty soon we'll be nothing more than memes as everything becomes virtual."

She had no idea what memes were, but she grinned and nodded agreeably.

For several moments they just stood there and smiled at each other, neither willing to end the evening. But one can only stand and stare so long before the circumstance becomes untenable.

"Well, I guess I'd better be going," Janice said.

"Yeh, me too. Got errands to run tomorrow morning!"

Without thinking, she leaned over and returned his cheek peck. His smile was broad and genuine.

"Good night!" she managed to toss-off as she ducked into her car. She moved so quickly and was so rattled she nearly took the top of her head off. When she looked in her rearview mirror to back up, he was already on his way to his car. She breathed a sigh of relief.

As wonderful as it had been, as promising their chemistry, her nerves were frayed almost to the breaking point. The battle that ensued as she drove home took place exclusively in her head, but it was no less violent than if her two selves had confronted each other in the real world.

'It was a good night. Can't you just leave it at that?'

'You barely know the man! Haven't you learned anything?'

'It's not the same.'

'How is it different?'

'He's different.'

'How can you be sure?'

'I can feel it!'

'Do you know how naïve you sound? Are you really going to do this?'

And so it went, back and forth, neither self giving an inch. By the time she arrived back at her house she was emotionally exhausted.

"How'd it go?" her mother asked chirpily as soon as she stepped through the door.

"It was fine," she answered, her tone as neutral as she could manage. She saw Jennifer's face curl into a question mark. "He's a nice guy."

"But…?"

"But I am who I am. I don't know if I'm ready for all this."

"All what?! It was only dinner, honey."

"Nothing is *only* to me."

Janice could almost hear her mother pondering. "If you want to talk about it…"

"Maybe sometime. Not tonight. I'm going to take a shower and go to bed." She started down the hallway.

"Okay, I understand. I'm sure you just need time."

Janice wished she was as sure.

*****

It wasn't a good night's sleep. Not good at all.

She might have dreamed of a second date with Mark (or 'non-date' if you will), or even just a picnic lunch with Jackie – possibly her mother too. But what she saw when she closed her eyes was that all-too-familiar taunting smile, stalking her in mirrors, storefront windows, the surface of a deep, black, beckoning depth – always just out of reach but never out of sight. She awoke in the middle of the night, her hair plastered to her forehead, her heart pounding in her ears.

It took her several seconds to remember where she was, but even then she felt compelled to get up out of bed and peek into the closet and under her bed – just to be sure. This was one of those times when the unreality of the dream seemed more real than the reality of her life. A reality that she dearly wished would morph into something much more… livable, and soon. She eventually convinced herself that all was well – as well as could be hoped for – and climbed under the covers determined to fall back asleep with a different feature film playing in her head. But although she tried all her tricks – the breathing exercises, the meditation, the visualization, even self-hypnosis – her subconscious wouldn't let loose of the notion that *he* would re-appear, or at least his most prominent, most disconcerting feature. And so she lay there, unable to drift off but unwilling to surrender the effort.

Until she glanced at her alarm clock and realized she'd been lying there for over an hour.

'*Enough of this,*' she declared silently and throwing off the covers she dragged her exhausted body across the bedroom to her closet, where she slipped into her terry-cloth robe. Then it was down the darkened hallway to the kitchen, where she made herself a cup of hot tea and grabbed two of Jackie's cookies. She began to tear-up when she thought of her son. '*What has he ever done to deserve a screwed-up mom like me?*' she blubbered. It took several minutes of sipped tea and deep breaths to bring her emotions back under control.

Even then, she looked up and saw herself reflected in a sliding glass door: hair bedraggled, eyes red and puffy, sitting bent over like some withered old hag, crying her eyes out in the middle of the night. She teetered on another crying jag, but this time her anger won out. '*I'm not going to let that son-of-a-bitch win!*' she promised herself. '*I'm not!*'

She wiped her eyes on the sleeve of the robe and carried her cup back to her bedroom, stopping just once: to peek-in on her son, and listen to his gentle, peaceful breathing. That sound did more to reset her emotional equilibrium than any self-help crutch Dr. Thurman had taught her. It was as if he pronounced that all was well in the world with every breath, if only for that moment. She shut his bedroom door with regret, yet with the motherly assurance that his sleep was more important than her momentary weakness.

Her own bed looked nowhere near as inviting, more a necessary evil than a welcoming safe-harbor. She read for a while, actually quite a while. The story was drivel – aren't they all? – but the physical act of turning the pages and focusing on something other than the horror of the past weeks gave her the slow-won sense of exhaustion (no, not serenity; never serenity) that she needed to fall back asleep. This time she slept the sleep of the just, untroubled by dreams, unburdened by fears.

And so she remained until morning.

CHAPTER 18

The morning arrived with an overpowering urge to see her son.

Jackie's excitement at seeing his mom emerge from her *den* - still wearing a robe - was slightly tempered by his evident confusion at seeing tears stream from her eyes while she hugged him ever so tightly as he sat at the breakfast table eating his cereal.

"Are you sad again, Mommy?" he asked, eyes wide.

"She's fine, Jackie," Jennifer answered when Janice was too overcome to speak. "She just hasn't seen you in a while."

"Just since yesterday."

His answer brought a chuckle from his teary mother. "I guess it seemed longer. Sometimes I miss you so much I can't hardly stand it!"

"Sometimes I miss you too, Mommy."

Slowly, almost painfully, Janice lessened her grip on her son and stood with a deep sigh.

"Rough night?" her mother asked.

She nodded. "Dark thoughts."

Jennifer shook her head. "You met the man of your dreams and you still have those thoughts?"

"Mark wasn't the man of my dreams last night." She went to get herself a cup of coffee.

"Same dream?"

She really didn't want to talk about it, but she felt she owed her mom an answer. "Pretty much, yeh."

"When was the last time you saw Dr. Thurman?"

Before she could answer, her son looked up from his cereal in alarm.

"You're sick?" Jackie asked, his face reflecting concern.

"No, no I'm fine, honey. This is a different kind of doctor."

"What kind?"

Janice looked to her mother who responded with arched eyebrows.

"The kind who tries to help people think right."

"Do *I* think right?" the boy asked after a long pause.

"Of course you do!" she said, hugging him once more. "You couldn't think wrong if you tried."

"Do you?"

At this, Janice hesitated. "Most of the time, Jackie."

"But sometimes all adults have bad thoughts," her mother jumped in. "It's nothing for you to worry about."

"Even you, Grandma? Even you have bad thoughts?"

Now it was Janice's turn to arch her eyebrows. "Yes, honey, even grandmas have bad thoughts every now and then."

Jackie stared solemnly into his cereal as if looking for a dead fly. "Does that mean I'll have bad thoughts when I grow up?" he finally asked.

"No, no of course not!" Janice said. "Not enough to cause you pain."

"Janice Greyson!" her mother bridled. "He doesn't need to hear the finer points of the argument!"

Actually, she thought he did. But she bowed to her mother's vehement assuredness.

"It's nothing for you to worry about," Janice went on. "So just finish your breakfast and go brush your teeth. We need to get goin' so you're not late for school!"

One of the wonders of young children is that they are capable of forgetting not only the finer points but entire arguments within seconds. Janice wished she had retained the same capacity.

*****

The ride to school featured no mention of bad thoughts. Not that some of them didn't continue to swirl in Janice's head, but she kept her smiling Mommy Mask firmly in place for the entire drive, allowing Jackie to return to his usual six-year-old bubbly self and pepper her with questions about super heroes, dogs and Doritos (he liked Doritos, but his grandmother didn't like him eating them at any time except lunch – "With a sandwich!")

He gave her his usual big smooch on the cheek and ran off without a care in the world. Janice just sat there trying to imagine her coming day in the office, but she couldn't quite picture it. A beep from behind reminded her that she was blocking the long line of mommies depositing their children at the school. With a sigh, she pulled away from the curb.

She drove aimlessly, her thoughts so knotted they proscribed a clear line of reasoning. At one point she scanned the city street she found herself driving down, and was both shocked and a little frightened to realize she had no idea where she was. She wanted to pull over, to clear her head, but in her current state of mind everything seemed dangerous, so foreign she didn't dare stop. After several minutes of growing tension, she found a spot where a number of well-dressed people were going about their normal day. Just as she began to pull over and park, however, she thought she saw…

someone. *Was it **him**? Could it be him? How could he be there?*
She jerked the wheel back toward the street, only to be
greeted by screeching tires and a blaring horn. She waved
meekly without ever meeting the other driver's eyes and
drove off.

By this point her nerves were so frayed she maintained no
illusion of being capable of spending eight hours behind a
desk at work. Instead, she let the car take her in a familiar
direction.

When she walked into the reception area, three other
patients were already waiting patiently.

"I need to see the doctor, right way," she whispered to
the young woman behind the desk.

"Do you have an appointment?"

"No, no I don't have an appointment. But this is an
emergency!"

Whether it was something in her eyes, or the way her
voice rose from barely audible to a near-shout, the
receptionist got the message. "Okay, all right, just take a deep
breath and have a seat." She pointed to a chair as far removed
from the other, flustered patients as possible, and hurried into
the inner office with barely a knock. In seconds Dr. Thurman
emerged, her trademark smile noticeably askew.

"Janice! Come in, come in," she beckoned, waving toward
the open door with professional urgency. She started to
follow her patient inside, before turning back to the other,
waiting patients.

"I'm so sorry. An emergency," she explained before
disappearing inside.

Janice was so upset she was shaking.

"Come here, lie down," the psychologist said, pointing to a worn brown leather couch. "Let me get you something to drink." She went over to a water cooler in the corner, keeping a surreptitious eye on Janice the whole time.

"What is it, Janice? How can I help?"

"I… it…" The words would not come. It was like an ice dam: too many words colliding with no place to go.

"Here – drink this," Dr. Thurman said, handing her the glass of water.

Janice's hands shook so badly the water spilled over the sides as she gulped it down. She didn't seem to notice. The pain on her face said it all.

The doctor sat next to her on the couch, and after putting the water glass aside took Janice's hands in her own and held them lightly.

"Breathe slowly," she said in a soft, hypnotic voice. "Feel your muscles relax."

Ever so gradually, with incessant repetition, the doctor calmed the shaking hands and eased Janice back to a prone position.

"There – is that better?"

Janice nodded. She still didn't trust her voice.

"Ready to talk about it?"

Janice took a deep breath.

*****

Thirty minutes later, Dr. Thurman walked Janice to her door.

"Ellen, see if you can work Janice into the schedule – tomorrow or the next day at the latest," she said to her receptionist before turning back to Janice. "Just keep in mind what we talked about – you are bigger than this. You are in control."

Janice nodded, her smile a thin forced arc.

"Good. Then we'll see you again as soon as she can find you a spot." She turned and picked up a manila file sitting on Ellen's desk. "Mrs. Williamson?"

After agreeing to return the next afternoon, Janice made her way outside into the warm summer sun. She felt... better, but in a qualified, half-hearted way. She moved through a world just slightly out of focus, just slightly unreal. She forced herself to not scan the parking lot – he wasn't there. He couldn't be there. Nonetheless, she couldn't avoid peeking left and right as she approached her car – *just to be sure,'* she justified.

She drove straight home. Dr. Thurman had made her promise to jot down her thoughts whenever she could find the time. With Jackie in school, she should have the time *if* she could convince her mother to give her the space.

Driving into her driveway she felt the slightest sense of panic reaching for her throat. As soon as she'd turned off the engine, she closed her eyes and repeated the very basic meditation techniques the doctor had demonstrated to her. Slowly, almost imperceptibly, her breathing deepened and the trembling in her hands lessened. Once she felt she'd re-established control, she got out and marched up the walkway.

She paused once again at her front door, steeling herself for the barrage of questions she knew her mother would launch as soon as she set foot inside. But to her great relief, the house lay silent. She wasn't sure where her mother had gone – grocery shopping, probably.

The weight of the anticipated inquisition fell away immediately, leaving Janice with a sense of independence she'd never realized she'd missed since *that* day. It was as if an interminable low-grade headache had suddenly stopped – you only noticed how much it hurt when it disappeared. She felt guilty that her mother's absence could stimulate such relief, but she couldn't deny the fact.

She brewed herself a fresh pot of coffee and carried a steaming cup into her bedroom office. She'd planned to type her journal on the computer, but now that she was faced with the task she decided to hand-write her thoughts and feelings on a yellow legal pad, hoping the physical connection with the pen and paper would ground her and allow for both more honesty and more detail.

She sat poised over the yellow pad for quite some time. *'Where to begin?'* she wondered.

*****

I could say it all began on __that__ day – the day of the attack. But I would be lying.

It began, in every real sense, with my divorce. **Our** *divorce. Mine, Jackie's, and yes, my ex's. All of us were impacted in various ways, some more immediately evident, some not noticeable for months, even years. For me, in retrospect, the two major impacts were guilt and self-confidence: too much of the first and not enough of the second.*

There was no way I could remain married to the man – we both knew that. Although few people go into a marriage expecting their significant other to change, well, significantly, it happens. In fact, I'm not sure it cannot happen. The key factor is not if change will come, but how much and what kind?

For us, it was too much, too fast. On both sides. I know I changed.
Especially after I became pregnant, I became much more conservative,
much more frightened of the world around me. A world of criminals and
terrorists, viruses and car crashes. A world of uncertainty and
unpredictability. Not so much for me, but for my child. I felt, if not
helpless, then overmatched. But I was determined to try. I stopped
drinking, I changed my diet, I became insistent that my husband do the
same. (I say insistent; he'd say I nagged.) I saw the changes as they
occurred, but I wasn't worried. In fact, I was amazed that my husband
didn't see the necessity himself. In retrospect, I suppose I was naïve, and
yes – selfish. Not selfish for myself, per se, but selfish for our child.
Selfish and stubborn. I wanted things done my way, on my schedule.
After all, I was the one carrying the baby, not him.

His changes? He became tense, irritable, not as giving. I
rationalized it to be due to the pressures of coming fatherhood. In fact, it
was probably just as much, if not more, due to the pressures created by
the changes in me.

For a few months, or was it weeks, we declared an unspoken truce
when Jackie was born. We were both thrilled, genuinely, totally, over-the-
moon thrilled. But even such a wonder, such a blessing, can't change the
immutable laws of human nature. I remember one night, maybe three or
four weeks after our son was born. I'd taken leave from my job,
obviously, but my ex- was still working. There was no paid paternity
leave at his workplace. Not that we could've gotten-by without his
paycheck.

He'd smoked when we first met. For the first couple of years of our
marriage, actually. But with the pregnancy I'd asked – insisted – that he
no longer smoke in the house. He'd complained a little, but not much.
The back porch of our little rental house was the designated smoking
zone.

This one night, however, it was cold, rainy and windy. Jackie woke up somewhere around two needing a change, and I crawled out of bed, half-asleep as usual, to do it. I didn't turn on a light, and so I didn't notice that my husband was already up.

When I'd calmed Jackie for a few minutes, I went into the kitchen to get a new pack of diapers. There, with a shot glass of whiskey in one hand and a cigarette in the other, sat my ex-. He scared the living bejesus out of me.

"What the hell are you doing?!" I asked. Maybe yelled.

"Smoking. Having a drink," he said with guilt-tinged calm.

I didn't think, just reacted. "You know you can't smoke in the house."

"It's raining outside. And pretty damn cold besides."

I heard him, but I didn't **hear** *him. "Couldn't you wait until morning?" I pressed.*

"No, I couldn't. I was wide-awake and needed something to put me back to sleep. And you know I don't drink without a cig."

"Then maybe you should've had a cup of hot milk."

Well that set him off. He told me the house was his house too, and that he was the one working to pay the rent, and 'Goddamn!' he should be able to have a smoke every once in a while without feeling like a criminal in his own house.

I gave as good as I got. I told him he was selfish, thinking only of himself and not his son. We were yelling back and forth, getting into it pretty good, when off in the distance I heard a wail.

Jackie! I suppose I panicked a bit, being a brand new mom and all, and I guess I didn't handle it well. "You asshole!" I screamed. "You don't deserve a son like Jackie!"

"At least I'm not some nervous-Nelly nutcase!" he yelled after me as I ran back to our son's room.

By the time I got Jackie calmed down, changed, and made my way back to the kitchen, he was gone. No note, no announcement. Nothing. Oh, he came back all right, the very next day. But things were never quite the same. He stopped joking, rarely smiled, never really showed much interest in me sexually like before Jackie arrived. Then he started going out at night with his 'buds' two or three times a week, and the next morning his clothes smelled like smoke and beer. It was like when you get a cut — it all heals over, but there's still a scar. And under that scar it can still hurt.

Looking back, that was pretty much the beginning of the end. It played out for more than a year, but that was the turning point. We weren't really a couple after that, just two people living together for the sake of... Jackie? That's what he said, and what I believed, but now I'm not so sure. Now it seems to me that people do whatever they do to satisfy something within themselves. There may be collateral benefit, but down deep we all do what we need to do to make ourselves happy. At least part of ourselves, since neither of us was very happy at the time.

So all that's happened since then really started all those years ago. I changed, no doubt. I wasn't as trusting, wasn't as open. For those first few months after the divorce I couldn't even look at Jackie without thinking of his father, as horrible as that sounds. My own son was a source of pain, and guilt. Oh yeh, plenty of guilt. How could a mother turn away from her beautiful baby boy and spend three, sometimes four nights a week at bars? Coming home drunk; sometimes not coming home at all until morning. I was a mess, and maybe I never stopped being one.

I got over the sharp, burning pain, all right. Took six months and more tequila and rum than I want to think about. But the dull pain, that never went away. Even now I can still feel it under all the crap that's been piled on top since then. Worse yet, I've spread the same crap to everyone I love, everyone I care for: Jackie, Mom, Patrice Daniels, even Detective Willard. They all reached out to help me and got a handful of crap for their pains. How can I let anyone else reach out, ever?

When I was standing out in my backyard hanging clothes on that day, I was probably thinking back to the way it used to be, or wondering if it would ever be that good again. I can't honestly say what I was thinking. But I remember what I was thinking later that day, not so much while it was happening as immediately afterward. During the attack, I was numb – from fear, from shock, from everything. (NOTE: Dr. T. wants me to stop calling it an 'attack.' It was a rape, plain and simple. I still haven't managed to do that, obviously.) Afterword, all I could think of at first was Jackie: was Jackie okay? When I found that he was, when I had nothing to think about other than myself, that's when I fell apart. And all the king's horses, and all the king's men…

I told myself it wasn't my fault, but that wasn't quite true, was it? I was at that bar when I met him – Archer. I was drunk. I talked to him. I pretended to give him my number. Am I so innocent? I could have been at home – should have been there. If I'd stayed with Jackie instead of farming him off to a sitter, I would never have met that asshole, and none of this would've happened.

That's where the guilt comes from, I suppose. I know I didn't invite him to my house. I didn't even give him a real phone number. But I started the whole thing. I made it possible. And isn't that what fault is all about?

And now? Everyone wants me to 'get on with your life'. They think it's a question of will-power, or determination. Do any of them honestly think there's anyone on this planet who wants me to get on with my life any more than I do?

But it's not a question of will. I know that now. It's deeper, more elusive. How to do you un-see something once you've seen it? How do I forget that smile, forget the evil, self-satisfied smile that haunts me? How do you not see threatening movement in the shadows? Not hear random sounds that once meant nothing and now mean everything. How do you believe in people?

I'm not sure I can.

But I can try.

www.ingramcontent.com/pod-product-compliance
Lightning Source LLC
Chambersburg PA
CBHW020215260626
47156CB00002B/395